CU00763817

THE MURDER ON THE ORDINARY EXPRESS

The Curious Case of The Butcher of St. Mary Nook

A Verbal Animation

em.thompson

1

Night was fast falling by the time that Simon 'Naff' Robinson and Heather Prendergast left North London. Overtaking anything and everything that got in the way, Naff's powerful Triumph Bonneville motorbike covered the fifty or so miles to Tunbridge Wells in as many minutes.

After ringroading the small market town, Naff branched off onto a quiet country lane. As he blurred past a sign . . . *St. Mary Nook Welcomes Careful Drivers* . . . he saw a blue light flashing in his wing mirrors. 'Bollocks,' he mouthed and freewheeled to a stop.

A police Panda car pulled up behind him and a policewoman got out. She strolled over, took out her pocketbook, said, 'all right, sir, where's the fire?' and pointed to a sign half-hidden by an overhanging branch. 'You were exceeding the speed limit. This is a built-up area.'

Naff flipped up his visor, peered into the night and gave his stubble a scratch. 'Call a cowshed and two barns built-up?' he said. 'Still, never mind, eh? Ain't as if there's any traffic round these parts this time of night. Hardly Piccadilly Circus, is it?'

If the officer's humourless expression was anything to go by, she was in no mood to bandy badinage. 'Please get off the bike, sir,' she said. 'Do you have any means of identification?' She raised an eyebrow when Naff showed her his warrant card. 'North Huddshire Undercover Crime Unit, eh?' she said. 'Bit of a long way from your patch.' Pen and pocketbook at the ready, she turned to Heather, looked her up and down and said, 'so, who have we here?' in such a way as to suggest that she could guess. 'Do your parents know you're out this time of night, miss?'

Although affronted by the ageist slur, Heather bit her lip and held her tongue. Aunt Elizabeth had taught her to respect her elders and betters when not on duty. And to be fair - as she went to great pains to be – it was an easy mistake to make; she wasn't wearing any makeup as she had left home in the mother of all hurries. So she swallowed her pride and showed the officer her CID ID. But behind an obsequious smile, she was seething and for good reason. She had lost count of how many times she had told Naff to slow down, but as was so often the case she had been hissing in the wind.

The officer gave Heather's warrant card a cursory glance, took a closer look, frowned and shone her torch in Heather's face. 'Buy this online did you, miss? You don't seriously expect me to believe you're old enough to be a detective in the Metropolitan Police.'

Despite being highly umbraged to have her probity impugned, Heather feigned an air of casual indifference. 'Oh, I've been at New Scotland Yard for ages,' she said. It might have slipped her mind, but she neglected to say that in her case CID stood for Catering Induction Detail and that she worked in the staff canteen. But why muddy the waters with petty irrelevances? To use a technical term employed in her line of duty, her lowly station was merely a red herring. So she settled for, 'we're visiting my aunt in St. Mary Nook.'

'Not on duty, then. In which case . . .' the officer wrote out a speeding ticket. 'And might I suggest you see to that, Detective Robinson?' She shone her flashlight at the Bonneville's rear tyre. 'Let's just pretend I didn't notice, shall we? This time,' she added with a hint of future menace.

'Aw, come on. Gimme a break,' Naff said with a roguish smile. 'We work for the same outfit, near as not.'

'I doubt that my duty sergeant would agree,' the officer said. 'In his book, anyone born outside Kent is a foreigner, a meddler or a troublemaker. Like as not all three. Now enjoy your stay, sir, miss. And mind how you go.' She tipped her cap, returned to the Panda car and drove off.

'Jobsworth,' Naff muttered as he ripped up the speeding ticket and tossed it in a handy ditch. 'Quite a looker, though, weren't she? Wouldn't mind being banged up by her.'

'Oh, please,' Heather groaned, duly disgusted if not unduly surprised by her boyfriend's boorish comment. 'If you want my opinion, I thought she was extremely diligent. I'm surprised she let you off with that bald tyre. I wouldn't have.'

'Bet you wouldn't,' Naff said. 'Hop on, honey. If we get a move-on, we should be there before you know it.'

Heather felt a rush of anticipation whistle through her hair as her boyfriend's motorbike banked into Trevelyan Hall's treelined drive. The historic mansion had once been her home and many of her most treasured possessions were mothballed in the attics along with an uncountitude of memories. Having said that, this was her first visit since Christmas, eight eventful months ago. From what she could see, nothing much had changed. Not that she imagined it ever had. And not that she imagined it ever would.

On the outskirts of the small village of St. Mary Nook, Trevelyan Hall with its half-timbered outbuildings and landscaped grounds was a historic local landmark. Dating back to Tudor times, according to Heather's aunt, Lady Elizabeth Trevelyan, a house on this site had been listed in the Domesday Book and she claimed to be able to trace her ancestors back almost as far, not that she professed to care. 'Blue blood?' she would scoff whenever her illustrious forebears were mentioned. 'Nonsense. Cut me and I bleed the same ghastly colour as the hoi polloi.'

Naff parked his motorbike beside a sporty Porsche in the gravelled carpark frontaging the house. 'Stone me,' he said as he surveyed the half-timbered mansion with its stable block, barns, bowling green lawns, tennis court and mature woods stretching far into the distance. 'So is this where you grew up?'

'Aunt Elizabeth took me in when I was ten, after mummy died,' Heather explained. 'I didn't see eye to eye with daddy's new wife. Must say, the feeling was mutual. Still is.'

Naff straightened his bandana and admired his reflection in a wing mirror. 'Got to say,' he said, 'if I'd known we'd be staying at a swanky gaff like this, I'd have shaved and changed me shirt.' Unusually for him, he seemed nervous.

'Don't worry, darling.' Heather took his arm and escorted him up the steps to the front door. 'Aunt Elizabeth will love you.'

Having reassured her boyfriend that her aunt was the most down to earth blueblood he could ever hope to meet, Heather rang the bell. A moment later the door was opened by an exceptionally handsome twinset-and-pearls woman with an aristocratic bearing and a striking family likeness to Heather.

'Spriggy . . .' Lady Elizabeth Trevelyan threw out her arms and smothered Heather in kisses. 'Thank you so much for coming, my dear,' she said with a tremor in her voice. 'I didn't know where else to turn.'

'Don't be silly, aunty. Of course we came. You sounded awful on the phone,' Heather said with all the niecely reassurance she could muster; she had never seen her aunt in such a state. 'What on earth is the matter?'

Lady Trevelyan sniffled back a tear, dabbed her eyes

with a monogrammed handkerchief and said, 'your uncle
Montague has been arrested for murder.'

2

'Thanks for coming, Isaac. Take a seat.' Chief Inspector Wheeler gestured to a chair in his office at New Scotland Yard overlooking the River Thames.

A large man with ebony skin and an easy smile, Detective Inspector Obafemi unbuttoned his sports jacket, sat down, crossed his legs and made himself comfortable. He nodded at a file half-buried in the paperwork on Wheeler's desk. 'So what do you think, Bill?' he asked. 'Good enough for the Crown Prosecution Service not to balls things up?'

'Exceptional work, Isaac, but no more than I've come to expect from you. Dare say you'd be doing my job if you had more ambition.' Despite his flippant quip, Chief Inspector Wheeler knew that his job was safe. Although his old friend might have an uncanny knack for solving the most intractable cases, ambitious he was not.

A legend in the Metropolitan Police, Inspector Obafemi preferred to work in his own time, at his own pace and in his own way. The top brass tolerated his pedantic plodology because more often than not he got a result. However, although he brought more felons to book than any other officer at New Scotland Yard, he was no pension-pusher. To the frustration of his longsuffering wife, he had turned down promotion on innumerous occasions and would no doubt continue so to do until he was the last man standing in the queue.

Obafemi cast an eye about Wheeler's office until it settled on a photograph of the Chief Inspector accepting an award from an unentitled nonentity. 'You know me, Bill . . .' He nodded at the photograph. 'Not my cup of tea, filling in forms, bossing people about and doffing my forelock to nobs I wouldn't want to give the time of day.'

'You don't have a forelock. You're as bald as a coot, you old goat,' Wheeler said with a good natured smile. Having shared a chuckle as old friends often do, he cleared his throat and came to the point. 'Think Sandra would miss you for a day or two?'

'I'm sure she'd be glad to see the back of me.' Obafemi disguised a bitter home truth behind a casual smile.

'We've been handed a hot potato I'd like you to run with.' Wheeler slid a file across the desk and sat back with his arms crossed.

Inspector Obafemi looked through the paperwork and shrugged. 'Don't see what this has to do with New Scotland Yard, Bill. Can't the local force take care of it? I'm up to my eyeballs in that cold case you asked me to look into.'

'That will have to wait.' Wheeler nodded at the file. 'Recognise any names?'

Under normal circumstances, Inspector Obafemi

would have dismissed Wheeler's request out of hand. At this particular junction in time, his team was short-staffed and the last thing he wanted was a run-of-the-mill murder enquiry to bottleneck his in-tray. However, what pricked his interest was the prospect of escaping from London for a few days. It would give him time to think about where his life was heading. Or rather, where it wasn't. So he took a closer look.

Chief Inspector Wheeler explained, 'the prime suspect is Montague Locke-Mortice, one of the country's top civil servants. He heads the Ministry Without Any Portfolios, no less. More to the point, he also chairs the National Security Council. If word of this leaks out, the press will be all over him like a rash. Stands to reason Whitehall want to keep the matter under wraps, so I'm under strict instructions to send my best officer to brush the affair under the carpet.'

'See what you mean, Bill,' Obafemi said. After eighteen years on the force, he knew the ropes like the back of his hand. 'Any idea where St. Mary Nook is? Never heard of the place.'

'Near Tunbridge Wells in Kent. But it's not about the where, Isaac. It is about the who.'

Inspector Obafemi gave his chin a pensive scratch. On the face of it, this seemed the kind of mundane murder hardly worth an inkblot in the local paper. Or it would, were it not for a nebulous connection to various nefarious security agencies. 'Right you are.' He tucked the folder under an arm. 'PC Bottomley is on maternity leave so I'll take Chambers.'

'No can do. We need to keep a low profile so you'll be flying solo. There are a couple of local coppers who can give you a hand. Looks an open and shut case, so I'm sure you'll have it wrapped up in no time. Oh, and Isaac . . .' Wheeler stood up, walked round the desk and placed a hand on Obafemi's shoulder. 'I don't need to tell you how sensitive this matter is, so be discreet. Nobody must know that New Scotland Yard is taking an interest. If anyone asks, say you're from Kent County Constabulary headquarters in Maidstone. They've agreed to cover for us.'

'I'll wear a shepherd's smock, suck a straw instead of my pipe and pass myself off as a local yokel. Say I've been out in the sun too long. Ooh-arrr,' Obafemi quipped.

But despite his scoffy repost, Detective Inspector Obafemi was intrigued - and with good reason. For with every new turn of the twist, he was to find that this hot potato, as Chief Inspector Wheeler had so earthily dismissed it, was far from being a damp spud. On the contrary, it was to prove the most baffling case the great detective would ever be called upon to crack.

3

Heather Prendergast licked a corner of her travelling handkerchief and scrubbed the kissage off her freckled cheeks - Guerlain KissKiss Candyapple Gold if she was not mistaken, or possibly Christian Louboutin Rouge Velvet Matte if she was. 'I must say, aunty,' she said as she re-shoulderbagged her waxy hanky, 'you're bearing up remarkably well in the circumstances.'

'Thank goodness you didn't see me earlier, my dear,' Lady Trevelyan said. 'I went completely to pieces. Let's just hope you can sort out your uncle's spot of bother before the press gets wind of it.' She stepped back and looked Heather over as if she were a daughter rather than a prodigal niece. 'But I can't begin to tell you how marvellous it is to see you. You have no idea how much I've missed you. And haven't you grown?' she said. 'You are the very image of my sister when she was your age. She was also a late developer.'

Having aired and graced her only niece, Lady Trevelyan turned to Naff and greeted him with an informal hug rather than a formal handshake. 'So you are the young man who has swept my darling niece off her feet,' she said with a twinkle in her eye. 'She is head over heels, don't you know? Gals tend to be at that age. Soon wears off.'

Naff frowned and tapped his chin. 'Ain't we met

before?' he said, stricken with a nagging sense of déjà vu.

'Possibly at Will and Kate's,' Lady Trevelyan suggested. 'Isn't Kate a sweetheart? For a commoner. We must forgive her lack of dress sense,' she said with a patronising smile. 'Or maybe we met at one of the Obama's little soirees. Don't you think Michelle is a heavenly cook? A little heavy-handed with the paprika perhaps, but rest assured I intend to have a quiet word next time she and her delightful husband come to stay.'

Ignoring Naff's blankety blink, Lady Trevelyan nodded at his motorbike. 'Ah, a nineteen sixty-nine Triumph Bonneville, if I am not mistaken,' she said. 'You must take me for a spin while you are here. Better still, give me the keys and I'll help meself.' Chuckling as Naff's jaw dropped, she shouted, 'Guany,' and a moment later a diminutive Chinese woman with a long black pigtail, side-slit mandarin-collared dress and breakneck heels padded out of the house.

Lady Trevelyan pointed to Heather's overnight case and clicked her fingers. 'Take my niece's things to the Blue Room, Guany. Chop, chop.' When Heather gave her a questioning look, she said, 'silly me, haven't introduced you. This is Guan-Yin, my new secretary. I took her on to translate my novels into Chinese but she hardly has a mo, what with organising the house, taking care of the alpacas and answering all my tiresome fan mail. Must say, I would be lost without her.'

Guan-Yin rested her hands on her thighs and bowed

her head. 'Lady Trevelyan revered in China,' she said. 'She who brings romance is the joy of the people. Is great honour to work for her.'

In response to Naff's raised eyebrows, Heather explained, 'Aunt Elizabeth writes novels under the pen name Melissa Moncrieff. You've probably heard of her.' The question was, of course, rhetorical. Moncrief's latest tear-jerker, The Proud, The Passionate and The Possessive, had been perched on top of True Fiction Weekly's best seller's list for months.

'A little hobby of mine, don't you know?' Lady Trevelyan told Naff modestly. 'I only wish Spielberg hadn't cast that ghastly American gal as Amelia Duggan in the film adaptation of Friends And Others. What was the silly old fool thinking? Can you honestly imagine that Lord Thomas would have fallen hopelessly in love with a serving wench with a whiny Brooklyn accent and platinum hair extensions?' She tossed her head in a righteous show of literary contempt. 'Last time Steven came to lunch, I suggested that he stick to directing mindless piffle about spacemen and fish. When I said that I had a good mind not to let him butcher any more of my scripts, he went down on his knees and begged me to reconsider. I do so hate to see a grown man cry, so I relented.' She gazed into an imagined distance and sighed. 'I suppose I'm just a soppy old softy at heart. But enough about me,' she said with a purposeful clap of the hands. 'You must be starving. Why don't I rustle up a quick snack? I am dying to hear what you have been up to.' She took Heather's arm and set off down a corridor talking nineteen to the dozen.

Naff followed at a distance, trying to work out where he had seen Lady Trevelyan before. Try as he might – and he tried with all his might - he hit a blank wall, so turned his mind to the here and now, particularly the here. Needless to say, he would have expected the mansion to be musty, dusty and crusty but nothing could be further from the fact. If called upon to express an opinion, in all likelihood he would have said that the decor was more Frank Lloyd Wright than clumpy tenpole Tudor. Modern and stylish was the word, or words, that came to mind.

When he joined Heather and her aunt in the kitchen, he was astonished to find another world, as newpin-bright and airy as the fabric of the house was olden daub and wattled. As large, if not a small bit larger, than his spacious open-plan loft apartment in Huddersford, he imagined the kitchen - or rather the main kitchen, for it was but one of several - would not have been out of place in a three-tyred Michelin restaurant. Oaken-floored with sunken ceiling-lights, much of one wall housed an extravagance of kitchenary appliances - ovens, hobs, refrigerations and deep freezers - and most of another homed a spoke of bespoke fitted kitchen units. To one far end of the other, a floor to ceiling picture window overlooked a spot-lit pond on a lawn the size of a football pitch. Teaming with ornamental carp, it boasted a floatilla of water lilies and a magnificent Rococo fountain bordered by a marbled balustrade colonised by screechy fan-tailed peacocks.

While Lady Trevelyan rustled up a quick snack, Naff sat down at the table, rocked back in his chair with his hands behind his head and stretched his legs to unwind them after the powerdash from London. 'So what you prefer I call you?' he asked as he watched Lady Trevelyan whisk essence of turmeric, clots of almond cream, a drizzle of veganitarian parsley-stock and a pinch of garlic-pepper into a hastily improvised sauce. 'Lady Trevelyan or Missus Locke-Mortice?'

'Please . . . I never use my husband's ghastly name. Sounds like a sexually communicable disease.' Lady Trevelyan shuddered at the very idea. 'Lady Elizabeth will do just fine,' she said. 'After all, you are virtually one of the family. Just be a good egg and don't get Spriggy pregnant. Now,' she clapped her hands. 'Autumn Green Risotto with Pear, Asparagus and Fennel do you?' she said in such a way as to suggest that it would be Autumn Green Risotto with Pear, Asparagus and Fennel or nothing. 'I grow everything meself, don't you know, although Guany gives me a hand when she has a mo.' She kissed the air and said, 'her beansprouts and water-chestnuts are to die for.'

As Lady Elizabeth bent over to put the risotto in the oven, Naff's eyes strayed to a framed photograph on the cheeserie - an incongruous splash of Hollywood glitz in the nouveau-kitchenary surrounds. 'Hey, that's from Die A Different Day, ain't it? It's me favourite James Bond movie.' Smirking like a smitten kitten, he gazed nostalgically at the image of Bond and his beautiful heroine walking out of the sea. 'Used to have a poster of the co-star, Veronika Vivendi, on me bedroom wall.' When Lady Elizabeth looked round and winked, he sat up, rubbed his eyes, did a double take and rubbed his eyes again. 'Hang about,' he said. 'Don't tell me that were you?'

'Well spotted, Simon. Veronika Vivendi is my stage name. If you must know, I did a bit of acting in my med school days.'

'To pay your way through college?'

'Great Scott, no. Daddy was filthy rich and spoilt me to death. I could twist him round my little finger. It was just a hobby, don't you know?' Lady Elizabeth flicked a wrist to suggest that starring in Hollywood blockbusters had merely been an adolescent dalliance. 'Sadly, I had to put my acting career on hold when I landed a neurosurgery post at the Royal Free Hospital. And when my ghastly brother-in-law parked little Spriggy on me after my sister died, I decided to give up the theatre. The operating theatre, I mean. I still do the occasional movie if I am offered a challenging role.' She gazed unseeing into the mists of time. 'Vanity, I suppose,' she said with a wistful sigh. 'I would rather like another Oscar. The one I have looks so sad all on his own in the servant's cloakroom.'

Her cookery duties done and peppered, Lady Elizabeth took off her pinafore, slung it on the back of a chair and decanted a bottle of vintage claret. She filled three glasses, handed one to Naff, another to Heather and helped herself to the third.

Heather took a sip and turned up her nose. To her way of taste, it was a little musty. Given a choice, she would have preferred a glass of sparkling something. But minded that wine sipping was not the primary purpose of her visit, she turned to her aunt and asked, 'so what exactly did Uncle Monty do?'

Lady Trevelyan stared into her glass, shook her head and said, 'that is what I need you to find out, my dear.'

4

Cramped though Detective Inspector Obafemi's office was – pokey would be another word, incommodious a third – it was the epitome of order, reflecting his fastidious persnicketiness. He detested sloppiness, abhorred messiness and despised slovenliness. Although some might dismiss the room as dingy, to his mind any and all shortcomings were outweighed by the near-proximity of the staff canteen. And in that his legendary appetite for work was only matched by a legendary appetite for all things fried, boiled, baked, fricasseed, stewed or poached, he spent almost as much time in the cafeteria as he did at his desk.

It might have been his imagination - he imagined that it probably was - but Inspector Obafemi had a sneaking suspicion that catering standards had slipped somewhat of late. Embarrassingly for a detective of his standing, he could not quite work out quite why. However, he had a gut hunch that the culinary plummet had coincided with the arrival of a new kitchenary assistant, a pretty young redhead with a trim figure and a humourless disposition. Admittedly, topping the rice pudding with black pepper instead of nutmeg was the kind of mistake that any novice might make. But adding prunes and Senokot to the lamb curry? His stomach churned at thoughts of the inedible mush and the unedifying aftermash.

There was something about the new girl that reminded Obafemi of his younger self. An eager curiosity, perhaps, coupled with an air of brash self-confidence that bordered on arrogance. But although PC Disasterzone - as the new canteen assistant had been monikered by her colleagues - held herself a cut above her fellow kitchenery minions, she was the last person at The Yard he would dream of turning to for advice on the dish of the day. Despite that, he had developed a sneaking regard for her devotion to duty; he found her dedication to her menial job laudable. And if shove came to push, he had to admit that on occasion she brightened his day, albeit unwittingly. He allowed himself a subtle chuckle as he recalled the time she tripped over a bootlace and emptied a jug of piping hot custard into Bill Wheeler's lap. The Chief Inspector might not have been amused but everybody else was, particularly when PC Disasterzone vociferously insisted that Wheeler only had himself to blame for being in the wrong place at the wrong time.

In recent months the inhouse catering had proved a boon as Obafemi rarely went home these days. It wasn't so much that he and Sandra no longer saw eye to eye as that they rarely saw one another's eyes at all, and when they did, they didn't speak other than an occasional grunt. Indeed, when Chief Superintendent Wheeler asked if Sandra could spare him for a few days, he felt like suggesting that Wheeler contact her solicitor.

A private man, Obafemi kept his work at arm's length from his dyslexic domestic life. It wasn't that he no longer cared for Sandra but rather that she despised his lack of ambition, his workaholic tendencies and his easygo attitude towards their marriage. To be brutally frank - and frankness was Inspector Obafemi's stock in trade - he welcomed a chance to escape the cacophonic chaos of London and do some serious thinking about his life. Nevertheless, he regretted that the murder hadn't taken place in Brighton or Bournemouth. From what little he knew, rural Kent was the last place on earth he would be likely to meld in with the retired snoots and misforgotten snobs who populated the sleepy backwaters of commuterland.

Inspector Obafemi sat down at his desk, shuffled an overflow of tiresome paperwork aside, booted up his computer and onlined train timetables. In his assistant's absence - she was currently on maternity leave but hoped to return as soon as the triplets were born - he would have delegated the task to the team's junior detective. However, following the ambitious young bootlicker's promotion to the Organised Grime Squad, that was no longer an option. Needless to say, he was keeping an eye out for a suitable replacement but his standards were impeccably high and to date none of the applicants had passed his muster. Until he found the right cog to crank into his demanding wheel, he was resigned to the fact that if he wanted something doing, he must do it himself.

He was pleasantly surprised to find that St. Mary Nook was on the direct line from London to Brighton, although not all trains stopped at the small station. He would need to catch what was colloquially known as the Ordinary rather than the Mainline Express, an hourly service departing from St Pancras Station. Accordingly, he booked an early morning reservation and settled back to think. He kept a clean shirt, a change of underwear, a toothbrush and a razor in a suitcase in the office as of late he slept there more often than he didn't. After leaving a message on Sandra's voicemail to say that he would see her when he saw her so don't wait up – as if she would – he put his feet up on the desk, closed his eyes and nodded off. And why not?

Detective Inspector Obafemi was famed for solving the most difficult cases in his sleep and had little doubt that this would be a slice of cake.

5

Lady Elizabeth topped up Naff's glass and dribbled the last few drops into her own. She propped her elbows on the table, cupped her chin in her hands, gazed into his eyes and asked, 'so what is the verdict?' although if his plate was anything to go by, the answer went without asking. 'I have a confession to make,' she said with a mirkish smirk. 'You are a guinea pig. It was an experimental recipe for my new cookery book. Vegan Cordon Bleu for Beginners. I wasn't sure whether I had overdone the Essence of Fragrance in the balsamic sauce.'

'What, you mean you made this up yesself?' Naff gave her a sceptical look. 'You're pulling me leg,' he said. 'It were ten out of ten. Eleven, even.'

Heather narrowed her eyes at her aunt as if to say, go easy on the booze . . . and keep your hands off my boyfriend. 'Didn't I tell you?' she told Naff in such a way as to leave him in no doubt that she was keeping a tether eye on him. 'My old aunt writes cookery books.'

'I would hardly call twenty-five old, Spriggy,' Lady Elizabeth said with a syrupy smile.

'Aunty, you have been twenty-five since *forever*,' Heather pointed out as diplomatically as she knew how.

'You would do well to bear in mind that age is just a

number, my child. A state of mind.' Lady Elizabeth told her with a note of saccharine aloof.

Sensing a glacial chill in the air, Naff tacked the conversation onto balmier waters. 'You write cookbooks, Lady Elizabeth?'

'Just a little hobby of mine, don't you know? Keeps me out of mischief,' Lady Elizabeth said with a throaty chuckle. 'Must say, the Bethany Baker Culinary Cuisine series has proved a spectacular success. Mediterranean Meals for Vegans has been reprinted six times, would you believe? Flies off the shelves almost as fast as Irish Vegan Cuisine for Beginners. Not that there is much you can do with a potato, a sprig of seaweed and a knob of rapeseed lard. Still, eco-friendly millennials love that kind of twaddle,' she said with a condescending smile. 'More wine?' Without caring for an answer, she shouted, 'Guany, be a treasure and fetch another bottle of the decent vintage from the cellar. Chop, chop,' She ratcheted her tipsy gaze at Naff and said, 'you must tell me all about yourself, Simon. Life, loves, dreams. Don't hold anything back. Start with how you met my niece. You must be extremely proud of her. A detective at New Scotland Yard, no less, and only twenty-one.' She looked at Heather from the corner of an eye. 'Whoever would have thought it? She used to be such a dreamer.'

'Heather telled you she was a detective?' Naff gave his girlfriend a sideways look. He cleared his throat and embarked upon an altogether different truth. 'Yeah, well,' he said, 'see, the thing is . . .'

'Guany, you clumsy oaf.' Lady Elizabeth leapt up from her chair when Guan-Yin knocked over her glass while trying to uncork a fresh bottle of brainfuddle. 'Just look what you've done, you chump.' She stripped off her sodden blouse, handed it to Guan-Yin and said, 'fetch me something clean to wear and be quick about it.'

Scandalised beyond the bounds of all decorum by her aunt's brazen barechestedness, Heather hissed, 'aunty, behave,' and averted her eyes.

But rather than spare her niece's blushes, Lady Elizabeth winked at Naff and said, 'you don't mind, do you, Simon? Dare say you have seen plenty of naked flesh in your time,' with an expression of virtual-virtue. When his face turned an acute shade of embarrassment, she threw back her head and roared with laughter. 'Anyway, as I was about to say,' she slurred between sips of inhibition uninhibitant, 'my pathetic excuse for a husband has rather blotted his copybook. To cut to the chase, seems he was involved in some kind of fracas on the Ordinary Express. The local constabulary are making a right old song and dance about it. Ah, thank you, Guany,' she said as her personal assistant returned with a clean blouse.

Naff pinched himself to make sure he wasn't dreaming. A few hours ago he had been arguing with his girlfriend in her cramped bedsitting flat in downtown Crouch End. But now, unless he had died and gone to bliss, he was chilling in the kitchen of a stately home after wolfing down a cordon-bleu meal cooked by an Oscar-winning former sex-kitten who used to be his fantasy pin-up. Actually, if lust be told, in his more bloodredded moments, she remained his standby fantasy, and in all bestiality probably always would. Age had not withered her nor custom staled her infinite allure. He looked from Lady Elizabeth to Heather, for a moment imagining them sisters rather than guardian aunt and niece. Dry of throat and shy of eye, he croaked, 'what you mean, song and dance?'

Seemingly unaware of Naff's bulging eyes – seemingly being the pre-emptive presumptive – Lady Elizabeth explained, 'PC Plod is keeping Monty in custody overnight. I have been trying to contact his solicitor but I'm told he is currently in Tunbridge Wells Infirmary,' she said as she buttonupped the rescue blouse and fussed her luxuriant tumbles of long red hair over her slim shoulders. 'Still, I'm sure it is all a ghastly mistake. My husband wouldn't hurt a fly. He wouldn't dare.'

'You said Uncle Monty has been arrested for murder,' Heather said. 'Do the police have any evidence?'

'Hardly,' Lady Elizabeth scoffed. 'But they don't need any, do they? For goodness' sake, you are a member of the profession so you must know better than anyone that if you give the plebs an inch, they will take a mile.'

'So there's no actual evidence as such?' Naff asked, more in hope than expectation.

'Nothing to speak of. The wretched little man wouldn't

say boo to a goose. You only have to look at him to see that he is no more capable of stabbing anyone in the back than Guany is. And the silly woman faints at the sight of red nail varnish, never mind blood. More wine?' Lady Elizabeth ignored her niece's scowl and topped up Naff's glass with another injudicious measure of hangover accelerant. 'I am rather hoping that you can pull rank and tell the local constabulary to stop wasting everyone's time,' she said. 'I am more than happy to make a modest contribution to the police benevolent fund if the authorities turn a blind eye. How much would you suggest, Simon? A hundred thousand pounds, or should I say guineas?' she asked in all apparent innocence. 'So, can you two take care of the formalities or should I telephone the Home Secretary and come to a mutually agreeable arrangement? His wife was my best friend at school, don't you know? Ghastly woman. Common as muck. I am given to understand that her father was something in the city. A nouveau riche pleb, I wouldn't wonder, or a street sweeper. Much the same thing, really. I ask you, what is the world coming to?' she said with a despairing shake of the head.

By now little more than a passenger on her aunt's befuddled train of thought, Heather raised a hand to stifle a yawn. The long and winding day had taken a toll on her flagging energy reserves. 'Let's discuss it in the morning,' she said. 'I'm bushed.' She reached for Naff's arm. 'Come on, darling.'

'Be with you soon as I've done the dishes.' Naff drained his glass, gave his stomach a pat and set about clearing the table. But as was so often the case when his hormones went jogging, his selfless willing masked a hidden agenda. By offering Lady Elizabeth a hand, he hoped to ingratiate himself into her favours as a precursor to ingratiating himself somewhere else entirely.

'Don't be so politically correct, young man.' Misinterpreting Naff's offer to help as an offer to help, Lady Elizabeth said, 'that is woman's work. Let Guany do it. You two love-birds could do with an early night. Feel free to exercise the bedsprings to your heart's content. There is no one in the room next door.' She blew them each a kiss as they headed for the door, arm in arm.

Naff paused midway up the broadoak staircase to look down at the loomy entrance hall with its hub of spokey corridors leading to the far flung wings. 'Bit different from your bedsit in Crouch End, ain't it, honey?' he said as if Heather didn't know, which she most certainly did.

'Oh, do get a move on, darling. I'm whacked,' Heather said irritably as she chivvied Naff up the last few stairs to the first floor landing. She led the way to their allotted guestroom and, beaming with pride, opened the door and gestured to the many splendored things within - a medieval French tapestry pressed into service as a throw on the chaise longue, an emperor-sized four-poster bed, a rosewood Chippendale tallboy, smallboy and matching crawlboy, several dreary ancestral portraits and a plethora of other Trevelyan family heirlooms, including a priceless blue antique Isfahan carpet to which the room owed its name. 'We're honoured,' she said. 'Aunty usually reserves the Blue Room for royalty. Believe it or not, King Charles once slept here.'

'Hope he changed the sheets,' Naff quipped as he followed Heather in. 'Stone the crows,' he gasped. 'It's near as not big as Wembley Stadium.' He crossed to the window and looked down at the floodlit pond. 'Bet the view is spectacular at dawn,' he said. 'Just as well I bought me camera.'

But Heather wasn't listening. She was already in the ensuite shower. 'Pass me a towel, darling.' She reached through the door and double clicked her fingers.

'So what's with your uncle?' Naff asked as he attended to his girlfriend's towelitary requestments. 'Bit of a Jack the lad, is he?'

Heather raised her voice to be heard above the billowing steam. 'You must be joking. He is the most innocuous little man you could hope to meet, though to be fair I hardly know him,' she said as she emerged from the shower togaed and turbaned from hair to toe in monogrammed towels. She sat down on the far side of the bed and as she dried her long hair, explained, 'Aunt Elizabeth packed me off to boarding school when I was eleven so I only saw Uncle Monty at weekends during the school hols. He stays over at one of Aunty's Westminster townhouses during the week.'

'What's he do?'

Heather shrugged. 'To be honest, I'm not really sure. High up in the civil service, I think, but he never talks about his work. He's very security conscious. His passion is collecting.'

'Let me guess,' Naff said with an infantile grin. 'Stamps?'

'Train timetables,' Heather said, puzzled why Naff should be smirking like a virtual turtle. 'He has pretty much every Great Western regional timetable since the year dot and knows them all by heart. Can't recall him having any other interests except clay pigeon shooting. Come to think, that's how he met Aunty.'

'On a shooting range?'

'No. At the Olympics. He was managing the English clay pigeon team and she was competing in the show jumping. Or was it dressage? Both maybe. I forget. It's a bit of a sore point actually, so please don't let on that I told you. She retired in disgust because she only won two bronze medals. Not that she claims to care. It seems that equestrianism was . . .'

'Just a hobby, don'tchya know?' Naff said in a crude parrotry of Lady Elizabeth's cultured accent.

Heather flung a sopping towel at him. 'You are an evil, evil man, Simon Robinson,' she giggled. 'That is so cruel.'

'Any hot water left?' Naff asked over his shoulder as he headed for the shower. 'So your uncle don't have no hobbies to speak of except train timetables.' He struggled to keep a straight face.

'I think he used to collect antique weaponry,' Heather said. 'I'm not sure.' Unaware that Naff was staring at her with his mouth wide open, she flopped down on the four-poster bed, stretched her arms in the grandmother of all yawns, snuggleupped beneath the duvet, closed her eyes and drifted into default dreams of a glittering career as Prendergast of The Yard.

6

Detective Inspector Obafemi sat down on a rustic bench to take the weight off his bunions - an occupational hazard in his line of work. As was his habit when in a thinking mood of mind, he packed his pipe with roughcut shag, lit up, took a few relaxing puffs and sat back pondering the vicissitudes of life.

He allowed his thoughts to idle as he watched The Ordinary Express locomotive from St. Mary Nook Station, if two brickconcrete platforms and a ticket vending machine could be so described. In days gone by, he suspected, the neatly flower-bedded rail-tweezer would have branded itself St. Mary Halt, or words to that effect. Although not a pedant, he took pride in his command of language and spoke several fluently, including French and his mother's native tongue of Welsh.

Obafemi accepted that he was overqualified for an officer of his middling rank. As his wife never tired of reminding him, not many coppers have a postgraduate degree in Medieval English Literature. Still, not by nature an ambitious sort, he was content with his lot. His clear-up rate was such that, by and large, he was granted free rein to plough his own furrow in the criminal pastures of the great metropolis. Although the powers on high regarded him as a throwback to a plodding age, what mattered was results, and in that respect he rarely disappointed.

Obafemi was old school and proud of it. The tools of his trade were legwork, experience and an uncanny sixth sense when it came to humankind. No fan of modern technology, if he wanted information, he asked and could tell by the shift of the eyes if someone was telling the truth. To his way of thinking, old-fashioned common sense and gut instinct stood the test of time and always would, whereas computers were a passing fad. Who remembers the Antikythera Mechanism or Charles Babbage's Difference Engine was his stock response whenever Chief Superintendent Wheeler suggested that he take the Metropolitan Police Information Technology refresher course. That said, if need be - and needs often must - he could find his way around a computer if he had to, as long as nobody was looking. Having learned to type on a pre-century golfball typewriter, his heavy-handed two-fingered technique left much to be admired.

Stoically resigned to being out of step with the digital age, Inspector Obafemi scrunched out his pipe and slipped it into into a pocket. He picked up his suitcase and set off at a leisurely pace to find his lodgings, of a mind to knuckle down to work as soon as he had unpacked.

From what he could see, St. Mary Nook was picture-postcard picturesque. The sum total of the chocolatebox village amounted to a couple of dozen half-timbered houses overlooking a narrow street. He imagined that most would have been modernised to satisfy the all-mod-con requirements of day-return commuters. Recreationary activities would doubtless be confined to the golf course where the menfolk would regurgitate the same-old-same-old over a snifter at the nineteenth hole. Meanwhile, their wives would sozzle themselves to a stupor in the fitted kitchen of a dream home that had become a lonely, lingering Stepford-stone to dementia or, for the lucky ones, an acrimonious but alimonious divorce.

According to his assiduous researches - and Inspector Obafemi was nothing if not assiduous - St. Mary Nook's one and only shop served as a post office, a grocery provisioner and, of late, a fancy delicatessen. The village pub, The Crossed Arms, afforded accommodation for the occasional visitor. Its restaurant received regular plaudits in Sunday colour supplements, in no small part because the landlord had perfected the art of getting journalists drunk before serving them traditional Kent fare such as pate de foie gras, fillet mignon, spaghetti arrabiata and couscous. To cater for the coarser pallets of a handful of generational locals, the public bar offered ploughman's lunches, farmer's loaves, poacher's pie and, in season, peasant's pheasant. Other than the railway station, a shop, a church, a pint-sized cafe and the pub, the only notable amenity of note was a small community police station. A breezeblock eyesore incongruously shoehorned between two half-timbered dwellings, he was given to understand that it comprised a receptionary, various miscellany stores, an interview room and two cells housed in a prefabricated annex abutting a pig farm at the rear. According to Chief Inspector Wheeler, the police station was manned by a Sergeant Burt Gummidge, a local man of questionable age, and a single policeman, or rather a singular policewoman, PC Samantha Ingham.

Obafemi found The Crossed Arms without much ado. He could hardly not. The foursquare redbricked building stood out from its half-timbered neighbours like a poker in a pack of jokers. He waited patiently in reception while the man behind the counter scraped grime off his fingernails. After what seemed an age, the receptionist looked up, scowled and returned his attention to his dishygienic nail proclivities.

'Excuse me,' Inspector Obafemi said with a personable smile. 'I reserved a room.'

'Not here, you didn't,' receptionman grunted without looking up.

'Think you'll find I'm in the book.' Obafemi nodded at the reservation diary.

'Not any more, you're not.' Receptionman scored a thick line through Obafemi's name with a felt tipped pen. 'The girl must have made a mistake. I was thinking of letting her go, anyway. Try down the road.'

'Ah, I get it,' Obafemi said as an all too familiar penny dropped. 'It's because I'm black, isn't it?'

'Can't say I noticed.'

'Need some identification?' Obafemi took out his wallet and showed the man his warrant card.

Receptionman gave it a quick look, unhooked a telephone from the countertop and nine-nine-nined a number. 'Burt,' he said. 'Got a comedian here impersonating a copper. Better come quick.' Hardly had he put down the phone than the door burst open and an elderly policeman in a shabby sergeant's uniform strode in, brandishing a truncheon. He balanced a pair of spectacles on the knobble of his nose, squinted at Obafemi, barked, 'all right, son. Let's be having you,' and cocked a thumb at the door.

Obafemi looked the uniformed knobsworth up and down and tapped his chin. 'You must be Sergeant Gummidge,' he said, 'or should I say, ex-Sergeant Gummidge.'

At that moment, or possibly a moment later, a young PC raced in, puffing and panting. 'Sarge,' she wheezed. 'You best tidy up reception and take down that flag of Saint George. Just had a call from Maidstone. They're sending a bigwig to head up the murder enquiry. He's got a funny name. Inspector Obi-something.'

'Inspector Obafemi?' Obafemi suggested.

'Crickey.' The young officer sprang to attention and tipped her cap. 'PC Ingham, sir. Let me know if there's anything I can do for you.'

'You can start by explaining the Race Relations Act to the bigot on reception. If he doesn't get it, read him his rights. That goes for Sergeant Gummidge too.' Inspector

Obafemi picked up his suitcase, helped himself to a pigeonholed room key and headed for the stairs. His parting words were, 'see you at the station. We could do with a word.'

Heather Prendergast surfaced from her slumbers with the hebetude of a slowdiver. For a time she lay on her back with her eyes closed listening to a feathery chorus tweetering in the cedar tree outside the bedroom window. It brought back memories of her first day at Trevelyan Hall when, as a teary ten-year-old, she had been taken in by her aunt after her mother died and her father, Sir Freddie Prendergast, disowned her like a peckless parrot.

Kind and caring though her aunt had been, Heather had missed her mother every second of every minute of every hour of every day. The only rock the anchorless teenager found to cling onto was a dream of future fame and glory as Prendergast of The Yard, the most renowned detective the world would ever see. And still the dream remained undimmed. As did the yearning for her mother

She reached out to smuggle an arm around her boyfriend but drew a pillowed blank. After a thorough fumble, she sat up, rubbed her eyes and glanced at the bedside clock. 'Golly,' she gasped, alarmed to see that the clockwork ticktock mechanism had wound down to a slack. But then she breathed a sigh of relief as she remembered that her aunt rarely went to bed before lark rising and seldom rose before midday. It reminded her of one of Lady Elizabeth's oft-repeated sayings . . . "If early to bed and early to rise makes a man healthy, wealthy and wise, why is my wretched husband so feeble, impecunious and moronic?"

Whereas Heather's uncle-in-law went to bed at nine and was at his desk by crow of dawn, Lady Elizabeth claimed to be at her most productive during the wee-small hours. Heather suspected that this explained her prodigosity. And her childless marriage. The thought of a fleshy grey skeleton of vacuous impersonality trampolining on her aunt did not bear thinking about . . . which is why she tried not to bear thinking about it. Ever.

When she saw that Naff's leather jacket was nowhere to be seen, Heather assumed that he had slipped out to photoarticulate the dawn. Feeling wonderfully relaxed, she rolled out of bed, showered and wandered downstairs for a late breakfast.

'Ah, there you are.' Lady Elizabeth gestured for Heather to take a seat at the breakfast table. 'Sleep well?' she asked.

Heather rubbed her eyes and yawned. 'Like a log, thanks, aunty. Must be the country air.'

'I am so pleased you came. I have missed you awfully. I only wish the circumstances were different.' Lady Elizabeth stiffed her upper lip in a show of resolute resolve. 'Must say, Simon is quite a catch,' she said. 'Do you intend to live in sin or tie the knot?'

'Please, aunty,' Heather said with a rosebud blush. 'I only met him a few months ago. I hardly know him.'

'I have been married to your uncle for thirteen years and still wouldn't say that I know him. Not as such. I thought I did, but . . .' Lady Elizabeth braved a smile. 'Vegan sausages and curdled beansprouts do you?' Without waiting for an answer, she poked her head through the door and shouted, 'breakfast, Guany. Chop, chop.'

A moment later, a pinafored Guan-Yin padded through the door carrying a tray, followed by Naff with a camera slung over a shoulder. He draped his leather jacket on the back of a chair and sat down next to Lady Elizabeth. 'Took a wander down the village to score some backy,' he said. 'Not exactly matey, are they? The locals. Anyone would think I were from Mars or somewhere.' His smile was more of a grimace than a smile as such. 'Saw that woman copper with the attitude so made mesself scarce. Still, got some cool snaps in the woods down by the tennis court. Some of them old oaks must go back forever.'

'My niece tells me that you are a talented photographer when you are not setting the world to rights, Simon.' Lady Elizabeth gave Naff an overfamiliar pat on the hand. 'Photography is a little hobby of mine, don't you know? You may have seen some of my holiday snaps in National Geographic magazine. If you can spare a mo after you have sorted out my husband's spot of bother, you must give me some tips. Now eat up. You have a long day ahead of you.'

Needless to say, Lady Elizabeth monopolised the breakfast conversation with a running docucommentary about her life, her little hobbies, herself, her times, her thoughts, her little hobbies, herself, herself and most of all, herself. When she eventually paused for breath, Heather asked, 'can you tell us about Uncle Montague's run-in with the police?'

Lady Elizabeth stared out of the window at a peckhopper on the lawn and, after a long few moments, said, 'ah, yes. Monty. From what I understand, he is due to be interviewed today under caution. Thankfully his solicitor is back at work. He phoned this morning to say that Monty should be released on bail while the police make further enquiries.' She took a sip of freerange coffee and gazed into a distance of abstraction. 'It is all a bit of a puzzle, really,' she said. 'From what I have been told, Monty was sitting in his usual seat in the first class compartment of the Ordinary Express, happily minding his own business when the chap in front of him keeled over. Dead as a dodo.'

Heather exchanged a glance with Naff. 'Dead, eh? Don't mind if I take a few notes.' She unshoulderbagged her offduty pocketbook, wrote DEAD on the first page in capital letters and underscored it several times. 'Last night you said the police claimed to have evidence that Uncle Monty was responsible.'

Lady Elizabeth batted Heather's frown into the long grass with a flick of the wrist. 'Purely circumstantial,' she said. 'Monty's fingerprints on the knife, the victim's blood on his suit, opportunity, a few witnesses - that kind of thing. Hardly what one would call evidence. Not as such.' She arched an eyebrow when she saw Naff run a finger across his throat. 'I say, is that a problem?'

'Ain't the best news I had all day, Lady Elizabeth,' he told her. 'So what's with these witnesses you said about?'

'No idea. I expect the police fabricated them. Par for the course in cases like this, Monty's solicitor assures me.'

Heather sat on the edge of her seat, pocketbook on knee, and poised her pencil. 'So who was the victim?'

'Ah, yes. Him.' Lady Elizabeth pushed her cup away and dabbed her lips with a monogrammed serviette. 'Some kind of colonial. He was staying at The Crossed Arms. Quite the nosy parker by all accounts. Always poking his nose into other people's business. Other than that, he seems to have kept himself to himself. Nobody knows a thing about him. The local wags used to call him the Isnot Man.'

'Guess that makes him the Wasnot Man now,' Naff muttered.

Despite her boyfriend's lame attempt at quippery, something in Heather's waters told her that her uncle-in-law was going to need all the help he could get.

If not more.

8

Detective Inspector Obafemi stepped across the threshold of the small community police station and caught his breath. To say that he was lost for words would hardly be over-egging the nog. Paint was peeling off the walls, the skirting boards were colonised by spiders the size of crabs, the front counter sagged in the middle of both ends and every other carpet tile looked to have been miss-laid.

When she saw Obafemi standing in the doorway with a thunderous glower on his face, PC Ingham stood nervously to attention and said, 'wasn't expecting you so soon, guv. Haven't had time to tidy up.'

'Tidy up?' Inspector Obafemi said, hardly able to believe his eyes. 'This sorry excuse for a police station needs blowing up.'

'Suppose it is a bit scruffy. Sarge has booked Murphy to sort it soon as he's free,' PC Ingham explained sheepishly. ''Fraid it don't work, guv,' she said when Inspector Obafemi tried the light switch. 'Hasn't done since don't know when.'

'You're waiting for Murphy to fix it, I suppose.'

Ingham shuffled on the spot and swallowed. 'As it happens, guv, you're not wrong. How did you know?'

'Just a wild stab in the dark,' Obafemi said punnily

as he looked up at the missing lightbulb. 'So who is this Murphy, anyway, when he's at home?

'The local handyman, guv. Thing is, he's not at home. He's serving a six-year stretch in Wormwood Scrubs for Grievous Bodily Harm. A farmer tried to pay him by cheque.'

'Rest assured, I will be having a few words in a few ears when I'm done here. Never seen anything like it in my life,' Obafemi said. 'Fetch the Mathers' File. Oh, and would you make me a cup of tea?'

'I'll send out for one, guv. '

'Suppose the kettle is broken.'

'No, sir. Works like a charm. It's the electrics.'

Inspector Obafemi cast a despairing eye around the dilapidated receptionary. He took off his jacket, draped it over the back of a chair, removed his cufflinks and rolled up his sleeves. 'Ah, Sergeant,' he said as Gummidge wandered in from the annex with his shirt tails hanging out. 'Might I ask what you were playing at earlier? I have a good mind to report your prejudiced behaviour.'

'With respect, sir.' The words grated in Gummidge's craw like a grind of rind. 'I find the suggestion that I'm prejudiced highly offensive. I will have you know that I been racially profiling foreigners since before you were born.'

'I will pretend that I didn't hear that, Sergeant. Anyway,

what makes you think I'm a foreigner?'

'Don't give me that, Sonny. Just look at you.'

'And what exactly is that supposed to mean?'

'Just stating the obvious, that's all.'

'Rest assured, I will see to it that you are sent for diversity training as soon as I've wrapped up this case.'

'Oh, really? Well let me tell you,' Gummidge told Obafemi with a jut of his bristly jaw, 'folk round here don't take kindly to outsiders pushing them around. This is Kent, not Kentucky.'

PC Ingham fidgeted with her cuffs, studiously avoiding Obafemi's eyes. 'Sarge don't mean it, guv.'

'Oh yes I do. Every word,' Gummidge said. 'It's bad enough they let women in the force, let alone the likes of you. No wonder we get pandemics.'

Inspector Obafemi took a deep breath to simmerdown his temper. 'Make no mistake, I will be drawing attention to your antediluvian attitudes in my official report,' he told the unrepentant Gummidge.

'Well make sure you tell the Head Squaw I'm English born and bred. Never been to Antediluvia in me life. Boris was right. Europe should stay where it belongs, and you can put that in your clay pipe and smoke it,' Gummidge grunted as he propped his elbows on the front desk and proceeded to roll a cigarette.

Determining that the sooner the better he could escape these Godforsaken backwoods, Inspector Obafemi turned to the task in hand. 'PC Ingham, I would like you to assist me with the investigation,' he said. 'One homicide on this patch is enough.' He narrowed an eye at Sergeant Gummidge. 'From what I've read, this is an open and shut case. Make no bones about it, Locke-Mortice is our man.' He made an effort to smile. 'The name sounds like an affliction, doesn't it?'

'And you're calling me a bigot, son.' In a remarkable act of multitasking, Sergeant Gummidge took a drag on his cigarette and sneered at one and the same time. 'There were Locke-Mortices in these parts when your lot were living up trees.' He tossed the fag-end on the floor and stubbed it out with a slipper. 'Best keep your head down, Inspector Mumbojumbo,' he said. 'Property prices in the village will take a tumble if word gets out you're here.'

It had been that kind of a day, Obafemi told himself, and it wasn't yet noon. His tummy grumbled whenever he sat down, stood up or paced the room,, struggling to hold his temper in check. The one glimmer of light in this otherworld of unremitting gloom was PC Ingham. Bright, breezy and efficient - if a little officious, as in his experience young officers often were - she took it upon her broad shoulders to make him feel at home. She cleared a space in a box room, rigged a makeshift desk and arranged for a hearty lunch to be delivered from the pub.

On the other hand, Sergeant Gummidge was gringiness

preamplified. He lapsed into a taciturn, not to say a surly, reticence, and on the rare occasion he deigned to acknowledge Obafemi, it was with a snide aside a hair's breadth from a slur. It came as no surprise that his one and only smile that morning was prompted by Obafemi's request that PC Ingham assist with the murder enquiry, leaving him to attend to the day to day duties of a chirpy-chappie village bobby. But first things first . . . Inspector Obafemi asked Ingham to sit in on the interview with the suspect.

Sergeant Gummidge showed Montague Locke-Mortice and his solicitor, Barry Mason, into the interview room. Locke-Mortice looked nervously around, mopped his brow and sat down opposite Obafemi. Mason chose to stand. In truth, he had little choice. Supported by two crutches, he was wearing a rigid neck brace, the result of a fracturous encounter with an ambulance he had been chasing. By all accounts, he had a narrow escape as the driver reversed at top speed in an attempt to run him down.

'Please be advised that this interview is being recorded.' Inspector Obafemi told Locke-Mortice. 'When you are ready, Officer Ingham.' He checked his watch. 'The time is thirteen hundred hours. Present are . . .'

Ingham leant over and whispered, 'a word in your ear, guv. We've not got a tape recorder. Sarge lent it to the Bowls Club for karaoke nights when theirs broke. They're waiting for Murphy to fix it.'

Annoyed though hardly surprised, Obafemi cleared his throat. 'On second thoughts, I will have PC Ingham take notes,' he said. 'Your solicitor can sign them after the interview.' As Ingham poised her pen, he told Locke-Mortice, 'if you are quite ready, I would like to ask you a few questions. Would you care for a glass of water?'

Mason prodded Locke-Mortice in the back and whispered, 'say no comment.'

Inspector Obafemi fixed the lawyer with a steely glare, then turned to Locke-Mortice. 'Now, according to the statement you gave Sergeant Gummidge . . .' He tapped the casefile. 'You caught the Ordinary Express from St. Pancras and occupied your usual seat in the first-class compartment. When the train pulled into St. Mary Nook Station, the passenger in front of you was dead. Run over the sequence of events again, if you would.'

'As I told your Sergeant, I was asleep and didn't see a thing. Can I go now?' Locke-Mortice gave Obafemi the look of a puppy dog accused of snaffling a Sunday roast that was still in the oven. 'My solicitor spoke to my good lady wife this morning. She is beside herself, isn't she, Mister Mason?'

'No comment,' Mason said.

Inspector Obafemi leant forward, propped his elbows on the table, bridged his hands and knotted his fingers. 'Now, apart from you and the victim – a Mister Trevor Mathers – you said there were three other passengers in

47

the first-class compartment.

Locke-Mortice nodded. 'That's right. Reverend Bragg, Colonel Dangerfield and Miss Decora.'

'Would that be Elouise Decora, the newspaper columnist?' Needless to say, Obafemi recognised the name. Decora's bigoted diatribes in The Sunday Rant scandalised all right-thinking left-leaning people. To call her opinions fair-minded would be akin to describing Homer Simpson as erudite.

As he turned the page, Obafemi noticed that Locke-Mortice was sweating. Concerned that he might be suffering a panic attack, he asked, 'would you like a cup of tea?' and scowled when Mason tapped his client on the shoulder and whispered, *no comment*. Keen to press on, he said, 'very well, maybe you can tell me how your fingerprints came to be on the murder weapon and why there was blood on your suit?'

Before Locke-Mortice could answer, Mason said, 'my client tried to pull the knife out of the victim's back. Jolly public spirited of him, I would have thought.'

Inspector Obafemi glowered at the smug solicitor. 'Mister Mason, would you please let your client speak for himself?'

'No comment,' Mason said with a shrug, then fingered his neck brace and grimaced.

'I tried to pull the knife out of the chap's back,' Locke-

Mortice said and mopped his brow. 'I am the pubic-spirited sort.'

'Are you quite sure you don't want a drink?' Inspector Obafemi asked, concerned that Locke-Mortice's face was growing pastier by the minute.

'I say, old chap, jolly decent of you.' Mason stuck up a thumb. 'I'll have a Scotch and soda. Make it a double. Gummidge knows how I take it,' he said. 'So how about a plea-bargain?'

'How about a what?' Inspector Obafemi stared at the solicitor, stunned by the man's brazen brass-neckedness.

Mason propped his crutches on the desk, sat down, crossed his legs and twiddled his thumbs. 'I'm not supposed to be able to flex my back,' he said, 'so if that chap from the insurance company comes sniffing around, be a good sport and tell him I screamed every time I moved.' He gave his nose another tap. 'Right you are, let's get down to brass tacks.' He leant forward and lowered his voice. 'Strictly off the record, my client's wife is prepared to make a modest contribution to the police benevolent fund if you reduce the charge to Sleeping Without Due Care and Attention. She is also prepared to donate ten thousand pounds to an offshore account of your choosing as a mark of appreciation for your diligence. Doesn't need a receipt. To be frank, she would rather not have any paperwork. Scratch her back and she'll scratch yours, know what I mean?' Taken aback when, too stunned for words, Inspector Obafemi glared at him, he gulped and said, 'dreadfully sorry, Inspector. Please accept my profound apologies for propositioning you in such a disrespectful manner. What was I thinking?' He cleared an awkward tickle from his throat, glanced about and whispered, 'I mean, ten grand will hardly cover a night out at a casino with a hooker, what with inflation, the price of tea in China and all. How about twenty? Thirty? Sixty? Why don't we call it a hundred - that's a nice round figure, wouldn't you say? And if you forget all about it and drop the charges, my client's wife will throw in an all-expenses paid holiday on her luxury yacht in the Caribbean with an accommodating young lady, no strings attached - unless you have a thing for bondage. Can't say fairer than that, can I?' he said with a nod and a wink. 'Come on, old boy, don't be shy. I'm on commission and my client's wife is hardly strapped for cash. Fact is, she's got more than she knows what to do with.'

'Where exactly did you study law, Mister Mason?' Obafemi asked with all the good natured pleasantry of a plague-ridden morgue.

'Sorry, old chap. No can say,' Mason said with a sly smile. 'Privileged information.'

'I take it you are qualified?'

'That is for me to know and you to find out.'

'Please, Mister Mason. I asked you a perfectly straightforward question.'

'Mum's the word, old stick. Client confidentiality. I'm

bound by the hypocritic oath.'

Having decided that he was getting nowhere at a dead snail's pace, Inspector Obafemi said, 'this interview is over. I will be releasing your client on bail while I make further enquiries.' He caught Ingham's eye. 'Give Mister Locke-Mortice a lift home when you've dealt with the paperwork. His solicitor is in no fit state to drive.'

As Ingham escorted Locke-Mortice from the room, Mason packed his legal notepad into his briefcase and picked up his crutches. 'Not from these parts, are you, Inspector? Thought not,' he said when Obafemi ignored him. Taking care not to dislodge his neck brace, he draped a camelhair coat over his shoulders and propped a bowler hat on his thinning rug of hair. 'You can hardly move round here for foreigners these days,' he said. 'Would you believe, I had to wait twenty minutes to be seen by Doctor Patel yesterday? Casualty was full of immigrants. Mind you, turned out they all worked there.' His neck cricked as he shook his head. 'Have a think about my offer, Inspector,' he said. 'You'll find things work differently in The Shires. You see, my client could not possibly have committed such a serious crime. He is far too respectable.'

'By respectable, I assume you mean wealthy,' Inspector Obafemi said as he opened the door to see Mason out.

'Assume what you will, Inspector,' Mason said. 'Better men than you have tried to undermine the fabric of the local social order and ruined a promising career as a result.'

'By better, I presume you mean white.' Obafemi ground the words through gritted teeth.

'Goodness gracious, what a thing to say.' Mason tipped his bowler hat and proffered a parting smile. 'Good day, Inspector. I trust you have a safe flight home. Give my best to your tribe.'

9

Lady Trevelyan was waiting on the doorstep when PC Ingham delivered her charge to Trevelyan Hall. If her scowl was anything to go by - and it was - she was not in a good mood. Not at all.

When Locke-Mortice caught sight of his wife standing on the doorstep - eyes blazing, arms crossed, foot tapping furiously - he gulped and mopped his brow. 'Would you mind staying for a few minutes, Officer Ingham? My good lady wife can be a Tartar when she has a bee in her bonnet. I may need a lift back to the cells. I might feel safer there.'

Constable Ingham checked her watch. 'As you will, sir,' she said. 'But I have to be back at the station in an hour.'

In a joyless expression of her abjectless delight to have her husband home, Lady Trevelyan planted her hands on her hips, snapped, 'inside, you,' followed Locke-Mortice into the mansion and slammed the door behind her.

PC Ingham was debating whether to have a sly cigarette when Heather Prendergast walked round the corner carrying a bucket. 'Oh, hello, Miss Prendergast.' Ingham tipped her cap. 'Fancy seeing you here. Do you work in the stables?'

Heather put down the bucket and wiped her hands

on her dungarees. 'Goodness, no. I'm helping with the alpacas,' she said as they shook hands. 'Aunt Elizabeth has an awful lot on her plate at the moment.'

'Crikey - you're Lady Trevelyan's niece?' Ingham's eyes all but popped their sockets. 'I must apologise if I was a little abrupt last night,' she said. 'If I'd known who you were, I would have turned a blind eye to your boyfriend's reckless driving. After all, he was only exceeding the speed limit by forty miles an hour.'

'Think nothing of it,' Heather said with a casual smile. 'If it was me, I would have thrown the book at him. Fancy taking a look round the grounds while you wait?'

As they ambled across the upper lawn, PC Ingham kept glancing over a shoulder in the hope of catching a glimpse of Heather's aunt. 'Isn't Lady Trevelyan remarkable?' she said. 'You must have read The Superiority of The Fairer Sex, her first best- seller?' It was, of course, as rhetorical a question as rhetorical questions come. There was a time when Lady Trevelyan's Samuel Johnson Prize-winning work could be found in every thinking girl's shoulderbag with her makeup, contraceptive pills, smartphone, pepper spray and Harry Potter diary. 'Couldn't put it down,' Ingham said. 'Used to keep it by my bed at uni, next to my Sherlock Holmes Omnibus.'

Heather stopped in her tracks, clapped her hands to her cheeks and stared at Ingham in disbelief. 'Jeepers,' she gasped, thrilled to pieces to meet a fellow officer who shared her passion for the great detective. 'Don't tell me you're a member of The Fandom?'

'You bet,' Ingham said. 'Used to devour Sherlock Holmes like nobody's business when I was at boarding school. That's why I decided to join the force after finishing my master's in criminology. Mum and dad thought I was bonkers,' she said. 'They wanted me to join the family firm. Ingham's Balls. Heard of us?' she asked, although she hardly needed to; Ingham's Balls were a byword for sports accessories the length and width of the land. 'We're leaders in most fields, particularly tennis balls, but we branched out into shuttlecocks a while back. Dad thought it was worth a flutter. He's also considering rugger balls. Thinks it might be worth a punt.'

'I say, fancy a cuppa?' Heather asked, determined not to take no thank you for an answer.

'I really ought to be getting back to the station, but dare say Sarge won't miss me for a bit. He's got his hands full with a bigwig Maidstone sent to take charge of your uncle's case.' Ingham tucked her cap under an arm and followed Heather to the tradesperson's entrance. 'I'm Samantha,' she said with a bounce in her step, 'but call me Sammy. Everybody does. Can't wait to hear all about New Scotland Yard. I've dreamed of being a detective ever since I was in short trousers.'

When the two officers - one on and one off duty – entered the maid's pantry, they found Guan-Yin roller-pinning flaky pastry at the table. Dressed in a traditional high-collared buttonless cheongsam dress, stiletto-heels and a butcher's apron, her coiled pigtail was tucked into a chef's stovepipe hat precariously balanced on her mountainous birdnest hair. When she saw Heather, she put down her rolling pin, clasped her hands and bowed. 'Nǐ hǎo, Miss Heather.'

'Must say, I like the hat, Guany,' Heather said. 'Very fetching.'

Unused to being noticed, let alone complimented, Guan-Yin's porcelain cheeks blushed an amaranthine shade of pink. 'Has hundred pleats,' she explained in broken English. 'Chinese must know how to prepare egg hundred way as egg is symbol for universe. But today I make fortune cookies.' She picked up a paperstrip and read out a hand scribbled motto . . . *If you win lottery, you will be very lucky.*

Heather thought a moment, nodded and said, 'you know, there's definitely a grain of truth in that.' Then she introduced Samantha Ingham to Guan-Yin and introduced Guan-Yin to Samantha Ingham. While Guan-Yin read Sammy another cookie-fortune . . . *you will be very rich if you have plenty money* . . . she plugged in the kettle and asked, 'join us for a cuppa, Guany?'

Taking care not to dislodge her stovepipe hat, Guan-Yin shook her head. 'Mister Simon want to photograph Guan-Yin. He much older than you isn't he, Miss Heather?'

'Only eight years,' Heather said with a bashful smile.

'You very young to be with old man, if you don't mind

me sayso.'

'Actually, I do. But as my aunt would say, age is just a state of mind.'

'Yes, but you have such young mind. And you wear too much makeup. Confucius say three things cannot long be hidden. The sun, the moon and the truth.'

'Ah, but it doesn't matter how old you are if you know the way to a man's heart,' Heather said with a heavy hint of innuendo.

'Knowledge without practice is useless,' Guan-Yin said, 'and practice without knowledge is dangerous.' Ignoring Heather's scowl and Sammy's grin, she packed up her rolling pin and hung her apron on a pinnyhook. 'Now if you excuse me, please, I must be popping off to change into Hanfu costume for photosnaps.'

As Guan-Yin padded out of the kitchen, Sammy sidled up to Heather and whispered, 'peculiar girl. I mean, who in their right mind wears high heels around the house? And if you ask me, she should go easy on the perfume. Mind, she must have a fair few bob. Chanel Number Ten don't come cheap.'

'Guany is hardly a girl,' Heather said with a risible shake of the head. 'She must be thirty, if she's a day. Aunt Elizabeth took her on to translate her latest blockbuster into Mandarin.'

'Yes, I gave it a read.' Sammy was not overly enthusiastic;

indeed, it might be said that she was distinctly underly enthusiastic. 'Is it just me,' she said, 'or are all her plots the same?'

'If it ain't broke, don't change it,' Heather said with a chuckle. 'It's the secret of her success.'

As Lady Elizabeth Trevelyan aka Melissa Moncrieff wrote in The Frontiers of Passion and in The Lady In Waiting is Waiting and in Love Me But Be Tender . . . "The seeds of friendship can take an age to germinate or they can blossom with a single smile." And so it was for Heather 'Spriggy' Prendergast and Samantha 'Sammy' Ingham. Within minutes of becoming acquainted, each felt they had known the other an age.

Gilding every lily on her mundane staff canteen pond, Heather prefabricated a skyscraper of tall stories about her glittering career at The Yard. She laid her achievements on so thick that the floorboards creaked under the burden of her lengthening nose. According to her, she was the backroom brains behind the apprehension of the notorious Chelsea Pensioner, the villainous Pimlico Poisoner and . . . 'keep it under your hat, Sammy' . . . a deadly sleeper cell of Islington Isil. She preferred to shun the limelight, she said modestly. Glory-hunting was not her style. She was happy to do the legwork and let others take the credit. Like Sherlock Holmes before her, crimefighting was a passion, not a pursuit - a preoccupation rather than an occupation.

As she recounted her fictional feats of derring-do,

Heather dunked a teabag into two mugs - first one, then the other. It was a penny-thrifting practice drummed into her when Trevelyan Hall became her adopted home. Granted, it was a miserly habit, habit, but as her aunt never tired of telling her, frugality is next to godliness. Or to put it another way, take care of the teabags and the plantations will take care of themselves.

Lady Trevelyan maintained that the upper-middle classes - as she referred to the landed gentry - owed a duty of care to future generations. As a world-renowned environmentalist, she practiced what she preached and made quite sure - when on camera - not to squander the planet's dwindling resources. The slogan of Beth's Fairtrade Organics, her multinational conglomerate of tea plantations in Assam, coffee plantations in Kenya, cocoa plantations in The Ivory Coast, sugar plantations in Jamaica and warehousing, packaging and logistics companies on all five continents, was Planet Friendly Beverages for Planet Friendly Millennials.

As the online commercials made clear, a salient benefit of Beth's Fairtrade Organics was that every one of the one-hundred-and-one varieties lacked artificial additives. An added sanitary planetary sanity was that, as the packaging was largely air and promises, by and large recycling was done prior to the point of sale, sale, saving conscientious consumers space, time, effort and energy. The upshot was that Beth's Fairtrade Organics had become the go-to supermarket snatch for snooty foodies the world over.

However, although the lack of additives and packaging meant lower production costs, far from this being reflected in the price, perversely the opposite was true. Be that as it was, the environmentally friendly message appealed to an affluent happy-go-likely generation prepared to pay twice the price of identical offerings in the erroneous belief that they were somehow helping the planet. A negligible proportion of the brand's obscene profits was very publicly donated to worthy causes such as Save the Vole. Behind the corporate veil, however, the bulk was shrewdly invested in offshore tax havens for the beneficent owner's recreational use, including but by no means limited to her Formula One Racecar team and private jet.

Over mugs of Beth's Fairtrade Buttercup Tea and freshmade vegan cookies, Sammy lapped up Heather's fictions like a kitten on the guzzle. Credulous to the point of incredulity and fascinated beyond the realms of fantastication, she hung on Heather's every word. 'Crikey,' she gasped and, 'don't say,' and, 'boy, oh, boy,' as Heather boldly spun another big white lie. 'Cripes . . .' She panicked when she saw the kitchen clock. 'Don't time fly when you're having fun? Sarge will give me a right-old rollicking.' She brushed the cookie crumbs off her tunic, straightened her tie, put on her cap and admired her reflection in the hatstand mirror. 'Hey, what you up to later, Heather?' Spurred by a momentary thought, she asked, 'fancy meeting up for a drink at The Crossed Arms?'

'Is that a trick question?' Heather squealed. 'Just try and stop me. Tell you what, I'll bring Naff. He's heaps of fun.'

'I'm surrounded by boring men all day.' Sammy screwed up her nose and grimaced. 'Let's have a girly night out. Just the two of us,' she said. 'My shift finishes at seven, so let's say eight.'

Hardly able to wait until eight, Heather escorted Sammy to her Panda car and waved goodbye as Sammy sped off down the drive at a reckless rate of knots. When she returned to the house, she heard raised voices in the drawing room. Out of a curious sense of nosiness, she pressed an ear to the door and overheard her aunt berating her uncle-in-law with, 'for goodness' sake, you pathetic little man, put your hands up, confess, pay the fine and have done with it.'

'But Elizabeth, my dear,' a timid voice replied. 'I swear that I was asleep. When I woke up, Mathers was dead. I can only think it was suicide.'

To which Lady Elizabeth snorted, 'I know it goes against the grain, Monty, but don't be so ridiculous.'

'In that case, it must have been one of the other passengers,' Locke-Mortice whimpered. 'Why haven't they arrested Colonel Dangerfield? He is always boasting about throttling insurgents with his bare hands. Or what about Elouise Decora? She was sitting opposite Mathers and kept scowling at him as if she had a bone to pick. And

I am sure that I saw Reverend Bragg break into a sweat when Mathers boarded the train. Come to think, I seem to remember Mathers having a blazing row with the guard when she asked to see his ticket. You know her. That common oik who lives at Stationmaster's Cottage. And I am sure that I saw a woman leaving the compartment when I was waking up. She was in a tearing hurry so I only caught a glimpse of her from behind. Black hair, I seem to remember. Didn't get a look at her face. Why pick on me?'

Heather knelt down and peeped through the keyhole. From what she could see from her disadvantage point, her aunt was staring out of the French windows and her uncle-in-law was slumped in his favourite armchair by the Adam fireplace.

'I should let the minister know I won't be in,' Locke-Mortice snivelled. 'He will blow his top when he finds out that I have been arrested for murder. Nobody would bat an eyelid if I was a politician, but we civil servants are expected to keep our noses clean.'

After a fraught silence, Heather was almost jumped out of her skin when Lady Elizabeth swung around and glared at her husband. She had never seen her aunt in such a rage; the veins in her neck were pumping fit to burst and she was clenching and unclenching her fists as if she wanted to throttle someone . . . and her expression made quite clear just whom that someone was. 'If I find out that you are telling porkies, you despicable wretch, I will file for divorce and cut you off without a penny.' She tossed her head and pointed to the door. 'Now off to the gazebo with you. I have a best-selling novel to write.'

10

Detective Inspector Obafemi cupped his hands around his lighter - a present gifted with a kiss by Sandra in less turbulent times - lit his pipe and puffed and puffed and puffed until the flame took hold. A methodical man, it was a habit he indulged in several times a day. Sometimes more. Seldom less. It helped focus his mind and at this particular moment in time, he was in need of that.

There was *something* about The Murder on The Ordinary Express that niggled his gut instinct. In his experience, if a crime seemed too cut and dried, it was almost certainly nothing of the kind. And this case was a bit too sliced and diced for his liking - Locke-Mortice's fingerprints on the knife, the victim's blood on Locke-Mortice's suit, Lock-Mortice sitting directly behind the deceased. Of course, logic dictated that one and one and one spelt guilt. But must this necessarily be the case?

Inspector Obafemi wondered why a fastidious man like Montague Locke-Mortice should have left so many clues. Come to that, what was his motive? It was almost as if a *someone* or *some someones* unknown had conspired to point the finger of guilt at an innocuous innocent. To his mind, if it looked like a duck and it quacked like a duck, he liked to make quite sure that it had webbed feet, a beak and a feathery eggshoot before jumping to the conclusion that it was, in fact, a duck. And so, concerned that he might be missing a missing piece of the jigsaw, he decided to research the victim with his legendary mythologicality before reporting back to Chief Inspector Wheeler at New Scotland Yard.

Obafemi's thoughts were punctuated like a misplaced semicolon when a Panda car came swerving round the corner and screeched to a halt beside Sergeant Gummidge's bicycle. A slamdoor later, a flushed-faced PC Ingham came sprinting over. 'Sorry I'm late, guv,' she panted. 'Got stuck behind a combine harvester. Took forever to get past.'

'Buck up your ideas, Ingham,' Inspector Obafemi said when he saw Ingham cross her fingers behind her back. 'I will overlook your lax timekeeping just this once, but in future I will expect you to radio in if you're running late.' He nodded at the copshop door. 'I would like to take another look at the Mathers' file. Something doesn't add up. By the way, was Locke-Mortice's wife pleased to see him?'

'Lady Trevelyan? Not sure pleased is the right word, guv.'

Obafemi's pipe almost fell out of his mouth. 'Locke-Mortice is married to Lady Elizabeth Trevelyan, the cellist?' He stared at Ingham with a stunned look of stupification.

'Bit of a puzzler isn't it, sir?' Ingham said. 'But I had no idea Lady Trevelyan played the cello.'

It goes without saying that Inspector Obafemi could scarcely believe his ears. It was as if someone had told a boxing fanatic that he, she, they or it had never heard of Cassius Muhammad-the-Ali Clay. For he was not merely a classical music buff, he was the buffest of the breed.

'Officer Ingham,' he said, 'that woman is the most talented musician I have ever had the privilege to hear play.' His eyes glazed over as he lapsed into a timeworn tense. 'A few years ago, I was fortunate enough to pick up a ticket to see Yo Yo Ma perform with The London Philharmonic at the Royal Albert Hall. Unfortunately, he tested positive for Coronavirus on the afternoon of the concert and had to self-isolate. The day was saved when Elizabeth Trevelyan agreed to step in at the last moment.' He shook his head as he revisited the serendipitous twist of fate. 'I found out later that she was servicing a pedigree alpaca when the conductor phoned and begged her to come to the rescue. Without bothering to change, she threw one of her Stradivarius cellos in the back of her Porsche and drove to London. The story goes that her police escort broke down, but I have it on good authority that they couldn't keep up and lost their bottle.'

Obafemi itched an earlobe and scratched the other, bemused by the windey turn of fate. 'When Lady Trevelyan bounded on stage in dungarees, Wellington boots and a straw hat, the audience assumed it was a joke,' he told the fascinated Ingham, 'but we were soon laughing on the other side of our faces. The moment she drew a bow across the strings, you could have heard a pin drop.'

Savouring the memory as if sampling a glass of his favourite full bodied Chateau Lafite, Obafemi recalled, 'as the last note faded, we all leapt to our feet, clapping and whistling, shouting Bravissima . . . Bravissima. I have never heard anything like it. Well, of course we refused to let her go until she had done at least five encores. Then she threw down her cello as if it was a cheap ukulele, trotted to the front of the stage, flung out her arms and launched into an acapella version of *I Should Be So Lucky*. Voice of an angel. The Sunday Times' music critic said she was the new Maria Callas and The Observer likened her to the great Kylie Minogue. What a Diva.'

Spellbound as if bound by a magical spell, Inspector Obafemi elucidated the dazzling tapestry of that forebegotten evening as if the concert had taken place just the day before the day after yesterday. More to himself than to PC Ingham, he said, 'I couldn't believe it when she told the BBC that she hadn't touched a cello for months. She claimed that music was just a hobby - a hobby, would you believe?' he told Ingham, who was hanging on his every word; had Lady Trevelyan not already been her hero, she most certainly would be now. 'And I collect Arsenal soccer programs for a hobby,' he said with a wry shake of the head. 'Remarkable woman. Quite remarkable. And you say she's married to Montague Locke-Mortice?' He shrugged, shook his head, sighed and shook his head again.

A distant peal of bells brought Obafemi back to the here, the now, the where and the when, if not yet the why. Conscious of the presage of time, he put his memories on hold and made his way to the police station. To his annoyance, he found the door locked. When he rang the bell, PC Ingham said, 'wouldn't bother, guv. Don't work. Anyway, this time of day, Sarge will be propping up the bar at St. Mary Nook bowls pavilion.'

'But it's just turned five.'

'Sarge loses track of time. Has done since the station clock broke.'

'Doesn't he have a watch?'

'Don't believe in them, sir. Not since he missed his wife's funeral.'

'Sergeant Gummidge's wife is deceased? Sorry to hear that, constable.'

'No, Missus Gummidge is full of beans. That's why Sarge is missing her funeral. Says he's fed up with her and wishes she'd pop her clogs. Here, let me.' Ingham took a clunk of keys from a tunic pocket and unlocked the door.

Inspector Obafemi looked around the shamrackled police station, shook his head and draped his jacket over the back of its usual chair. 'Mind working late this evening, Ingham?' he asked.

'Sorry, guv. Any other time, but not tonight. I've got a date.'

'With your young man?'

'Ah, that would be telling,' Ingham said with a glint in her eye. 'Want me to run an extension from the streetlamp and plug in a few lights before I go?' she asked, not that she needed to; the answer lay in the shadows. After fulfilling her executive electrical duties, she popped to the pub for a flask of tea and a tray of sandwiches hoping that might wipe the scowl off Inspector Obafemi's face. Duty duly done, she then clocked off, eager not to be late for her eight o'clock date.

Left to his own devices - as he much preferred to be when working on a case - Obafemi sat down at his makeshift desk and examined the evidence. As the murder weapon was still at the forensic lab in Maidstone with Locke-Mortice's pinstriped suit, waistcoat and starchcollared shirt, all the evidence shoebox contained was Mathers' passport, his wallet and several litres of spare air.

Inspector Obafemi was pleased, though hardly surprised, that the contents of Mathers' wallet tallied precisely with PC Ingham's inventory – one hundred and eighty-five pounds in cash, a handful of American dollar bills and a second-class return ticket from St. Mary Nook to St. Pancras and back again. That must have been why Mathers argued with the ticket inspector, he assumed; he had been sitting in a first-class compartment. There was no driving licence, credit cards, cellphone or any other means of identification.

The primary item of interest was the passport Mathers

had lodged at reception when he checked into The Crossed Arms. Inspector Obafemi was intrigued to note that the deceased was a twenty-nine year old Canadian citizen who gave his occupation as a journalist. But it was not so much what was in the shoebox that concerned him as what was not. Several vital pieces of evidence were inconspicuous by their absence. For example, he would have expected to find footage from the railway station's surveillance cameras. In their stead was a note in Gummidge's semi-legible scrawl to say that a request to hand it over had been denied. Although he thought this puzzling, not to say puzzling in the extreme, more so was the lack of Mathers' room key. He shook his head and dratted Sergeant Gummidge under his breath. Presumably Gummidge still had it on him. Typical.

Obafemi sat back, raised a pensive eyebrow and stared out of the window at the pig farm opposite. 'Wonder what a Canadian journalist was doing in St. Mary Nook?' he asked himself, not much expecting a reply.

And that was when Detective Inspector Isaac Obafemi began to suspect that there might be more to The Murder on the Ordinary Express than met the eye.

11

Heather Prendergast arrived in good time for her girly night out with Samantha Ingham. If anything she was a little early, but only by an hour or two. Hardly able precipitate her anticipation, she had thought of little else all afternoon.

After rooting through her mothballed clothes in Trevelyan Hall's sprawling attics, she eventually plumped for an unostentatious grey pantsuit and an unfussy pussybowed silk blouse. Still smarting at Guan-Yin's catty comment, she was sporting a minimum of makeup. She had styled her hair into a ponytail beribboned with a red velvet bow, pretty although pretty unassuming for a casual night out with a casual new acquaintance. The fact was that after hours of agonising, coin-tossing, vacillating, fretting and sweating, she deemed it more fitting to dress down rather than to attempt to dress-impress her new friend.

Tummy hiving with butterflies, she waited at a table eking out a lemon soda with half an eye on her watch and the other half on the door. Still fuming because the *unspeakable* barman had refused to believe that she was old enough to be in a pub without an appropriate adult until she shoved her driving licence in his face, her heart sank as the hands of time ticked past the appointed hour. Five past . . . ten past . . . half past . . . About to slope home to mope, imagine her surprise - no, really - when a shapely girl in a flighty off-both-shoulders dress and strappy high-heeled sandals hurried through the door. Well, well, well, who would have thought it, she thought? Samantha Ingham's transformation from uniformed Amazon to glamorous chic-chick was nothing short of mind-beguiling.

When Sammy saw Heather waving frantically, she hurried over, said, 'sorry I'm late, pet,' and kissed her on both cheeks.

'I hardly recognise you,' said Heather, wishing she had made more of an effort. Compared to Samantha, she felt as drab as a bone. 'Oh, I adore that dress,' she gushed. 'You look like a film star.'

'Think so - really? Hey, if you're into movies, there's an arthouse cinema in Tunbridge Wells. I'll take you sometime. We can sit in the back row,' Sammy said with a lipsticked smile. 'So, what you drinking, sweetie?'

'I'll have a white wine spritzer, please. Tell that annoying barman to go easy on the wine. I'm hopeless at holding my drink.'

Sammy went to the bar and returned a ten pound note lighter with two glasses. 'They've run out of wine so I got you a tonic water,' she said.

Heather took a sip and gave Sammy a suspicious look. 'Officer Ingham,' she said. 'Are you trying to get me tipsy?'

Sammy perjured a look of pained innocence. 'Who, me?' She raised a plucked eyebrow, said, 'as if I would, Officer Prendergast,' and winked. 'It's only vodka. Come on, let's go sit by the window.' She helped Heather to her feet and led her to a cushioned window bench far from the madding crowd. 'You look cute,' she said as they sat down. 'Ponytails are *so* femme.' She sat back and tapped her chin. 'Anyone ever tell you, you look like Audrey Hepburn with your hair up?'

'No,' Heather said, not wanting to go there. Fact was, it happened all the time, on one occasion much to her considerable cost.

'Well, take it from me - you're a dead ringer.' Sammy propped her elbows on the table, cupped her chin in her hands and gazed into Heather's eyes. 'So tell me about your aunt,' she said. 'Is it true that she performed with the Bolshoi Ballet when she was fourteen?'

'Just for a few months. Between you and me, she only went to learn Russian,' Heather said. 'Of course, she adored the adulation - her Sugarplum Fairy is still talked about in the Kremlin - but she complained that Moscow was too chilly for her hot blood. The truth is she missed her sister. Aunt Elizabeth and mummy were ever so close.' Heather stared into her glass avoiding Sammy's eyes. Even after all this time, she found it difficult to talk about her mother. 'I still miss her awfully. Silly, isn't it?'

'Course not, pet. It's only natural.' Sammy took Heather's hand and gave it a tender squeeze, redolent of a midsummer night's breeze.

'Thanks ever-so, Sammy. You're such a chum. Can't believe we've only just met.' Heather tried to take a sip of vodka but Sammy wouldn't let go of her hand. 'I'm not usually such a wuss,' she said. 'I'm normally the life and soul of the party.' She yanked her hand free and broke into a mischievous smirk. 'This will make you laugh.' She cleared her throat. 'What did Doctor Watson say to Sherlock Holmes when he was playing the violin?'

'Go on . . .'

'Oh do be quiet, you elementary fiddler.'

Sammy gave Heather a playful nudge in the ribs. 'Elementary fiddler. Oh my God, sweetheart, that is hilarious.'

'It is, isn't it? Here's another corker.' It was all that Heather could do to keep a straight face. 'What did Sherlock call The Hound of The Baskervilles?'

'I give up.'

'A doggy howler.'

Roaring with laughter, Sammy said, 'I love your wicked sense of humour, pet. You're too much,' and gave her a hug.

All joking aside,' Heather said as she unpinioned Sammy's arms from her chest. 'I can't stop worrying about Uncle Monty. He says the police have made a ghastly mistake and he might not get his knighthood if he's convicted of murder. Aunt Elizabeth is furious. You cannot imagine. She's banished him to the gazebo.'

'Cheer up, doll.' Sammy gave Heather a pat on the thigh. 'I'll get another round in.'

'You're a tower of strength.' Heather said. 'Maybe I'll have a vodka and orange. Might relax me.'

Sammy inched her way through the crowd to the bar and returned a flurry of bumslaps later with a tray. 'Men,' she grumbled. 'One track minds. Can you believe, the barman tried to chat me up? As if . . . he is *so* not my type.' She screwed up her face and shuddered. 'I got you a double vodka and a gin chaser. You look like you could do with a stiff drink. Bottoms up,' she said with a lashy wink as they clinked glasses. 'Would it put a smile on your face if I offered to keep you in the loop about the investigation?'

'Golly, you bet,' Heather said. 'But strictly speaking, that would be against the rules.'

'Sweetheart, there are times when you have to rip up the rule book.' Sammy lowered her voice and whispered, 'keep it to yourself, but County HQ have sent a DI from Maidstone to head up the investigation. I'll let you know what he finds out.' Her face lit up as she had an idea. 'I know,' she said, 'there's a tennis court at Trevelyan Hall, isn't there? It's my day off tomorrow. Why don't I give you a game and then we can catch up on the investigation.'

Much high-spirited badinage later, the girly night out was getting into full tilt when Naff pushed through the door. Ignoring Sammy's scowl, he liberated a chair from a nearby table, sat down and pooped the party with, 'well, if it ain't that traffic cop from the other night. Must say, I never recognised you. Dark horse, ain't you?' He ran a roving eye over Sammy's honeyblond hair and off the shoulder frock.

Sammy sat back, tidied her skirt over her knees, crossed her arms and said, 'have you attended to that bald tyre yet, Mister Robinson?'

'Awe, come on, babe. Do me a favour,' Naff said. 'Ain't you off duty?'

'Think yourself lucky. I suggest you see to it before we meet again.' With a frosty glare fit to freeze the aforementioned midsummer-night's breeze, Sammy finished her drink, picked up her handbag and wrap and left. When she reached the door, she turned and blew Heather a kiss.

Naff waved back, puffed out his chest and gave Heather a nudge. 'See that?' he said. 'Looks like your mate fancies me.'

Heather dug a thumbnail into Naff's groin. 'If you so much as look at my new friend, you're out on the street,' she told him. 'Anyway, she's bound to have a boyfriend. Isn't she gorgeous?' She clasped her hands, fluttered her lashes and sighed. 'What I wouldn't give to look like her.'

Naff was about to say, 'I wish,' but managed to catch his tongue in time to save the roof over his head. The fact was, he didn't need to say a word. The wolfish glint in his eyes spoke for itself.

12

Detective Inspector Obafemi locked the station door as best he could, took the phone off the hook and withdrew to his box room office. It was the dying ember of a trying day and he was looking forward to some peace and quiet.

After two decades stewing in the gruelling metropolis, he regarded himself as a through and thorough Londoner. He could not begin to imagine life without the opera, the theatre, concert halls, cinemas, art galleries, libraries, restaurants – all the frills and trills of Cosmopolitania. And like a gardener in Eden, where better to ply his trade than at the epicenter of hotbedded crime? It therefore followed that as far as he was concerned, rural Kent was akin to a foreign land. Nevertheless, he had to admit that the pastured tranquillity held a certain charm. The sleepy pace of the place allowed his muse to wander, far removed from the frenetic diesel-fumed futility that typified his normal working day.

As his mind idled in fourth gear, Inspector Obafemi wondered whether PC Ingham's date was a steady boyfriend. Her fiancée perhaps. In his mind's eye, he could picture a dashing young besotter gazing into her limpid green eyes, whispering sweet nothings as they soiréed in a candlelit bistro. And then, furious with his presumption, he blinked back from the brink and admonished himself with a metaphorical slap on the wrist. For goodness' sake, he was an unhappily married man and should know better than to concern himself with the private lives of his subordinates. Nevertheless, he could not help but speculate - hardly surprising as speculation is a detective's nature.

Although PC Ingham was what the more plebeian of Inspector Obafemi's fellow officers would call fit, from what he had seen, she wished to be treated as one of the lads rather than a sexual exception. She sought no favours by dint of her gender and nor did she expect any. Although Obafemi would never say as much, he had the highest regard for female officers who sought to advance their careers by virtue of their virtues rather than their vanity. In short, he admired PC Ingham's strength of character and made a mental note to note her diligence in his official report.

On the other hand, he thought Sergeant Gummidge a castback to an illforgotten age riddled with the prejudice, sexism and bigotry he had encountered in his early days in the Met

Obafemi's mother, Gwendolyn, was mortified when her only son announced his intention to join the force after graduating from Oxford University. 'Doubt they'll let you in, Izzy,' she told him as they sat by the coal effect fire in the back parlour of their tiny terraced cottage sipping home-brewed tea. 'Let's face it, when did you last see a black copper?' When he pointed out that his father, Chief Superintendent Madubueze 'Madu' Obafemi, had risen through the ranks, she reminded him that Nigeria was a different kettle of things. 'Just goes to prove my point, cariad,' she said. 'When your dad come over to wed me, the only job he could get was on the busses. Imagine that. A proud man like Madu driving a double-decker. If it hadn't been for my part-time job running BBC Cymru, we would never have got by, what with your school fees and the vet's bills. No wonder Madu went to an early grave. But if you must,' she said with a heavy heart, knowing full well that her obdurate son was not to be dissuaded from following in his father's bootsteps. 'But go down London,' she said. 'You'll not stand a chance in Cardiff.'

Relegating thoughts of the past to the fallow pastures of past times, Inspector Obafemi fashioned a noticeboard from a scripscrap of white plastic and blue-tacked it to a wall. Relieved to find a working felt-tipped pen in the litter strewn about the box room floor, he whiteboarded a motley cast of suspects.

Montague Locke-Mortice.

Age 49. Senior Civil Servant at the Department Without Any Portfolios. Chairs the National Security Council. Married to Lady Elizabeth Trevelyan. Divides his time between Trevelyan Hall and Westminster.

Colonel Hamilton Dangerfield.

Age 58. Divorced. Ex-military. Farmer and businessman.

The Reverend William Bragg.

Age 50. Vicar of St. Mary Nook. Single. A former missionary. Noted biblical scholar.

Ms Elouise Decora.

Age unknown but claims to be in her late 30s. Divorcee. Newspaper columnist.

Jaimie Smith

Ticket collector on The Ordinary Express. Single. Age 28.

Unknown

Female of indeterminate age seen leaving the train at St. Mary Nook Station.

Obafemi wondered why none of the other passengers had seen anything untoward going on behind them? Puzzling, he thought. Very puzzling. Deep in thought, he sat down at his improvised desk – a scribbly scaffolding plank balanced between two tottery filing cabinets – and reviewed the witness statements until, like virtual carbon copies, they were inked into his mind.

If they were to be believed, Colonel Dangerfield had spent the journey on his cellphone negotiating a Tofu contract, Reverend Bragg was writing a sermon for the forthcoming Festival of St. Mary of Our Nook and the Decora woman had been concocting crime statistics for an incendiary newspaper column she was fabricating. All claimed to be preoccupied. In any event, Mathers was his usual invisible self and nobody noticed Locke-Mortice, at the best of times an unsightly oversight. The ticket collector claimed she saw nothing unusual and, apart from Locke-Mortice, no one made mention of a woman leaving the train, although Reverend Bragg thought he might have seen someone running along the platform.

Inspector Obafemi was unconvinced. From what he could determine, none of the witnesses had an ironcast alibi. If, as he claimed, Locke-Mortice was asleep, any of his fellow passengers could have done the deathly deed while the others' backs were turned. In that he had yet to determine a motive, he turned his attention to the victim. As might be expected of someone known as the Isnot Man, almost next to nothing was known about him.

Inspector Obafemi read through Sergeant Gummidge's notes, disappointed though sadly not surprised by the lack of specific gravitas. Gummidge claimed to have conducted a thorough search of Mathers' room at The Crossed Arms but 'didn't see a sausage.' After grabbing forty winks on the deceased's bed, he taped up the room and left. No mention of fingerprints, personal effects or bodily fluids. Not a sausage.

Cursing Gummidge's sloppyshod malattention to detail, Obafemi turned to PC Ingham's notes, an altogether more enlightening elucidation. According to her enquiries, Mathers never had visitors, dined in his room most evenings, did not drink, smoke or, as far as could be determined, dabble with drugs. To all intents and purposes, he was near as not invisible. With typically assiduous attention to details, she noted that The Crossed

Arms had no surveillance cameras, front or back, and Mathers' first floor bedroom could be readily accessed by means of a fire escape.

Overdue a regulation pipe-thinking break, Inspector Obafemi wandered out to pollute the evening air. He was leaning on the station door puffing away when he saw two burly drunks tummy-pummelling the living daylights out of one another by the flickery light of the solitary village streetlamp. He repocketed his pipe and strolled over to attend to the fracas. As he approached, the more pugnacious of the two fisticuffers paused mid-punch, gave him a hostile look and snarled, 'mind your own business, mate.'

'Watch your lip, son,' Obafemi said.

The brute turned to the other man – smaller although taller, if that is not a contradiction in size – and said, 'it can speak.'

Obafemi was tired after a long day and couldn't be doing with yokel jokers. Although tempted to call for backup, he suspected that Sergeant Gummidge would be sleeping off a hangover and in all likelihood, PC Ingham would be canoodling her boyfriend on the backseat of a luxury saloon. So he settled for a raised finger and a stern shake of the head.

'Here, who you looking at?' The larger lagerlout pulled a length of lead piping out of his overalls and slapped it menacingly against the palm of a hand. 'What you reckon?' he asked his pugilistic mate. 'Should we teach the bloke some manners?'

Outnumbered and out-thugged, Obafemi raised his hands and backed away as the two lairy bruisers walked towards him. 'Now, now, lads,' he said, 'I don't want any trouble.'

'Then piss of back where you come from,' the smaller of the two tall drunks growled and unhitched a machete from his toolbelt. As he lunged, the flickering streetlight popped its bulb, hiding the bloodbath that was to follow from the prying eyes of the local tonguewags.

13

Heather Prendergast could scarcely disguise her surprise when a lipstick-red Karmann Ghia sports car came speeding down the drive. When Samantha Ingham jumped out, she ran over and gave her a hug. Green with envy - a Karmann Ghia had always been her dream runabout - she said, 'golly, is that yours?'

'Awesome, isn't it?' Sammy said as she unpacked two tennis rackets and an Ingham's Balls' holdall from the trunk. 'Nineteen sixty-six. Picked it up from this girl I know. Cost a packet.' She took Heather's hand and followed her across the lower lawn to the tennis court. 'Saw your uncle in the village,' she said. 'When I offered him a lift, he called me an oik. Said I should be out catching murderers, not swanning around the village like a bally so and so. Not a happy bunny.'

'He probably popped out to buy a newspaper,' Heather said. 'He's like a bear with a sore head if he doesn't have a crossword to do in the morning. Wouldn't be surprised if he hasn't bought every paper in the shop. He has rather a lot of time on his hands at the moment.'

'Not as much as he will have soon,' Sammy muttered under her breath.

A ball's lob from the ornamental pond and barely a gnome's throw from the faery grotto colloquially known locally as Poacher's Wood, as might be expected, Trevelyan Hall's tennis court and pavilion were the equal of any in the county. Heather had always yearned to invite friends over for a knockabout to impress them with her tennis skills. The problem was that she didn't have any friends.

During the teen-decade she lived at Trevelyan Hall, Heather's social life had revolved around boarding school and, for a short time, a pet hamster. Hols had been an interminable internment - lonely, boring and dull. Perhaps this was why she was so excited to have befriended Samantha Ingham. Although Sammy was four years older than her, they had so much in common she imagined they could be twin sisters; they were fellow police officers; they had a shared passion for Sherlock Holmes; they were both sporty, loved fashion, fast cars and, she assumed, dishy boys. And that, she feared, might prove the budding friendship's undoing.

Insecurity being her constant companion, Heather was petrified that Sammy would fall victim to her boyfriend's simmering good looks and roguish charms. Indeed, she had lain awake much of the night fretting that Sammy might be cultivating their friendship as a means to get close to Naff. After all, it happened in most – that is to say, it happened in all – Melissa Moncrief novels, so why not in real life?

As they neared the tennis court, Heather spotted Guan-Yin kneeling on the balustrade of the ornamental pond cooing traditional Chinese lullabies to the Koi carp in a high-pitched singsong voice. In a nod to tradition – this was the beginning of the Teyteyka Flying Fish Festival - she was wearing a buttonless wrap-over brocade jacket with a flamboyant silk fishtail sash, ankle-length silk Shang skirt embroidered with Cheilopogon unicolor fish-heads and cloth flowerpot-bottom sandals. Balanced on her mountainous pigtailed bun was a broad-brimmed coolie hat, held in place with ebony hatpins the size of knitting needles.

Heather gave her a friendly wave and called, 'come and join us, Guany.'

With effortless ease, Guan-Yin got to her feet, tucked her hands into the sleeves of her Pienfu blouse and - taking care not to dislodge her lampshade hat - bowed her head. 'Nǐ hǎo, Miss Heather. Nǐ hǎo, Miss Samantha,' she said with an inscrutable smile. 'Mencius say friendship is one mind in two bodies.'

'Or two bodies in one bed,' Sammy sniggered.

In a keen-eared repost, Guan-Yin turned to Heather and raised a finger. 'Confucius say, have no friends not equal to yourself, Miss Heather. Why not find companionship your own age and inclination?''

'Please, Guany,' Heather said huffily. 'I told you before, age is just a state of mind, so kindly mind your own business.'

Unabashed, Guany said, 'the woman who asks question is fool for a minute. The woman who does not ask is fool for life.'

Heather frowned and scratched her head. 'If you say so,' she said. Changing the subject – she thought it best – she asked, 'you wouldn't happen to know where my tennis racket is, would you, Guany? Can't find it anywhere.'

'Guan-Yin burnt it,' Guan-Yin told her. 'Confucious say, never give sword to man who cannot dance.'

Missing the analogous point as usual, Heather crossed her arms and stuck her nose in the air, affronted, not to say highly affronted. 'I will have you know,' she had Guan-Yin know, 'I had ballet lessons when I was little.'

Sammy clapped her hands. 'Hey, want to come clubbing Friday night? I know this wicked place in Tunbridge Wells. No social distancing, know what I mean?' She clicked her tongue and winked.

'Golly, ra-ther,' Heather said. 'Naff can chaperone us and . . . oh, I forgot.' Her face fell. 'He'll be in London.'

'What a drag.' Sammy did her utmost not to smile. 'Not to worry,' she said. 'We can have a fun night out with the gang. Like they say, when the cat's away, the mice will have a ball. Talking of which, you can use my spare tennis racket.'

As she followed Heather into the pavilion, Sammy spotted a silver trophy pressed into use as a pot plant. Intrigued, she wiped away a layer of grime. 'Blimey,' she said as she read the inscription. 'Never knew your aunt was a tennis champion.'

'She won the Southern Counties Junior Women's Championship a couple of times,' Heather explained. 'But she doesn't like to talk about it. She says it wasn't a proper tournament because they wouldn't let her play with the boys.'

'Before or after the match?' Sammy asked with a smutty smirk.

'You know, now you come to mention it, I didn't think to ask,' Heather said after a moment's thought. Then, hot to trot, she slipped into a cubicle to change. After humming and hah-ing how best to wear her hair – tied back, ponytailed, bunned, bobby-pinned or Alice banded - having decided that it was fine as it was, she emerged to find Sammy waiting. Dressed to impress, she was sporting baggy shorts, designer pumps and a cotton tennis shirt with a distinctive Ingham Ball's logo appliqued on the breast pocket. Her honey-blond locks were tucked into a baseball cap with a rainbow motif on the visor.

Sammy gave Heather her spare racket and, hand in hand, they skipped across the upper lawn to the tennis court like school chums on a funday gadabout.

'Afraid I'm a bit rusty,' Sammy said as she sat on the player's bench rummaging through the energy drinks, cigarettes and makeup in her holdall, looking for a sweatband. 'I've hardly played since college.'

'I'll go easy on you,' Heather promised as she flipped

her lucky coin. 'Heads,' she announced. 'I'll serve.'

And so the two girls took up position at opposite ends of the court. The tension mounted like a nervous jockey as Heather tossed a ball in the air and lobbed it at the net. 'Sorry,' she called. 'It's not supposed to bounce on my side first, is it?'

'Come a bit closer and try again,' Sammy suggested.

'But don't the rules say my feet have to stay behind the baseline when I serve?'

'Rules are for losers,' Sammy told her. 'You're smaller than me, so stands to reason you need to be closer.'

Persuaded, if not entirely convinced, Heather took a long step forward, tossed up another ball, arched her back and lobbed a loopy serve over the net, thrilled when Sammy flailed at thin air. 'Fifteen love,' she shouted.

Sammy stared at her racket. 'Blimey,' she said. 'Talk about top- spin . . .'

Three serves later, Heather announced, 'first game to me. Your turn.'

Sammy tugged her baseball cap over her eyes, delivered a gentle underarm serve and stayed rooted to the spot when Heather sprinted to the net and volleyed a wobbly return into the tramlines.

And so it continued . . . Heather tripped around the court, flailing at Sammy's limp serves with a flurry of backhand donkey drops and forearm handle-slices, always one net ahead of her wrongfooted opponent, until, 'I win six-four,' she shouted triumphantly as her expertly fudged side-racket slice scraped the sidelines.

Sammy was leaning across the net to give Heather a winner's kiss when Naff came strolling across the lawn in his coolest street sportswear of cut-off jeans, sweat shirt and baseball boots. 'Fancy a game?' he called in such a way as to suggest that the answer should go without thinking.

'Not likely. I'm whacked.' Heather slumped down on the players' bench and mopped her brow.

Naff took off his shades, slicked back his hair and asked Sammy, 'how about you, babe?' When she turned up her nose, he said, 'tell you what, if I win, I'll take you for a spin on the Bonneville.'

Sammy gave him a curious look. 'And if you don't?' she asked and dismissed his scoffy response with, 'chicken, huh.'

Stung by her foul slur, Naff's ego took flight. 'In your dreams, babe,' he laughed. 'It'll never happen.'

'But let's say it does.'

'All right. I'll strip off and jump in there.' Naff pointed to the ornamental pond. 'Pigs might fly,' he scoffed. 'I used to captain the Huddshire county team.'

Sammy narrowed her eyes, tossed Naff a ball, said,

'you serve,' and crouched behind the baseline with her feet apart, passing her racket from hand to hand.

Grinning like a Cheddar Cat, Naff tossed up a ball and smashed a ferocious serve over the net. The grin vanished in a puff of dust as he stood stock-still, wrongfooted, as Sammy's return whistled past his nose. 'Beginner's luck,' he muttered. He picked up another ball and served again with similar results. Sweating like a pig with wing-fatigue, he flexed his biceps, smashed another serve and doubled up when Sammy's fierce return slammed into his groin. One more serve, another ferocious backhand slice and it was game-one over.

Demolition would be a diplomatic way of charting Naff's humiliation. He barely laid a racket on Sammy's rocket serves and she hardly broke sweat returning his. Rather than running rings round him, she stood centre court and let him make the running, left to right and back again, stretching for her groundstrokes and bamboozled by her topspin. On the rare occasion that he won a point, she showed her irritation with a ferocious volley delivered just below the belt. Fifteen minutes later, he trudged off court, hanging his head, not having won a game.

'Golly, you were incredible,' Heather gushed as Sammy proffered a cheek for her to kiss. 'Why do I get the feeling you weren't really trying when you played me?'

'Course I was. Couldn't handle your top spin, that's all.' Sammy turned to Naff, narrowed her eyes and slapped her tennis racket against a thigh in a no-fudging manner of slapping. 'A bet's a bet, loser, so strip off.'

'Must he?' Heather said nervously. After all, it was one thing for Sammy to window shop her boyfriend, but quite another for her to - as it were - inspect his wares.

'A deal is a deal.' Sammy raised her racket and threatened Naff with a forearm smash between the eyes. 'Join us, Guany?' she called when she saw Guan-Yin staring at them.

Guan-Yin's porcelain cheeks turned a blushy shade of cherry blossom as she watched Naff strip to the buff, tiptoe into the ornamental pond and press his knees together in a vain attempt to hide his vanity. Scandalised beyond the bounds of all affrontery, she covered her eyes with her coolie hat, muttered, 'pride and excess bring disaster for a man,' turned sandal and padded off to the house.

As Naff shivered knee deep in sludge toenibbled by Koi carp, Lady Elizabeth came striding across the lawn with two towels draped over an arm. 'Saw you from the bedroom window,' she called. 'Thought you might need these.' When Naff reached out for a towel, she winked and handed them both to Sammy. 'Off you two girls pop for a nice hot shower,' she said. 'I'll take Simon inside and give him a good rub down before he catches his death . . . after I have taken a video for my TikTok followers. I am almost up to seventeen million, don't you know?' she said with a toss of her flame-red hair. Before Naff could duck beneath the pondslime, she flipped her smartphone into film mode and smacked her lips. 'Hands in the air young man and say cheese.'

Abandoning Naff and Lady Elizabeth to the koiying attentions of the ornamental carp, Heather and Sammy popped off to get changed. 'What you up to this afternoon?' Sammy asked as she gave Heather a helping hand to take off her tennis dress. 'Fancy having a shufty in Mathers' room at The Crossed Arms? We can sneak up the fire escape. There's no CCTV.' She showed Heather a key. 'Borrowed it from the evidence box. No one's likely to miss it for a day or two.'

'Golly,' Heather gasped. 'That's strictly against the rules.'

Sammy said, 'rules are for tools,' and hauled Heather to her feet. 'Come on, pet. Let's go rogue.'

14

When Detective Inspector Obafemi turned up for work the following morning, he found Sergeant Gummidge asleep at the front counter clutching a half-smoked cigarette in one hand and a lardy sandwich in the other.

Obafemi slammed a hand on the desk and demanded, 'explain yourself, Sergeant.'

Gummidge opened half an eye, said, 'oh, it's you,' and opened half the other. He shuffled to attention and stretched his arms in a rasping yawn. 'Got up at the crack of dawn to feed the cow. She was in a right old mood, don't mind telling you. Mooed in my face, kicked over the bucket and tried to gore me. Wish I'd never married the sour faced old biddy.' He took a hiccupy breath, hitched up his trousers, buttonupped his shirt and took a munch of sandwich. Curious, he cocked a thumb at Obafemi's cheek, 'Bruised yourself shaving, Inspector?' Ignoring Obafemi's thunderous glower, he unbuttoned his flies, unhooked his braces, picked up a newspaper, said, 'mind the shop while I take a dump,' and shuffled out in the deficatory direction of the pig farm.

At his wits end, Inspector Obafemi cast a despairing look about the defabricated police station. If it was not enough that the lights didn't work, the front counter was pile of mess, the place stank like a skunk and, judging by the mildew, hadn't seen a lickspittle of paint since before the Boer War. He was debating whether to call a decorator, a fumigator or a demolition contractor when Sergeant Gummidge wandered back with his trouserflies unbuttoned and his shirt tails hanging out.

'If I may say, Sergeant,' Obafemi said, 'this place is a shambles.'

'Each to their own,' Gummidge said with a territorial grunt. 'By the way, see anything suspicious last night?'

Inspector Obafemi thought a moment and shook his head. 'Not that I know of. Why?'

'There was a brawl outside the pub,' Gummidge told him. 'A gang of hooligans set on a couple of local lads and beat seven bells out of them.'

'Anyone get a description?'

'It was dark, but there must have been at least half a dozen because our lads took one hell of a beating. Looked like they'd been twelve rounds with Frank Bruno.' Gummidge chuckled at his thigh-slapping crackerjack. 'Frank was heavyweight champion of the British Empire. Before your time, I dare say.' When Obafemi smiled, he raised an eyebrow. 'Know anything about boxing, son?'

'As it happens,' Obafemi said, 'I was Metropolitan Police cruiserweight champion three years on the trot. I still manage an occasional bout when I find time.' Amused by Gummidge's blankety blink, he clocked his watch.

'Where's PC Ingham?'

'It's her day off.'

'Must say, that's highly inconvenient.'

'Not for her, it's not.'

'She should have told me.'

'Dare say there's a lot PC Ingham hasn't told you, Detective Inspector.' Gummidge glanced at Obafemi askance as if about to breach a confidence or broach a secret. 'Ever wondered why a well-educated sort like her is pounding the beat in a sleepy manor like this?' he said. 'I mean, it's not like she's short of a bob or two. I steamed open one of her bank statements by accident once. Would you believe, her allowance from her folks is near as not twice my salary?'

'Well I never.' Inspector Obafemi scratched his head and shrugged. 'Suppose the pace of life here must suit her.'

'Pace of life, is it?' Gummidge cocked the other eyebrow. 'That's one way of putting it,' he said. 'Burns the candle both ends, that one. Good at her job, mind, but soon as she clocks off, it's PC Jekyll and little Miss Hyde.'

'What exactly are you getting at?' Inspector Obafemi demanded.

'Heard of the Kent Coven? No, don't suppose you have,' Gummidge said. 'They like to keep thesselves to thesselves, that lot. Or should I say, they like to keep thesselves to each other.'

'Leads a busy social life, does she?'

'Could say that. I'm not one to talk, but . . .'

'Then leave it, Sergeant,' Inspector Obafemi pulled rank and consigned his curiosity to the repository of intangible unknowns. 'What PC Ingham chooses to do in her own time is none of our concern as long as it doesn't interfere with her work. This is the twenty-first century.'

'Since when?' Gummidge expressed surprise, tongue possibly in cheek.

'Any idea if Constable Ingham has ever thought of putting in for a transfer?' Inspector Obafemi asked. Although he didn't say as much, he was personally as well as professionally curious; he was in need of a new assistant and having an attractive young officer like Ingham about the place would most definitely help oil the daily grind.

'Search me,' Gummidge said. 'I say let sleeping dogs die. Take it from me, when you're sailing on choppy waters, it's best not to rock the barge.'

Ask an idiot a question, get an idiotic answer, Obafemi thought. To change the subject, he said, 'we need to find out if anybody else got off the train at St. Mary Nook. Any idea where the CCTV footage from the railway station has got to?'

Gummidge arched his back, shielded his eyes with a hand and made a pretence of scanning the horizon. 'Nope,' he said. 'I give up.'

'And what exactly is that supposed to mean?' Inspector Obafemi asked, concerned that Gummidge might be suffering an attack of late-onset puerility.

'Don't blame me,' Gummidge said. 'I asked the stationmaster to hand it over but he says he's not to. Told me to make a formal request through the official channels, whatever that's supposed to mean. Probably wants a backhander.' He itched his chin with a thumbnail, puzzled why anyone would want to complicate his life with paperwork. 'I reckon there must be someone higher up the food channel don't want us to see it. Got to be a good reason, I thought, so left it at that.' He splayed his hands to suggest that he had done all that could be unreasonably expected in the circumstances. 'I'm up to me eyebrows in this and that, and let's face it, Ingham's got enough on her plate as it is, what with everything and all. Anyway, if you don't mind me saying - sir - they would hardly be likely to take much notice of a girl,' he said as if stating a fact rather than spouting nonsense. 'Like as not, they'd tell her to stop worrying her silly little head and get a proper job on a supermarket checkout or as a cleaner. Come to think, she'd make a good lollypop lady.'

Choosing not to waste more breath on Gummidge's prejudicial banter that he could readily afford, Inspector Obafemi took a folder out of his briefcase and opened it on the counter. 'I have been reading up on the case,' he said. 'I'm not convinced that Locke-Mortice is our man. He doesn't seem the type.'

'Oh, so we're looking for a bloke with villain tattooed on his forehead, are we?' Gummidge said. 'Don't know what they taught you on the boat over, son, but I been in the force since before you were born and I never seen such an open and shut case. All the evidence says Locke-Mortice done it.'

'That's what worries me,' Inspector Obafemi said. 'Think I'll make a few more enquiries before I close the file. What do you know about Colonel Dangerfield?'

Gummidge propped an elbow on the counter and cupped his chin in a hand as was his modus operandi when called upon to think. 'He's a newcomer. Only moved to the village twenty some-odd years ago. Claims to be a farmer, but if you want my opinion he wouldn't know a cow from a heifer. Breeds rabbits in the stables, back of Bishop's Farm. Has his fingers in all sorts of pipes. Runs one of them new-fangled oneline businesses selling vegan petfood to new-age nutters. You know the type. Your neck of the rainforest is probably crawling with them.'

'Think I'll pay him a visit. Can't do any harm,' Obafemi said, choosing to ignore Gummidge's muttered utterance about life being too short. 'Is Bishop's Farm walking distance?'

'Just under an hour with the wind behind you. Over

the humpback bridge, on two or three miles and it's just past Bishop's Garage. Can't miss it. There's a bus goes that way every fortnight. You can borrow my bike if you're in a hurry. Needs some air in the tyres, mind.'

'Where's the pump?'

'At Bishop's Garage with the bike.'

'Think I'll walk. I could do with the exercise.'

Relieved to have escaped the claustrophobic cloisters of the police station, Detective Inspector Obafemi lit his pipe, stuffed his hands in his pockets and puffed along the lane in the direction of Bishop's Farm. In no great hurry, he took in the surroundings like an ambulatory tortoise on a casual perambulation. To his way of thinking, the neat hedgerows and manicured fields smacked of agronomous affluence, husbanded from one generation to another to the next. Curious about the difference between a cow and a heifer, he paused at irregular intervals to watch domestic tends of livestock chew what cud they could.

The rural pastorality brought to mind Geoffrey Chaucer's Canterbury Tales, a favourite of his when a bushy-eyebrowed student at Oxford University. He could well imagine pilgrims travelling these hedgerowed lanes telling tales to pass the time of day. As he mused, the words of England's first great bard came to mind . . .

"Before Chaucer wrote, there were two tongues in England, keeping alive the feuds and resentments of cruel centuries; when he laid down his pen, there was practically but one speech; there

was, and ever since has been, but one people."

But one people, Inspector Obafemi thought with a wry smile. Were that truly were the case. For insofar as the Burt Gummidges of this world were concerned, the locals were one people and everybody else another. He remembered Gummidge's snarky remark about PC Ingham, supposing that Gummidge would likely liken emancipation to constipation - an affliction, not a predilection. For his part, he was impressed by the young officer's dedication to duty, although her timekeeping left much to be desired. But he was sure that that could be remedied given a firm hand and an occasional word in both ears. To now learn that she enjoyed a private income made him even more intrigued. It implied a commitment, if not a passion, for her chosen career. He made up his mind to sound her out about the vacancy on his team. He fancied she might fit the ball to a tee.

A couple of miles from the village, a garage loomed up ahead, or strictly speaking, Obafemi loomed up on a garage. A single petrol pump stood lonely and forlorn in a mashmish of uncombined harvesters, fractured tractors and mangled crashmobiles. As he strolled past, an overalled mechanic gave him a reflex wave then took a closer squint and put down his carjack. He shouted, 'that way, mate,' and pointed anywhere but there.

One hundred or so yards beyond the garage, Inspector Obafemi came upon a five-barred gate affixed to which was a sign announcing, *Bishop's Farm. No Admittance.*

Nailed to an adjunctive fence was a billboard with the slogan, *Nutri-Bella. Vegan Dog Food for Socially Conscious Pets. Tastes Just Like the Real Thing.* As he was unlatching the gatelatch, he was accosted by a burly man in a tweed jacket with a shotgun under an arm.

Colonel Dangerfield – for it was he – roared, 'hoy, you. Get off my land.'

Unfazed by the gratuitous show of inhospitality, Obafemi showed Dangerfield his warrant card. 'Mind if I ask you a few questions, Colonel?' he asked.

'You here about the Bunny Liberation Front?' Dangerfield uncocked his shotgun and lowered it to a less threatening angle. 'About time. I'll be bankrupt if you don't catch the buggers soon. Bloody tree-huggers.'

'Bunny Liberation Front? I take it you are joking.' It was all that Obafemi could do to keep a straight face.

'Do I look like a stand-up comic?' Dangerfield glared at him. 'It's those nutters who are the bloody jokers,' he said. 'Wanting to save the planet is all well and good but threatening me, trashing my fences and freeing my livestock is a criminal offence. Look . . .' He pointed to a ragged jag in a nearby fence. 'Soon as I patch them up, the vandals rip them down again. My business is haemorrhaging money like there's no tomorrow and at this rate, there won't be. I'll be in Carey Street before the month is out.' He triggerfingered his shotgun and scowled at the damage. 'Oh, I know what you're thinking. Why don't I install surveillance cameras and catch the lunatics in the act? Well I did but they stole the lot. Another two thousand quid down the bloody drain.' The blood vessels in his neck throbbed fit to rupture as he rolled his eyes to the heavens and ground his teeth to the cavities. 'I've lodged no end of official complaints, but until you showed up, none of your lot could be arsed to lift a finger. Don't know why I bother paying my taxes. They just get pissed up the wall on bone idle coppers and high-speed trains to shantytowns up north no one gives a damn about,' he said. 'So, Inspector, what do you intend to do about it, or must I take the law into my own hands?'

'What am I going to do about the high-speed trains?' Obafemi asked in all apparent innocence.

'Get a grip, man. This is no laughing matter. You know damn well what I mean.'

'I'll have a word with Sergeant Gummidge when I get back to the station,' Inspector Obafemi said, meaning that Colonel Dangerfield could go whistle. His stream of consciousless invective came across more like a hyperanimated delusion than an actual factuality as such. Pressed for time, he said, 'I'm investigating the murder on The Ordinary Express. I wonder if you would mind answering a few questions.'

'Think I care about Mathers? Think anyone in St. Mary Nook cares about that creep?' Colonel Dangerfield said. 'As I told your sergeant, I was on my cellphone negotiating a contract at the time of the murder. Check with Taylor at Tofu Temptations if you don't believe me. Didn't see a thing. Anyway, if you ask me, whoever killed the interfering busybody did the world a favour.' He made a show of cocking his twelve-bore. 'If you know what's good for you, Inspector,' he said menacingly, 'you will stop wasting my time. And yours.'

15

'Are you sure this is above board, Sammy?'

'No. But so what?'

'We'll be for the high jump if your sergeant - what's his name - catches us.'

'Gummidge? Fat chance. He's made turning a blind eye into a fine art. If anybody reports an offence round these parts, he gives them a raffle ticket and says he'll look into it if they win the annual draw. Seems to do the trick. Our crime figures are the lowest in the county. Have been for ages. Anyway, he's always asleep at his desk this time of day.'

'What about that Inspector Kent County Constabulary sent to head up the enquiry?'

'Don't worry. Gummidge will have packed him off on a wild goose chase to interview a goat or something. Got your gloves? Good. Come on.'

Making sure the coast was clear, Heather Prendergast and Samantha Ingham ducked into a blind alley behind The Crossed Arms and crept up the rickety fire escape. When they reached the first floor, they let themselves in and sneakerpimped along a dimlit corridor to a tape-upped door.

Sammy took a jangle of keys from her pocket and, with a quick look thiswaythat, tried them one by one until the lock clunked. Satisfied that nobody was looking, she serrated the Do Not Enter tape with a thumbnail and tiptoed in.

Much against her better judgement, Heather followed. Shocked beyond all reasonable doubt, she caught and held her breath as she ran an eye over the slum-ber of festering neglect that was Trevor Mather's bargain-basin hotel room. From what she could discern in the half-light of the semi-curtained window, the furnishings were a hodgepodge of utility futility and the haberdashery a mishmash of slapdash trailertrash. *Unspeakable* hardly did the room justice. With Aunt Elizabeth's words ringing in her ears - needs be as needs must in the line of trespass – she swallowed her colour-clash anathema, stiffed her upper lip and set to task.

A thorough search confirmed that forensics had removed everything deemed readily removable. The chest of drawers, wardrobe and bedside cupboard were empty, there was no cellphone or computer and if Mathers kept a notebook, it was notable by its absence. To put it in a nutkernel, Heather was convinced that they were wasting their time. 'There's nothing here, Sammy,' she whispered. 'Let's make ourselves scarce. If anybody catches us, we can kiss our careers goodbye.'

'Chill, pet. This is St. Mary Nook. There's a different set of rules round here,' Sammy told her. 'Let's just say,

Sarge will do anything for an easy life. If anyone reports an offence, he threatens to charge them with Disturbing His Peace and says he'll bang them up in pokey if they don't stop pestering him. Works a treat. The Murder on The Ordinary Express is the first crime on our patch worth getting out of bed for since I don't know when. Come on. I'll do the bedroom while you check the loo,' she said as she knelt down to rummage through a scruff of fluffy stuff under the bed.

Heather Prendergast had always held herself somewhat of a toiletry authority. In her time, she had encountered a wide variety of ablutionary amenities, but Mathers' ensuite toiletwreck defied relief. She was holding her nose with one hand and feeling gingerly behind the cistern with the other when Sammy summoned her from the bedroom. When she hurried through to see what the shout was all about, she found Sammy clutching a small blip of plastic.

'Found a memory stick taped under a drawer,' Sammy said excitedly. 'Forensics took Mathers' laptop but there was nothing on the hard-drive. I bet he downloaded everything on this.'

'Goody,' Heather said. 'Once we've handed it in, we can . . .'

'Whoa, hold on a minute. Think, sweetheart. Think. How we going to explain where we found it? Say we happened to be passing and it fell out of a window? Gummidge might buy it, but Inspector Whatshisname won't.' Sammy flipped the memory stick in the air, caught it one-handed and tucked it in a shirt pocket. 'Don't forget, as far as the official investigation is concerned, your uncle is near enough bang to rights. If we want to get him off the hook, we're going to have to pursue our own line of enquiries.'

And so it was that sometime later, should anyone care to ask, they might be told that Heather Prendergast and Samantha Ingham could be found huddled in front of a bureautop computer in the smaller of Trevelyan Hall's three libraries.

'Did your aunt write all those books?' Sammy pointed to a shelf of academic tomes.

'Don't be silly,' Heather scoffed. 'Only that one.' She nodded at a leather-backed volume entitled *Dung Beetles of the British Isles*. 'Don't ask,' she said before Sammy could.

Banishing most, if not all, thoughts of dung and beetles, Sammy inserted the memory stick into a computer port. Barely able to hold her breath, she squeezed Heather's knee as four icons appeared on screen – Montague Locke-Mortice, Hamilton Dangerfield, Reverend William Bragg and Elouise Decora. 'Looks like we got a full house,' she said. She was about to click on Dangerfield when Guan-Yin padded through the door.

In homage to her zodiacal deities, Nuwa and Fu Xi - siblings who saved mankind by choosing to marry when the world's population was scraping the bottom of the genomic barrel - Guan-Yin was wearing an ankle length Qipao robe embroidered with figurative dragons and snake-headed serpents. In a mark of respect for the bride, Nuwa, who had to hide behind a fan during the incestuous marriage ceremony, her face was masked by a delicate filigreed veil framed by two pendulous earrings and a blue brow-bauble the size of a quack-egg. Pigtailed as always, she was carrying a stack of books almost, but not quite, as tall as she was - geology, geography and genealogy in the main, with a smattering of geometry, trigonometry and Agatha Christie to add balance.

Afraid that Guan-Yin might spot what she was up to, Heather yanked the memory stick out of the computer and slipped it in a pocket. Assuming a casual pose - legs crossed, hands folded in her lap - she said, 'must say, you look pretty as a picture, Guany. Going on a date?'

'She who depend on herself will attain greatest happiness. Mencius say woman must keep distance from man,' Guan-Yin said with her back turned as she filed the books in alphaomegal order

'With you there, sister,' Sammy said with a lashy wink.

Guan-Yin looked over a shoulder, parted her veil and broke into an inscrutable smile. 'There are two kinds of perfect people, Miss Sammy,' she said. 'Those who are dead, and those who have not yet been born.' And with those words of oriental wisdom, she hitched up her Qipao, padded out of the library and eased the door to behind her.

Sammy tapped her temple. 'If you ask me, that woman's got a screw loose. Talking of which, didn't anyone ever tell you how to remove a memory stick?' She retrieved the pentop drive, inserted it into the computer and stared glumly at a flashing error message. 'Flip,' she said. 'You corrupted the data when you pulled it out. Bozo.' When Heather's bottom lip started to quiver, she gave her a chummy pat on the knee. 'Chin up, pet,' she said. 'There's bound to be some kind of software that can sort it.'

Heather took a steadying breath and rattled data recovery into Googoyle. After a quick net-surf, she credit-carded a likely site and sat back idly examining her manicured fingernails while she waited for a megagigitudinous programme to download. 'This is going to take *ages*,' she moaned. 'Oh, well - might as well do some online shopping while I wait.'

As she watched the digital hourglass upload at an e-snail's pace, for the want of anything more illuminating, Sammy stated the obvious. 'Well, at least we know who Trevor Mathers was investigating. Once we've fixed the removable drive, we'll know why. I've a hunch it'll give us the motive,' she said as a blinking message indicated that the memory stick was ready to reveal its secrets. Breath bated, she clicked the drive icon, gasped and turned to Heather with a wide-eyed expression of WTF?

'Golly, it's that dress I just ordered from Partygirl Online.' Heather clapped a hand to her brow. 'I must have pressed the wrong key by mistake. Is that a problem?'

'I'll say.' Sammy struggled to keep a cool face. 'You've only gone and overwritten Mathers' files, that's all. Now we'll have to find a geeky boffin to sort it.'

Struck by an incoming thought, Heather clicked a finger. 'Naff is bound to know a man who can fix it and won't ask questions. I'll ask him when he's back from London.'

'A man? Yeah, right. I've never met a man who can sort a problem without bragging about it in every pub from here to Timbuktu,' Sammy said. 'Oh well, suppose there's got to be a first time for everything.' She raised an eyebrow when she saw the virtual image of a flirty cocktail dress that Heather had erroneously downloaded onto Mathers' memory stick. 'Hey, babe - that's cute.'

Heather's cheeks flushed a blushy shade of cherry. 'Promise not to tell a soul, but I'm planning to surprise Naff with a romantic candlelit dinner for his birthday,' she confided. 'Trouble is, I'm terrified I might do something silly like forget to reserve a table or eat my soup with the wrong spoon.'

'Mum's the word.' Sammy pressed a finger to her lips. 'Hey, why don't we book into a quiet hotel for a dress rehearsal? I can pretend to be your boyfriend,' she said. 'I know just the place. It's run by two mates of mine, Felicity and Fiona. They're the complete package. Total fruit loops. Tell you what, I'll blag us a deal. Two nights for the price of one or whatever. You want everything to go without a hitch, don't you?'

Heather's eyes lit up. 'You know, I might just take you up on that, Miss Ingham. That is so incredibly thoughtful of you. I mean, you've hardly said a word to Naff since you met him, but here you are, offering to help make his romantic birthday treat a success.'

'Birds of a feather should stick together, sweetie.' Sammy gave Heather a sisterly cuddle. 'And the tighter the better.'

16

Inspector Obafemi cast a weather eye at the sky and shuddered. Moments later, raindrops started falling on his head. In no short shrift, the sporadic sputter mizzled from a spatter to a patter to a drizzle to a shower to a downpour to a deluge . . . and then all unmerry hell broke loose.

Cursing his negligence for forgetting to bring his trusty umbrella, Obafemi buttoned up his jacket, turned up the collar and hurried from overlopping branch to leeward wall in search of shelter - scurried might be a better word, or skeltered. To turn a coin of phrase, it seemed that when the heavens opened in these Godforsoaken climes, they did so with a biblical vengeance.

After minutes that felt like more, he burst into the police station looking for all the world like a drowning fish in need of a nice warm grill to toast its gills. Thankful to be home, if not yet dry, he shook the drips off his jacket and draped it over the back of an expectant chair. With a shiver and a shake, he towel-dried his bald head then took off his shoes and left them to dry in front of the Colourgas fire, the only appliance that applied a semblance of application in what was, to his mind, a travesty of imperspicuity.

'Wouldn't leave them there,' Gummidge said without looking up from his newspaper. 'Roof leaks. Put them in the dustbin out back with me wellies. Make sure to put the lid on.'

Why bother, Obafemi grumbled to himself. Judging by the state of the place, here was probably as dry as there. To call the police station decrepit would be doing decrepitude a gross disservice. Every other roofslate was missing and as far as the guttering went, it already had and was now no more than a drain on the imagination. Resigned to being confined with Gummidge until the storm passed, he asked, 'ever heard of The Bunny Liberation Front?'

Sergeant Gummidge turned to the bowls section in the bowels of his newspaper and shrugged. 'Might have,' he said. 'Depends who's asking.'

'Is that a yes or a no, Sergeant?'

'You tell me, Inspector. You're the detective.'

'For crying out loud, this is ridiculous.' Obafemi thumped a fist into the palm of a hand. 'Buck up your ideas, Gummidge,' he shouted. 'Colonel Dangerfield just told me that a bunch of trouble-makers are trying to put him out of business. Says he's lodged no end of official complaints.'

Unperturbed by Obafemi's rising hackles, Gummidge licked a thumb, turned the page and nodded. 'Well he would, wouldn't he?' he said. 'Anyone would think I care.'

'And anyone would think you are a bone-idle slacker,

Sergeant.' Inspector Obafemi said through gritted teeth, temper growing shorter by the fuse. 'If I may say, I find your attitude lax in the extreme.'

Gummidge scrunched up his newspaper and flung it on the floor. 'Oh you do, do you?' he harumphed. 'Well, let me tell you, my constipation is none of your business. We never had no trouble round here before you poked your nose in our affairs.'

Fast losing his tether, Inspector Obafemi clenched his fists. 'So I suppose you don't regard murder as trouble?'

Unflustered by the Inspector's bluster, Gummidge said, 'with all due respect, sir,' with a transparency that brooked all opacity, 'that weren't on my patch. Least, it weren't until The Ordinary Express pulled into St. Mary Nook, and by then Mathers were already a statistic. Anyway, don't know why you're getting so wet under the collar. Locke-Mortice done it. It's as plain as the nose on your face.'

Inspector Obafemi strode over to the front desk and glared Gummidge in the eye. 'Well I'm not convinced,' he said. 'Seems there was no love lost between Colonel Dangerfield and Trevor Mathers. I would like to know more about Dangerfield. Got anything on file?'

'Try in there.' Gummidge cocked a thumb at a rusty metal box behind the counter.

Obafemi knelt down, prised open the lid and caught his breath, appalled by the stinking mess of festering

116

verminary distress. 'Good grief. Looks like mice are nesting in here. Are all these files ongoing investigations?'

'Not unless one of the time-wasters wins the raffle, they're not,' Gummidge said. 'And for your information, we've not got mice. They're rats.'

Lost for meaningful words, Obafemi upended the box, separated the whiff from the chaff and arranged the files in alphachronological order. When he came across one marked Dangerfield, he brushed off the rat droppings and opened it on the counter. 'What's this?' He held up a scrap of paper with *Joker* scrawled on one side and *Ignore* on the other.

'You can read, can't you?' Gummidge said. 'Them's my conclusions after I looked into the Colonel's complaint.'

'So you investigated it?'

'Well, I give it a quick think.' Sergeant Gummidge raised a hand to smother the mother of all yawns and sighed, 'so much to do, so little time.'

Inspector Obafemi's eyes widened by the page as he looked through the file. 'Good grief,' he said. 'This is full of threatening letters, photographs of vandalised fences, damaged doors and goodness knows what. Looks like the Colonel has every reason to be concerned.'

'If I may say, that is only your opinion,' Sergeant Gummidge said. 'To my mind, he needs to get a grip and stop harping on like a moaning Minnie.'

Patience tested to the hilt, Obafemi read out a note scrawled in blood red ink . . . *All God's creatures deserve their freedom. We shall not rest until the last enslaved bunny hops free.*

'Dare say it's just kids larking about,' Sergeant Gummidge said with a cockeyed snook. 'Didn't you make mischief when you were a young-un? I know I did.' He broke into a distant smile, reminded of days of yore joyriding tractors, chucking housebricks at old age pensioners, stampeding livestock across neighbourhood gardens and countless other ribtickling japes before he joined the Kent Constabulary as a trainee jobsworth. 'Nothing a good clip round the ear can't sort. But, oh no. These days you're not allowed to raise your voice to the wife, let alone give a snotty-nosed brat a good hiding. Your do-gooder mates should never have abolished the birch.'

Inspector Obafemi pretended that he hadn't heard, a trait fast becoming a habit. 'Whoever The Bunny Liberation Front are,' he said, 'they have been making Colonel Dangerfield's life a misery for almost a month.' He leafed through the file, pausing every now and then to take a closer look at this or that or occasionally the other. 'Death threats, criminal damage, breaking and entering . . . no wonder the man is at his wits' end.' Struck by a thought, he asked, 'when did Mathers come to St. Mary Nook?'

Gummidge turned to look at the station diary chalked

on a wall behind the front counter. 'A month ago last Saturday, it says there. I like to keep a close eye on strangers.'

'Oh you do, do you? And why is that?' Obafemi asked, although he had a sneaking feeling that he might already know the answer.

'It's a well-known fact that strangers got criminal tendencies, present company excepted,' Sergeant Gummidge said with all the sincerity of a used car salesman offering a lifetime warranty on a cut-and-shut carwreck.

Inspector Obafemi bit his lip in an attempt to stem his contempt. 'So what do you intend to do about Colonel Dangerfield's complaint?' he asked, then instantly regretted squandering precious breath on such a flutterbrained question.

Sergeant Gummidge took off his tunic, pegged it on the back of the door and reached for his off-duty gabardine. 'Don't know how things work in your neck of the swamp, Inspector,' he said, 'but when you been on the job as long as I have, you'll know that if you ignore a problem, it'll like as not go away. A storm in a teapot, most of them. Take this bunch of nutters.' He rapped his knuckles on Dangerfield's file. 'Either they'll sort it out in the pub car park one night or the barmy bunny army will get bored and lose interest. With any luck, Dangerfield will go broke, piss off back where he come from and that'll be the end of the matter. No point kicking over an asp's nest and making work for PC Ingham,' he said as if it went without thinking. 'Anyway, it's not like anyone cares apart from the colonel and them funny-bunny warriors, and they're welcome to each other.' He peered through the windowgrime, said, 'it's stopped raining. About time,' hitched up his trousers, buttoned up his flies, put on a flat cap and shuffled out to the binzone to swap his slippers for his wellies.

Inspector Obafemi dusted a spider's web from a windowpane and watched Sergeant Gummidge make a beerline for St. Mary Nook Bowls Club whistling *A Copper's Lot is Not a Happy One*. He was breath-taken by the man's brazen laziness. Regretting that PC Ingham wasn't present to bring a modicum of correctitude to proceedings, he turned his attention to what Gummidge catalogued as "possible pending complaints."

After reading Colonel Dangerfield's file again, Obafemi looked for any connection between Mathers and the mysterious Bunny Liberation Front, as good a reason as any why Dangerfield might have wanted Trevor Mathers dead. Having drawn a blank, he examined the remaining box contents for complaints relating to, from or by Reverend William Bragg or Elouise Decora.

'Well, well, well, what have we here?' he said to no one in particular when he came across a sheet of foolscap paper stapled to a raffle ticket. 'So Decora wanted Gummidge to arrest Mathers for stalking, did she? Interesting.' He hoiked Elouise Decora's file out of the ratfodder box, put it to one side and dug a little deeper. Eyebrows raised, he unearthed a complaint lodged by Reverend William Bragg. If Bragg was to be believed - a distinct plausibility bearing in mind that he was the local vicar - Trevor Mathers had been seen hanging around the vicarage on numerous occasions. Moreover, Bragg claimed that Mathers had accosted him one night and threatened to physically defrock him unless he divulged some kind of confidential information.

What information, Inspector Obafemi wondered? Stumped, he put on his damp shoes and wandered outside to have a pensive smoke. Thankfully the rainclouds had passed. In their stead, a whimsical daffodil sun floated high in the afternoon sky patiently waiting to put her hat on and pootle off to bed.

Inspector Obafemi weighed the evidence between two minds. From what he now knew, it would seem that all Mathers' fellow-passengers bore the victim a grudge . . . all except one - Montague Locke-Mortice. He ticked off possible motives on the fingers of one hand: Colonel Dangerfield's livelihood was being threatened by a crackpot terrorist organisation that first appeared when Mathers came to St. Mary Nook; Elouise Decora claimed that Mathers was stalking her; and reading between the double-spaced lines, Mathers was threatening to commit egregious bodily harm to Reverend Bragg unless he spilled some confidential beans.

What could the local vicar possibly know that could

be of interest to a Canadian journalist, Inspector Obafemi wondered? Lost for an answer, he decided to ask the horse's mouth.

St. Mary of Our Nook Vicarage proved easiness defined to find; it was but a gravestone's haul from the medieval parish church to which the village owed its name. Set back from Tunbridge Road by a sturdy gardened wall, were Obafemi called upon to describe it in a few too many words, in all probability he would have said that it was a typically Victorian squarebricked slateroofed building with a gated gravelled drive, overarching windows and tall chimney stacks. He had little doubt that it had been splendid in its day but that day had long since gone. In dire need of a scrape of paint and brickworn at the extremes, like the dwindling congregation at the nearby church, it was barely fit for purpose.

Inspector Obafemi unlatched the gate and strolled up the driveway savouring his last few puffs of Virginia shag. As he approached the porch, a portly dog-collared man in a woollen jacket with patchy leather elbowcuffs came out to meet him, hand outstretched in greeting. After a brief exchange of irrelevant pleasantries and vacuous platitudes, Reverend Bragg - for it was he - invited Inspector Obafemi in.

'Dreadful business. Shocking. Truly shocking,' Bragg said as they sat in the sitting room sipping insipid tea and nibbling fruity nutcake surrounded by the trappings of the reverend's missionary past - carved and whittled crosses, faded photographs of smiling supplicants, dog-eared bibles in a variety of tongues and a grotesque shrunken head in a grotesque shrunken pith helmet. 'Hard to believe that Mister Mathers was murdered, may he rest in peace.' Bragg raised his eyes to the heavens and made the sign of the cross. 'Do help yourself to more cake, Inspector,' he said with a virtuous smile. 'It is a Bethany Baker recipe. I would be lost without The Vegan Vicar's Cookbook. To my mind, it is her tour de force.'

'Don't mind if I do. It's delicious.' Inspector Obafemi gave his tummy a pat and helped himself to another wadge.

'You must understand, Inspector Obe . . .'

'Obafemi,' Inspector Obafemi said as Bragg struggled to wrap his tongue around the name. But that was by no means unusual; Obi wan Kenobi and Isaac Aberfanny were foremost on a long list of miss-speaks.

'If I am not mistaken, that is Nigerian, is it not?' Reverend Bragg said. 'As you may know, I was a missionary in Abuja before I came to St. Mary Nook. Archbishop Ndukuba was a dear, dear friend of mine. Marvellous country. The wildlife is spectacular, especially the Bunyoro rabbits. And what wonderful people. So devout. Truly.'

'So I gather,' Obafemi said. 'But I've never been there. I'm from Cardiff.'

'What a wonderful country Wales is,' Bragg said. 'Marvellous people. The national dish, Welsh Rabbit, is utterly delicious. And of course the choirs are famous the world over.'

'Indeed.' Inspector Obafemi agreed. Although he didn't, he was tempted to tell Bragg that he had been a leading member of the Pontprennau Chapel boys' choir. Well, that is to say he was until his voice broke. Although keen to continue, the pastor demanded he leave following complaints from the dwindling congregation. Such is life, he thought with a philosophical shake of the tonsils.

Having sated his appetite with homemade cake, Inspector Obafemi posited his crumby plate on the gatekneed table and moved on to the reason for his visit. 'According to the statement you gave Officer Ingham,' he said, 'you didn't see anything unusual on the Ordinary Express on the afternoon of Mister Mathers' murder.'

'I have no idea who was responsible, if that is what you mean, Inspector,' the reverend said with a shrug of his bowed shoulders.

'Maybe you heard something. Raised voices, perhaps?'

'Goodness gracious, no. I am sure that Colonel Dangerfield would have rallied to Mister Mathers' assistance had he cried for help. Hamilton is always boasting about his military exploits. I certainly wouldn't want to get on the wrong side of the man,' Bragg said with a grimace.

Inspector Obafemi turned over a new leaf in his pocketbook and jotted down a note in his flying shorthand.

'I understand that you recently filed a complaint about Mister Mathers,' he said. 'Would you mind telling me what that was about?'

'More cake, Inspector? I have another in the pantry,' Bragg said in such a way as to suggest that he would rather Obafemi eat cake than ask questions.

Inspector Obafemi patted his paunch to indicate fullupness and cast a timely glance at his watch to suggest that he wished to press on. 'Now, according to your complaint,' he said, 'you claim that Mathers threatened you. Mind telling me why?'

Mindful of his duty as an upstanding citizen, Reverend Bragg explained, 'well, if you must know, Mister Mathers waylaid me outside the church one night after evensong. He said that he was researching an article for a Canadian magazine and demanded that I reveal certain facts that Colonel Dangerfield had confided in me. He was most insistent.' He sat back in his easy chair, folded his hands in his lap and gazed at a bamboo crucifix affixed to the far wall, gathering his thoughts. 'Of course, the idea was laughable,' he said after a moment, and as if to prove the pudding, chuckled to himself. 'I am a man of the cloth, Inspector. Anything I am told by a parishioner in confidence goes in one ear and stays there.' He tapped a temple to suggest that a multitude of sins lay between his ears.

'You told Sergeant Gummidge that you were concerned for your safety,' Inspector Obafemi said, choosing not to mention a note in Gummidge's spidery scrawl stapled to Bragg's complaint. It had *timewaster* scribbled on one side and *needs to get a life*, on the other. 'Did Mathers threaten you?'

'Not in so many words.' A note of hesitancy in Bragg's quietly-spoken voice suggested that the confrontation had indeed been physical as well as verbal. 'He said that he would come back later, but I didn't care for his tone of voice. That is why I felt I should report the matter, but I don't know if Sergeant Gummidge found the time to speak to him.'

'I doubt that he did,' Inspector Obafemi said diplomatically. 'Thank you, Reverend. If I have any more questions, I will let you know.' He started to get up but paused midchair. 'Oh, one more thing,' he said with a contrived air of vague-mindedness. 'Have you heard of The Bunny Liberation Front?'

About to show Inspector Obafemi out, Bragg paused midstep, thrown off his stride. Then he smiled and said, 'I see you know about Colonel Dangerfield's bête noire. He is convinced that somebody is trying to put him out of business. I must say, he was in a dreadful state about it when we last spoke. He told me that his partner had accused him of fabricating the story to explain the farm's losses.'

'Colonel Dangerfield has a partner?' Inspector Obafemi expressed surprise, although perhaps he shouldn't have. He only had Sergeant Gummidge's word that Dangerfield was a lone boar.

'Didn't you know, Inspector? Someone invested a tidy sum in Colonel Dangerfield's petfood business. Judging by his lifestyle, I assumed the venture must be doing well, although if I may be frank, I had my suspicions that things were not all they seemed.' Reverend Bragg glanced at the window and lowered his voice. 'Between you and me, the colonel is a compulsive gambler. Of course, it is a terrible affliction at the best of times, but in his case I fear it is an addiction. And unless things have changed since my days as an army chaplain, Her Majesty's Armed Forces are not known for their generous pensions.'

Inspector Obafemi made another note, underlined it and poised his pen. 'Would you have any idea who Colonel Dangerfield's partner is?'

'Now you come to mention it, that is what Mister Mathers wanted to know.' Bragg shrugged aside the question. 'I didn't tell him, of course. And I am afraid that I can't tell you either. Let me just say that I believe they are partners in both senses of the word.'

Having made clear that his lips were now sealed, Bragg saw Inspector Obafemi on his way with a plasticated container. 'A little something for your trip back to Wales,' he said. 'Homemade rhubarb tarts in case you feel peckish.' And with that act of benign charity, he bade Obafemi fare thee well and God speed.

As he strolled down the driveway nibbling a rhubarb

tart - utterly delicious, he thought - Inspector Obafemi had an uneasy feeling that he was being watched. He took a quick look over a shoulder and saw Reverend Bragg peering through the sitting room window. He couldn't be sure, but he had a distinct feeling that the mild-mannered vicar was laughing to himself.

17

A dedicated follower of plainclothes fashion, Heather Prendergast fingered the cuffs of her mutton-sleeved blouse and fiddled with the buckle of her svelte felt belt. To say that she was a bag of iterative nerves would hardly do her jangles justice. 'Golly,' she said, 'Colonel Dangerfield says he can see me at five o'clock. How did you know he was looking for a farm hand?'

'The job's been advertised in the Parish Magazine since forever, but the pay sucks,' Sammy told her.

'I don't know the first thing about livestock,' Heather said in all due honesty. Although she had a fondness for most, or almost most, creatures large, small and indifferent, it was an arms' length passion not shared by all, or almost all, of the animate objects of her affections. Indeed, apart from Harry Hamster, her only childhood pet - a bloodhound called Baskerville - used to bare his fangs and snarl at the slightest sniff of her name. 'Why don't you go?' she asked Sammy with a note of guarded panic in her voice.

'Wish I could, but he'd be bound to recognise me,' Sammy said. 'I've pulled his Bentley over for speeding more times than I've had hot dinners. He'd have lost his license yonks ago if Sarge could be bothered to do the paperwork.'

'Suppose I'll just have to risk it then. He is our prime suspect,' Heather mumbled with a reticence that brooked no enthusiasm. 'But my dungarees and jeans are in the wash and I can't go like this. He'll think I'm applying for a job as a receptionist.'

Sammy looked Heather over with what, for the want of a better adjective, might be described as a grimacey frown. 'Guess not,' she said. 'Pencil skirts, chiffon blouses and kitten heels aren't the best gear for mucking out barns. Tell you what,' she said, struck by an inspired stroke of common sense. 'I'll get Cassie to lend you something. She works on a farm.'

'Thanks awfully,' Heather said. 'Is Cassie a close friend?'

'We're like that.' Sammy pressed two fingers together and held them up for Heather to see. 'She's a bit of a chopstick tomcat, but she's Family.'

'A cousin?'

'More like a sister once removed.'

'Sounds like great fun.'

'She's a real sweetheart. Never a dull moment.'

'Can't wait to meet her.'

'She'll be at the nightclub Friday night with the rest of the gang. You still up for coming?'

'You bet. Wouldn't miss it for the world,' Heather

said, hardly able to bottle her enthusiasm. 'Naff will be in London so you might say I'll be off the leash. Hopefully there will be lots of dishy boys to flirt with.'

'Don't hold your breath,' Sammy muttered. 'I'll bell Cassie while you take a shower. You want to look your best, don't you?'

Some time later, a turquoise Saburu saloon pulled up outside Trevelyan Hall. A trim Heathersized girl jumped out, dashed over to Sammy, thrust a suitcase into her hand, gave her a quick hug said, 'must dash, babe. My other half's waiting,' dashed back to the Saburu and sped off.

While Heather was upstairs changing gear, Sammy took advantage of a lull in the narrative to spongebucket her Karmann Ghia. She was shammy-leathering the bonnet when Lady Trevelyan came striding across the front lawn. Looking every inch the itinerant dilettante in an artist's smock and beret, she had an easel tucked under one arm and an oil-colourist's palette under the other.

'Officer Ingham, isn't it?' Lady Elizabeth greeted Sammy with a smile and a wave. 'My, don't you look a picture in that leather jacket and those jeans?' She put down her easel, stepped back and cocked her head. 'I say, ever thought of modelling?' she said. 'The editor of Vogue tells me the androgynous look is all the rage this season. Let me have a few words in a few ears.' Alerted by a timid scuffle, she looked round to see her niece shuffling out of the house. 'What-ho, Spriggy,' she called. 'Off to a fancy-dress party?'

Heather narrowed her eyes at Sammy. It need hardly be said that she had been expecting Cassie to lend her some farmy overalls and bootwear rather than a lavender hipsway skirt, a brown satin shirt with suede shoulder pads and tasselled sleeves and a pair of fancy Cuban-heeled cowboy boots. And as for the polka-dot neckerchief, spurs, leather chaps, holster and broad-brimmed Stetson hat . . . *unspeakable* was not the word. Italics hardly did them justice.

As Lady Elizabeth stared at Heather, lost for words for the first time since her critically acclaimed role as Monsieur Bean in the Pedro Almodovar genderbending movie of Les Miserables, Sammy rallied to Heather's sartorial defence. 'She's auditioning for a new musical at Tunbridge Wells Hippoladium. Whip Crack Away,' she blurted out. 'She's up for the part of Calamity Jane.'

'Oh my word, Doris Day.' Lady Elizabeth tweaked an arched eyebrow. 'When I was a teenage sex-kitten, Miss Day was something of an icon for my fey theatrical friends.'

'Still is,' Sammy muttered. After air-kissy-kissing Lady Elizabeth goodbye, she squeezed Heather into the passenger seat of her sporty car, jumped in beside her and tried to ram Heather's knee into gear. 'Whoops. Sorry, pet,' she said. 'Thought you were the gearstick.'

'Dipstick, you mean,' Heather muttered darkly. 'Why

did you tell Aunt Elizabeth a fib?' she asked as Sammy accelerated down the drive in a cloud of oily tyreburn.

'You're undercover, remember?' Sammy reminded her, lest she forget - hardly likely bearing in mind her outlandish disguise. 'We don't want her to get suspicious.'

'I'm really not sure,' Heather said caught between two doubts as Sammy navigated the twisty lanes with her foot rammed to the floor like a dodgem diva. 'Maybe if I tuck the hem of my petticoat under my skirt, I'd feel less self-conscious.'

'Give it a go if it makes you feel better,' Sammy said with as straight a face as she was able. 'Trust me, sugar. That gear is what all self-respecting farmhands wear round these parts. St. Mary Nook is years behind the times.'

Twenty harum-scarum minutes later, Sammy pulled up in a layby by the driveway to Bishop's Farm. 'I'll drop you off here and wait,' she said as she shunted a reluctant Heather out of the Ghia and wished her, 'good luck. Break a leg.'

Colonel Dangerfield was pacing the farmyard checking his watch when Heather arrived for her appointment. 'Good grief. Where's the rodeo?' he gasped and rubbed his eyes when he saw her hobbling down the track, biting her lip - her chaps chafed, her holsters pinched and the spurs dug into her heels like peaky anklegrinders.

Silently cursing Sammy for sending her into the lion's

den dressed as a circus act, Heather improvised with, 'I came straight from the television studio,' and fingered her replica Colts. 'I do walk-on parts in TV westerns. Bit of a hobby of mine, don't you know?' she said as Colonel Dangerfield stared at her in stupefied bemusement. 'Work's been thin on the ground lately. That's why I need this job.'

Colonel Dangerfield frowned and checked his watch again. He said, 'I've got another appointment in an hour so let's get on with it,' and led the way to a corrugated concrete barn circumfenced by barbed wire. As he unpadlocked the gate, he nodded at Heather's replica six-shooters. 'Know how to use those?' he asked. 'The woods over by Bishop's Hill are infested with foxes. Bloody pests. I keep a loaded twelve-bore to see them off.' He opened the barn door, flicked a light switch and showed her in.

Never in all her born years could Heather Prendergast have imagined such a hoppalongitude of ragtag and bobtailed furriness. To describe the barn as a stinking mess of unsanitary bunnitary distress would be doing it an alliterative mercy. As far as her eye could see were rabbits, rabbits, rabbits, cowering in caged misery. She felt her heart rend into a thousand achy-braky pieces as they looked up at her with pleading eyes begging to be released from a blight worse than death.

'They eat, they fuck, they sleep, they fuck, they eat,' Colonel Dangerfield told her. 'Pathetic creatures. Your job will be muck them out and stuff dandelion leaves down their gullets until they're too fat to move.'

'What happens to them then?' Heather hardly dared but nevertheless asked.

'They're shipped off to loving homes,' Dangerfield said. 'I'm a dedicated environmentalist committed to preserving endangered species.'

'Rabbits - endangered?' Needless to say, Heather assumed that the colonel was pulling her petticoated leg.

'With global warming the way it is, rabbit numbers will plummet if we don't ground planes. And cars,' Colonel Dangerfield said as he led Heather through a carpetude of hopskipjumpies to an annex at the rear. 'Cows are the worst. They fart more methane than the House of bloody Lords.' He opened a cage, grabbed a rabbit by the ears and thrust it into Heather's arms. 'This one's ready to go. It's too fat to move. Take it to the transit hutch for grooming. I'll deal with it later. No, not that door, you imbecile,' he yelled as she poked her head into a dimlit room.

Aghast at the sight that met her startled eyes, Heather held her breath and clutched bunny to her chest. For before her lay a butcher's slab caked with blood. Dead center lay a bone handled knife with a bloodied blade.

Above the killing table hung rows of throatslit bunnies dangling by their hind legs. Scores of amputated paws were drying on a nearby table alongside glittered boxes labelled *Synthetic Lucky Rabbit Foot Charms.* In one corner of the morbid mortuary was a stack of tofu sacks and in another, a pile of cartons branded, *Nutri-Bella. Vegan Dog Food for Socially Conscious Pets. Tastes Just Like the Real Thing.*

Unsure whether to faint or scream, Heather clamped a hand to her mouth. 'Murderer,' she gasped through her fingers.

'It's not what it looks like,' Dangerfield assured her.

'Yes, it is,' Heather said as she snuggled bunny in her arms for mutual protection.

'OK, maybe you're right,' Dangerfield admitted. 'But they're only bloody rabbits, for God's sake.'

'Monster,' Heather gasped.

Colonel Dangerfield grabbed the bloodied dagger from the table, wiped it on his slacks, raised it menacingly above his head and snarled, 'so do you want the job or not?'

'Are you serious?'

'Is that a yes or a no? Make up your mind,' Dangerfield growled as Heather backed away.

Clutching bunny for all dear worth, Heather fled like a will o`the wimp with Colonel Dangerfield hot on her Cuban heels. Younger, nimbler and fleeter of foot than her pursuer, she sprinted into the yard and hid behind an upturned dirtbarrow. As Dangerfield lumbered past panting and wheezing like a clapped out buffer, she scrambled into the cab of a Goliathon Combined Hedgemower and ducked beneath the dashboard. Hardly daring to draw breath, she clamped a hand over bunny's mouth to stop it braying – she was, after all, a dyed-in-the-woods livestock novice - and crouched stockstill, frightened out of her wits. Chilled to the marrow, she crossed her fingers - she and bunny both - as Dangerfield stalked the yard, screaming blue-thunder at the top of his voice. He nosepoked into piggypokes, he opened barn doors and slammed them shut again, he kicked defenceless hay bales in a frenzied fit of fury. Unable to find her, he stormed back to the barn to prepare for his next meeting, cussing and blinding like the trooper he once was.

Making sure the coast was clear, Heather crept out from her hiding place. She looked warily about, kissed bunny on the whiskers and set it free. After throwing up in a pigslop and twice more in a barleybucket, she staggered up the track to impart the grim truth to her co-conspirator in sleuth.

'So what's the deal, pet? Tell, tell, tell,' Sammy gushed as Heather slumped into the Karmann Ghia's passenger seat, pale of face and bilious at gill.

Heather dabbed her mouth with her neckerchief and after taking a moment to collect her guts, told Sammy, 'Dangerfield is a fraud. His vegan pet food tastes just like the real thing because it *is* the real thing. Rabbit mixed with tofu. As if that's not enough, he sells bunny feet to superstitious new age cranks claiming they're synthetic lucky charms. Trevor Mathers must have stumbled across his fraud and threatened to expose him.' She took a deep – a very deep – breath and shuddered as a grizzly vision of a butcher's slab and a bloodied dagger came to mind. 'Colonel Dangerfield is our killer, Sammy,' she said with a certitude that brooked not one small shadow of a possible doubt. 'I'd stake my reputation on it.'

18

Detective Inspector Obafemi examined the defective fence and shook his head. This turn of events was, he thought, most ominous - most ominous indeed.

Had this been London, the crime scene would have been clodhopping with Bobbies. But it wasn't. So it wasn't. Needless to say, he had expressed cellularphonic disappointment when Chief Inspector Wheeler informed him that the Met couldn't spare any additional man or womanpower to assist with another murder investigation. When challenged, Wheeler resorted to technical jargon such as back of the beyond, sheepshaggers and country bumpkins.

And so, begrudgingly, Inspector Obafemi was resigned to having to pursue his own lines of enquiry assisted by Sergeant Gummidge - a hamfisted encumbrance if ever there was one - and PC Ingham. Talk of the devil . . . he nodded a cursory hello as Ingham staggered out of the barn clutching her stomach.

'Dicky tummy?' he asked.

'Sorry about that, guv.' Ingham mopped her brow and belched. 'Must be something I ate.'

'Not a pretty sight.' Inspector Obafemi nodded in the direction of the barn.

'You can say that again, guv.' Ingham tried her feeble best to smile. 'It's my first suicide.'

'Dare say you'll get used to it.' Obafemi pointed to a field hopping with liberated bunnies, burrowing, munching, jumping and humping as if every bonk was their first and quite possibly their last. 'Never seen so many rabbits in my life,' he said. 'They're over the moon to be free, and can't say I blame them. That barn was beyond belief.' He drew Ingham's attention to a yawning gap in the fence. 'Looks like the work of The Bunny Liberation Front,' he said. 'Colonel Dangerfield must have caught them in the act.'

'What - you think he was murdered?' PC Ingham expressed surprise. 'How come? The shotgun is registered to him and his finger was on the trigger. I'd have thought it was an open and shut case of suicide.'

'Yes, obviously suicide,' Inspector Obafemi agreed. 'A little too obvious for my liking. Take it from me, constable, the scene was staged. The shotgun was fired from at least six feet away. Any closer and the wound would have been star-shaped. I'll wait for the forensics report,' he said, 'but I can tell you now, they won't find any dabs on the shotgun or powder residue on Dangerfield's hands. Whoever did this will have wiped the place down. By the way, did you notice a pungent smell?'

'Not half, guv,' Ingham said, trying not to gag. 'Doubt I'll ever be able to look a bunny in the tail again.'

'Must say, the stench was pretty overpowering. But I'm talking about the perfume on Dangerfield's shirt.'

'Oh, see what you mean, sir. Actually, now you come to mention it, I did. If I'm not mistaken, it was Chanel Number Ten.'

'Well done, constable. That's what I thought. You know, I bought some for the wife's fortieth birthday, but it didn't suit me,' Obafemi joked. Or was he joking? We may never know. 'And what about those footprints in the yard?'

'High heels. I'd say we're looking for a woman.'

'Two.' Inspector Obafemi corrected her. 'By the looks of it, Colonel Dangerfield had two visitors yesterday. One was wearing stilettos and unless I'm very much mistaken, the other was wearing Cuban heels. Let's hope forensics get some casts before Gummidge tramples all over the crime scene.' He showed Ingham a polythene bag containing a few strands of hair. 'Judging by these, I'd say the killer was a brunette. Shame there's no surveillance cameras.' He pointed to a picture-book cottage browing a nearby hill. 'Come on. Let's see what the neighbours have to say.'

Inspector Obafemi and PC Ingham set off at a brisk pace, keeping to a well-trod path that cuffed a stalky cornfield before arboretuming a leafy copse and meandering across a clovered meadow. From there, it hugged a berried hedgerow before sloping up a hummock to a picturesque thatched cottage overlooking the valley.

Although PC Ingham made a brave effort to smile, she failed to convince. If her pasty pallor was anything to go by, Inspector Obafemi suspected that she was having trouble scrubbing the murder scene from her mind. That was hardly surprising, he thought, as Colonel Dangerfield's brains and gore and blood were spattered all over the bunnymorgue like a Jackson Pollock mural and what remained of his face was contorted into a Munchian scream. He could well imagine that the gruesome scene would have been a baptism of fire for the young officer. But like losing one's virginity, there always has to be a first time . . . unless the one in question is a hermit, a eunuch, a monk, a nun, wilfully abstemious or all of the above. And like losing one's virginity, seeing a first murder victim is all too often a traumatic experience. It certainly had been for him. Come to think, both were.

As they walked, Obafemi engaged Ingham in small talk to take her mind off the bunny barn. 'Not from these parts, are you?' he asked or rather he stated the blaringly obvious bearing in mind her accent.

'No, guv. Brighton.'

'I know it well. So what brings you to St. Mary Nook?'

'Came to visit a mate and liked it. When a vacancy cropped up on the local force, I applied and got the job.'

'Ever thought of moving to London?'

'Maybe one day, guv. Depends.'

'Depends on what?'

'Oh, this and that,' said Ingham with a non-committal shrug.

They continued in silence until Obafemi asked, 'so how was your date the other evening?'

PC Ingham cleared her throat. 'We had a lovely time,' she said.

'No hubble, bubble, toil and trouble?'

'Sorry, guv. Not with you.'

'Sergeant Gummidge said something about a Kent Coven.'

'Wouldn't listen to a word sarge says, sir. He's out of the ark.'

'So, your young man didn't turn up in a wizard's hat.'

'I'm not dating Harry Potter if that is what sarge told you,' Ingham said with a smile.

'Is he your boyfriend?' Inspector Obafemi asked.

'If you don't mind, guv, I would rather not say. It's early days.'

'Sorry. That was out of order. It's none of my business.'

'No, sir,' Ingham said. And there the conversation

ended.

Half-timbered, fully thatched and squat-chimneyed, Rose Cottage was typical of the area. As Obafemi and Ingham strolled up the garden path, a middle-aged woman in bri-nylon slacks and a prissy polyvested blouse opened the front door. She gave them a disparaging look and asked, 'may I help you?'

'I'm Detective Inspector Obafemi and this is my assistant, Officer Ingham. Can you spare a few minutes?' Obafemi gave the cottage-holder his card. 'We're investigating an incident at Bishop's Farm. I wonder if you would mind answering a few questions, Miss . . .'

'Patsy Gomersall, and if you don't mind, it is Mizz,' the woman said. 'Oh, well, if you must. But be quick.' She tapped her watch. 'I'm zooming in half an hour.' When Obafemi and Ingham exchanged glances, she explained, 'I work from home. Marketing. Frightful bore, but there you are.'

'May we come in?' Inspector Obafemi asked politely and peeked over Mizz Gomersall's shoulder at a cosy inglenooked sitting room at the far end of the hall.

'Certainly not. I have a gentleman friend staying. I don't know what he'll say if he sees me talking to a police officer. Particularly not one like you.' Mizz Gomersall scowled at Obafemi then hurriedly backtracked when he raised a finger. 'I didn't mean . . .'

'Of course not, ma'am. Perish the thought,' Obafemi

said with a misanthropic smile. Ignoring Mizz Gomersall's scowl, he nodded in the direction of Bishop's Farm. 'Tell me, do you know if Colonel Dangerfield had any visitors yesterday?'

Mizz Gomersall ignored him and asked Ingham, 'is the Inspector always so rude?'

PC Ingham stood smartly to attention, said, 'only to bigots, miss,' and tipped her cap. 'Now, would you mind answering the question?'

Thrown off her stride, Mizz Gomersall stuttered, 'well, I say,' and snatched a breath. 'If you must know, the Colonel had a couple of callers yesterday afternoon,' she said. 'There is a good view of Bishop's Farm from my bedroom if I stand on a box. I remember Dickie saying that the Colonel didn't just breed rabbits, he carried on like one. Quite a card, is Dickie.'

'And what do you suppose he meant by that?' Inspector Obafemi asked – as if he didn't know.

'Isn't it obvious?'

Obafemi gave Ingham a meaningful look. 'Am I to take it that the Colonel had a female visitor?'

'Two. In and out in a jiff. Both of them,' Gomersall said with a puritanical snoot.

'Can you describe them?'

Mizz Gomersall looked over a shoulder and shouted

up the stairs, 'won't be long, Dickie. Just chatting to a black detective about Hamilton. Don't forget, we're zooming at half past so you better put on a shirt. No need to bother with boxer shorts.' She turned to Inspector Obafemi and, when she saw him make a note in his pocketbook, exclaimed, 'goodness, what language is that?'

'Shorthand. Describe Colonel Dangerfield's visitors if you would.'

'The first was a young redhead. Slim. Medium height. That's all I remember. She didn't stay long.'

'Can you recall how she was dressed?' PC Ingham asked, doing her best to avoid Inspector Obafemi's eyes.

'Now you come to ask, she was wearing a bizarre costume,' Mizz Gomersall said. 'That's right. I remember Dickie saying that she looked like Calamity Jane from that film, Annie Get Your Gun. He's such a hoot, is Dickie.'

PC Ingham gave Inspector Obafemi a shifty look and cleared her throat. 'And the other woman?'

'Ah, yes. She came an hour or so later. I only caught a glimpse as she was in a tearing hurry. Older than the first girl, I'd say. Short skirt and high heels. Black hair. Too much makeup. You know the type. She had a floppy hat pulled down over her eyes. That's right.' She clicked two fingers. 'She was carrying a laptop. I remember because Dickie said he wouldn't mind sitting on top of her lap. He's such a one, is Dickie,' she sniggered.

'A regular Benny Hill,' Inspector Obafemi said, then stepped back sharply as Mizz Gomersall slammed the door in his face and slid across the bolt.

19

'Can you spare a mo, aunty?'

'Of course, my dear. What is on your mind?'

'A friend has invited me out this evening.'

'And you are worried what Simon will say. Well, have no fear. I will be the soul of discretion. Promise I won't say a word.'

'No, it's not that kind of date. It's a Great Gatsby theme party. Trouble is, I don't know what to wear.'

'I say, what fun.' Lady Elizabeth clapped her hands. 'You know, I believe I may have just the thing. Last year Tim Burton bullied me into starring as Daisy Buchanan in his remake of the Gatsby movie. You know what Timbo is like. Simply won't take no for an answer. And as for his adorable wife, Helena . . . what a sweetie,' Lady Elizabeth said with a throaty chuckle as she cast her mind back to those ne'er forgettable nights of Bonham-Carter bonhomie in her boarding school days. Several of Lady Trevelyan's best-selling autobiographies relate in gripping detail how, whenever Helena was at Ascot for the races, she used to sneak out of the dorm at the dead of night and rendezvous with 'Hell Baby,' as she called Helena, behind the celebrities' cycle sheds. They would make merry until dawn with a humidor of Cuban cigars, a magnum or two of Remy Martin Napoleon X111 Cognac and a few athletically configured stable boys. Happy days . . . oh, happy, happy days.

Although Lady Trevelyan, or rather Veronika Vivendi as she was known to her millions of devoted fans, was a modest and unassuming star of stage and screen - as long as she was given lead billing and the lioness's share of the box-office take - she had on occasion been known to throw a tantrum on set. It was, however, never her fault. Nothing ever was. And Burton's Gothic Gatsby remake was no exception. She explained, 'midway through dress rehearsals in Transylvania, Leonardo DiCaprio bit the head off a bat and stormed out. He was quite right, of course. The catering was hardly up to scratch. Well, when I heard that Tom Cruise had agreed to step into darling Leo's shoes, I resigned on the spot. There are limits.' She stuck her nose in the air, mortally offended by the very idea. 'Fortunately the production company allowed me to keep my costumes. They were far too delicate for my stand-in, Scarlett Johansson.'

In a rare display of auntly hospitality, Lady Elizabeth invited Heather up to her boudoir, a palacious bedchamber overlooking the ornamental pond on one side and Poacher's Wood on the other. Boasting an ensuite wetroom the size of a Turkish bath and a humungous walk-in wardrobe, the décor was part bordello, part town-and-county and part jetset chic.

Lady Elizabeth explained that she and her husband

occupied separate bedrooms and had done since their honeymoon; one night listening to him snore had been enough. 'No idea what he does when he goes to bed. I assume he has some kind of perversion. He is a man after all,' she said as if stating Newton's Fourth Law of Emotion. 'According to the cleaner, Missus Mopp or whatever the slovenly woman's name is, Monty keeps train timetables under his mattress. He stores all his other personal effects in the gazebo. His office, he calls it. Won't let anyone near the place.'

Slipping seamlessly into the role of fashionista seamstress, Lady Elizabeth traded her designer daywear for a common or garden Dolce and Gabbana housecoat and showed Heather into her dressing room.

Honoured and awed in equal measure, Heather gazed about what looked to every purpose and design a Hollywood wardrobery – glitzy lightbulbed dressing table, wall to wall closetry and multitiered drawers crammed to overflowing with every manner of tittilacious and bummapy underthings. Pinned to the walls were autographed photographs of Veronika Vivendi posing in a variety of made-for-pleasure haut-couture gowns arm in arm with a brogues gallery of well-heeled Hollywood stars including, but by no means limited to Sean Connery, Woody Allen, Barbra Streisand, Bruce Willis, Matt Damon, Mickey Mouse, Will Smith, Danny DeVito, Leonardo DiCaprio . . . in short, everyone and anyone in Tinseltown who might be said not to be nobody and no one.

Lady Elizabeth sat Heather down at the dressing table, tucked a towel round her shoulders and set to task with a comb, scissors and clippers. 'You have such lovely hair,' she remarked as she snipped and clipped. 'Just like your mother.'

'Tell me about her,' Heather said with her eyes glued on the mirror. 'I didn't know her. Not really. I was only ten when she died. From what I remember, she was a very private person.'

'Indeed. Other-worldly, one might say. A dreamer. She was extremely beautiful, you know,' Lady Elizabeth said as she fingered her niece's hair with the fondness of a surrogate mother rather than the snatch of a profligate aunt. 'It never ceases to amaze me that my Veronika Vivendi swimsuit calendar sells by the million, but as a gal I was considered quite the plain Jane,' she said, half with a chuckle and half with a sigh. 'I was a sporty tomboy whereas your mother was an elegant swan destined for a glittering future as a doyenne of high society. Do sit still, Spriggy. You are such a little fidget,' she scolded as she untucked the towel and brushed a wigsworth of hair off Heather's shoulders. 'Like it?' she asked as Heather examined her radical new nineteen-twenties bobstyle in the mirror.

'I'm not sure,' Heather said as she fussed with the fringe. 'It's very different.'

'Goodness me, you are such a stick in the mud, young lady. Just like your mother. Thank goodness you have inherited her looks as well as her personality,' Lady Elizabeth said as she slid open a multi-storey wardrobe and weaved a hand at a dazzling array of stage-screen garmentry.

'Golly, you've kept all your old movie costumes,' Heather said as a superabundance of silver-screen iconoclasms was revealed in all its frocky glory.

'Call me sentimental,' Lady Elizabeth sighed, 'but it would break my heart to part with a stitch.'

Dazzled by row upon row of sartorial wonders, Heather could hardly sublimate her thrall. 'Do you still have the costumes you wore in Die A Different Day, the James Bond film you starred in when you were a teenager?' she asked. 'I read somewhere that they influenced a generation of girls.'

'I most certainly do.' Lady Elizabeth pointed to a shelf at the top of a wardrobe. 'They are in that vanity case up there. Not the shoes, of course. I keep them in one of my warehouses.'

'What about all those gorgeous gowns you wore in the Movieflix serialisation of Princess Diana's life?' Heather asked. Along with half the nation, she had followed the series from start to finish.

'Sadly not,' Lady Elizabeth sighed. 'I donated most of them to darling Diana's favourite charities. Having said that, I did keep a few bits and bobs I couldn't bear to part with – lingerie mainly. I keep the negligees in an aircraft hangar at Biggin Hill with my Spitfire. The corsets and camisoles are in a barn in Essex. Not sure where the camiknickers are. Buck House, maybe. I must ask Charles and Camilla next time they pop round for drinkies. But enough about me,' she said with a purposeful clap of the hands. 'Let's find you something to wear.' She thumbed through her period dress collection until she arrived at the twentieth century. Twinkling an eye, she unwardrobed a slinky chiffon flapper dress. 'Dare say it is a little risqué so you better wear a slip underneath. I always say, never let a gentleman see what is on offer until he has earned the right of passage.'

Busybeeing like a fusspot on the boil, Lady Elizabeth helped Heather on with the dress and adjusted it to fit. When she finished, she said, 'slip these on,' and handed her a pair of silk stockings.

'If you don't mind me asking, aunty, why did you marry Uncle Monty?' Heather tried not to sound too dismissive but it wasn't easy. Her aunt's choice of husbandry was one of the great unsolved mysteries of the twenty-first century.

Lady Elizabeth turned to look at an autographed photograph of Jacqueline and Aristotle Onassis tacked to the bidet door. 'I suppose it seemed the thing to do at the time,' she said. 'You simply would not believe how tiresome it was being young, gorgeous, rich and unattached. I had suitors hounding me morning, noon and night, threatening to slit their wrists if I refused to marry them. Film stars, bankers, playboys. The worst were the titled nobodies with family estates in Scotland. Ghastly place. Would you believe, the national dish is boiled offal? Doesn't bear thinking about.' She screwed up her face - as legend has it, a face that launched a thousand ships. 'I told them all to go hang and married the first insignificant little worm I came across prepared to do my bidding without answering back,' she said. 'I suppose I took pleasure in humiliating all those ghastly billionaires. Rubbing their noses in it. Serves them bally-well right.'

Lady Elizabeth gazed wistfully into a misspelt passt, shook her head and sighed. 'I remember the headlines to this day. The World's Most Beautiful Woman Marries Nonentity in Whirlwind Romance.' Misty-eyed, she gazed at a photograph half hidden by the jars and phials and twists and puffs of cosmetic chemistry littering her dressing table. Taken at Canterborough Cathedral, the blushing bride and stuffy groom were exchanging nuptial vows at the altar. Halfway down the aisle, slightly out of focus, a score of titled bridesmaids could be seen struggling with the billowing train of her preposterously ostentatious wedding gown. To Heather's way of thinking, they looked like petticoated shrimps tangled in an organza fishing net.

'Whirlwind romance?' Lady Elizabeth scoffed. 'The only thing that gets Monty's dander up is a train timetable. That's why he is the ideal husband. Vanilla ice to my hot chocolate sauce. I can get on with my life without him interfering.'

Refocused on the material task at hand, Lady Elizabeth handed Heather an elasticated garter and chuckled when she blushed. 'To be honest,' said she as she squatted down to straighten the seams of her niece's stockings, 'can't remember when Monty and I last had a meaningful conversation, never mind an intimate evening together. Why would we? He doesn't have a thing to talk about except The Flying Scotsman. But at least he hasn't been any bother . . . until now,' she said wistfully. 'Nearly done, my dear.' She tucked a safety pin into a corner of her mouth and fiddled with Heather's sash. 'Righty-ho, let's have a look.' She ran an eye over her craftswomanlike handiwork and nodded. 'Splendid,' she said. 'Now sit still and stop fidgeting while I do your makeup.'

After pansticking her niece's face with foundation, puff-powder, lashliner, lip-wax, cheekblusher and lidfrost, Lady Elizabeth rooted through one of her jewellery trunks for a string of pearls, a pair of satin elbow gloves and a preposterosity of bling – bangles, dangly geometric earrings, a gold armband and a pharaoh broach. As a final coup de gras, the doyenne of the silver screen, Playmate of multiple months and serial Mann Booker Prize winning novelist, morphed into common-as-muck lady-in-waiting mode and mocked a servile curtsy. 'Well I do declare, me-Lady,' she did declare in the authentic Mockney accent she had perfected for her Oscar-winning performance as Eliza Doolittle in Kenneth Branagh's radical screen adaptation of Pride and Prejudice. 'You shall go to that-there ball.' Rollicking with laughter when her love-a-duck impression met with a scowl, she nudged Heather in the ribs and said, 'but seriously, Spriggy. That dress looks far better on you than it ever did on me. You have such a trim figure.'

'By that, I suppose you mean I'm skinny and flat chested.'

'Think yourself lucky,' Lady Elizabeth said with a busty flush.

Heather was strapping on her t-strap shoes when Guan-Yin padded through the door. In deference to her astronomical muse - the spirit of Xiwangmu, the powerful Chinese goddess who tends the Peaches of Immortality - she was wearing an orange silk Song dynasty comb hijab dress. Her jet black hair was swept back into a delicately ribboned high ponytail, which dangled down her back like a hairy snake. She tucked her hands into her sleeves and bowed. 'Miss Sammy is outside,' she announced. 'Numerous friends means no deep friendships. Water flows in only to flow out.'

To Heather's acute embarrassment, Lady Elizabeth clapped her hands and told Guan-Yin, 'I am so pleased that Spriggy has made a friend. She was always such a solitary child. I used to worry awfully that she would grow up to be a spinster or a virgin. Both quite possibly. But look at her now.'

Guan-Yin turned up her nose, said, 'happiness is best cosmetic,' and padded out, quietly closing the door behind her.

'You don't think this dress is too fleshy?' Heather said as she examined the fit in the mirror. 'I'm terribly self-conscious about my knees.'

'Humbug,' Lady Elizabeth snorted as she made a last minute adjustment to Heather's headband. 'You look more like Daisy Buchanan than Mia Farrow ever did.' She draped a feather boa over Heather's shoulders, pressed a beaded clutch into her hand, and tucked a small silver brandy flask into a garter. She winked and said, 'a little tease for your gentlemen admirers.' Delighted with her niece's makeover, she shooed her out with, 'now off with you before your stagecoach turns into a pumpkin.'

Feeling like a brand new self, Heather tripped down the stairs and skipped out of the front door. When she saw Sammy, she raised her arms, twizzled a twirl, shimmied her hips and gushed, 'like it?'

Sammy clapped her hands, said, 'doll, you look cute enough to eat,' and give her a hug.

Blushing like a rosebud, Heather wriggled free. She took a few steps back, the better to admire Sammy's beaded hipswing dress, fishnet tights and strappy high-heeled sandals. 'We look like a pair of flappers,' she giggled.

'Slappers, more like.' Sammy slapped Heather's backside and winked. 'Take it from me, sugar - you're going to be a catastrophic success.'

'Think so – really?' Heather said with a nervous titter. 'I wish Naff could see me now. Promise you won't tell him if I get chatted up by any boys.'

'Dream on,' Sammy said and winked. 'Hey, come and meet Cassie. She's our designated driver so we can let our hair down.' She took Heather's hand and, laughing and joking like schoolchums off to a prom, they flapped across the carpark to Cassie's Saburu.

'Golly, you look like a boy,' Heather said as she admired Cassie's tweed three-piece suit, spats, brogues, candy-stripe bow tie and short side-parted hair. 'If there's a fancy dress competition, you're bound to win by miles.'

Cassie took off her flat cap and flourished a gallant bow. 'Miss Daisy Buchanan, I presume,' she said in a low-pitched, faux New England drawl. 'Jay Gatsby. Would you do me the honour of the first dance?'

Heather fanned her face with a hand. 'Why, Mister Gatsby,' she said with a coy flutter of the lashes. 'I do declare, it would be a pleasure.'

The moment Heather's back was turned, Sammy dragged Cassie aside and hissed, 'hands off, bitch, or I'll bust you for dangerous driving.' Ignoring Cassie's moody sulk, she helped Heather into the back of the Saburu and wrapped a possessive arm around her feather-boaed shoulders. 'I got loads to tell you, pet,' she said. 'But it can wait. Tonight we're going to have ourselves a ball.'

20

Detective Inspector Obafemi rapped his knuckles on the copshop door. When there came no reply, he rattled the letterbox and then, fast losing patience, he rattled it again. Cursing like a navvy when the flap came off in his hand, he flung it into the neighbouring pigfarm with the ferocity of a promiscuous discus.

Obafemi was hardly surprised that the squalid apology for a police station showed no signs of life. After what he had seen in the last few days, nothing would hardly surprise him anymore. Regretting ever having set foot in St. Mary Nook, he sat down on the doorstep, unpocketed his pipe, packed the bowl with roughcut shag, lit up and fumed . . . in every sense of the word.

He had been in a foul mood from the moment he woke up and had grown evermore foulmooded as the day wore on. He was utterly fed up, but not in the substantive sense of the word. And therein lay the problem.

Very much looking forward to expanding his waistline with some traditional local fare, the previous evening Obafemi had parked his paunch at a vacant table at The Crossed Arms restaurant. He unbuttoned his jacket, put on his reading glasses and perused the mouthwatering menu. Decided, he rubbed his hands and told the waitress, 'think I'll have the poached salmon with garden vegetables and roast potatoes.'

'Poached Salmon's off,' the waitress told him with a witless smile. 'The poacher got collared by Sergeant Gummidge and was tagged. That's what them round here call a clip round the ear.'

'Shame,' Obafemi said. 'So what do you suggest?'

The waitress hovered at Obafemi's shoulder, nibbling the blunt end of her pencil. 'The Jugged Hare, Roast Pheasant and Grilled Trout are all off,' she announced, 'but we got Beer Braised Rabbit, Seared Rabbit with Potatoes, Rabbit Stew, Rabbit Fricassee, Italian Style Rabbit and Mash, Slow Roast Rabbit, Rabbit with Garlic and Chives, Savoury Rabbit Meringue Pie, Upside Down Rabbit Pudding . . .'

'Hmmm. They all sound delicious, but think I've had enough rabbit for one day.'

'How about the plat du jour? Traditional Kentish Hotpot with Canterborough Garnish.'

'OK. Let's go for that.' Inspector Obafemi clapped his hands and licked his lips. 'What is it?'

'Rabbit stew with nettle broth and dumplings. I take it you're insured?'

'Unfortunately not. Well, in that case, I'll have the Seared Rabbit and potatoes with extra potatoes and no rabbit. Oh, and a bottle of house wine.'

'Red or white, sir?'

'What do you suggest?'

'Red or white.'

'Think I'll go for the red as long as it's palatable.' Despite the trials and fibrillations of the last few days, Inspector Obafemi had not entirely lost his sense of humour.

'So that's the Seared Rabbit and potatoes with extra potatoes and no rabbit and a jug of water.' The waitress jotted down Inspector Obafemi's order on her squigglepad. 'Want a starter?'

'Got anything without rabbit in it?'

'So that's no starter, then.' The waitress pinafored the order, popped a stick of gobblegum in her mouth and slouched off to the kitchen.

After tucking into a breadstick-in-a-basket washed down with a carafe of house tapwater, Inspector Obafemi retired to his room to take a shower. Or try to. The cranky plumbing was barely fit to dribble. Typical, he grumbled; to describe the room as spartan would be pushing the boot out or putting the boat in - he fancied either euphemism equally inept. The three square metres of perspirational penury brought to mind his digs back in his days as a squalorly scholar. Both rooms bore a similar must of neglect, but whereas his student lodgings had been strewn with half-read books, dirty clothes, sweet wrappers and orphaned CDs, his hotel room was almost quite the opposite. Barren bar a solitary stick of scruff furniture, the creaky floorboards, saggy curtains and lopended mattress granted the room an air of cloistered claustrophoby. The frayed thread that bound the two rooms across the loom of time was that both seemed purposelessly designed to encourage the occupant to spend as much time elsewhere as day, and particularly night, allowed.

Mind buzzing like a faulty refrigerator, Obafemi sat down on the cushioned window seat and gazed out at the lamplit street. He cursed New Scotland Yard for refusing to send reinforcements or better still a replacement or best still, both. When pressed, Chief Superintendent Wheeler admitted - albeit off the record - that he had been instructed to brush the murderous events at St. Mary Nook as far into the undergrowth as the official broom would stretch. It seemed that the Commissioner of Police was concerned that the tabloid press would have a field day should word leak out that Lady Elizabeth Trevelyan, Montague Locke-Mortice and Elouise Decora were tangled up in what was now a double homicide. And in that the Home Secretary was keen to remain on speaking terms with his good lady wife, Lady Trevelyan's old school chum, he had let it be known that a highly invisible profile must be the order of the day. He maintained that one murder squad detective should be sufficient to solve the case. Let's face it, he told Wheeler, Hercule Poirot managed perfectly well on his own and he was Belgian - Belgian, for Christ's sake.

As Inspector Obafemi's mind shunted from The Murder on the Ordinary Express to The Carnage at

Bishop's Farm, he asked himself, had Trevor Mathers and Colonel Hamilton Dangerfield been dispatched by the same unseen hand? Not one to store much place in coincidence, he deemed it reasonable to assume that he was looking for a serial killer. And if that was the case, the other passengers might also be in danger. All except one - the perp.

As was his wont, Detective Inspector Obafemi marshalled his thoughts orderlogically. He deemed it feasible that Trevor Mathers might have unearthed some kind of scandal and was threatening to expose the scandaler. If so, it did not take a giant leap of elucidation to work out that this must have something to do with Locke-Mortice, Dangerfield, Decora or Reverend Bragg, to his way of mind a motley crew of suspects if ever there was one. And now that Colonel Dangerfield had been rubbed out of the equation, those four had become three.

Of course, Montague Locke-Mortice was the front-runner in the finger-pointing stakes. But Inspector Obafemi's famed gut instinct told him that Locke-Mortice was not his man. There were too many clues, almost as if a *someone* was trying to point the finger of guilt in Locke-Mortice's direction. So that left Elouise Decora and Reverend Bragg, on the face of it unlikely villains. But Isaac Obafemi was sufficiently long in his remaining teeth not to take faces at face value.

Tired, not to say exhausted, not to say knackered, Inspector Obafemi put his speculations on hold and slumped into bed. He was just nodding off when his ears were pierced by a cacophony of high-pitched squeals, shrieks and carhorn tooting in the street outside. Unamused to say the least, he trudged to the window. When he drew back the curtains, he saw two girls staggering down the road in hoots of drunken laughter. From what he could make out by the gentle glow of the village streetlamp, the shorter and skinnier of the two was wearing a flimsy chiffon dress and what looked to be an Egyptian headband. Unsteady on her feet, her head was slumped on the shoulder of her scantily-clad companion. A turquoise saloon was following at a first gear crawl. The driver – a fresh faced young man in a flat cap and a candy-striped bow tie – had one hand on the horn and was waving the other out of the window.

When Obafemi saw the taller of the two girls turn and birdy a finger at the driver, he narrowed his eyes and muttered, 'right you are, young lady. We will have words in the morning.' Relieved when the party revellers clambered into the backseat of the Saburu and honked off down the road, he crawled back into bed. He was at one and the same time desperate to drop off yet, in the literal sense of the verb, hoping that he wouldn't - the mattress inclined precipitately to one side. Unable to dim his speculations, he lay awake much of the night with his mind churning like a virtual tombola trying to unpuzzle a cornucopia of convoluted conundrums.

So it was that, suffering from acute overnight starvation and not having winked much sleep, the following morning Inspector Obafemi arrived at the police station more moody and broody than bright and breezy. He was sitting on the doorstep smoking his pipe when PC Ingham came sprinting down the road buttoning up her tunic.

When she saw Inspector Obafemi glaring at her, Ingham stumbled to a halt and snatched a breath. 'Sorry I'm late, guv,' she said. 'The alarm didn't go off.'

Obafemi tapped an eyelid. 'Glitter,' he said.

PC Ingham swallowed. 'See, it was my sister's little girl's birthday party last night. Must have forgot to . . .'

'Think carefully, Officer Ingham. I saw you staggering down the High Street at three in the morning. Must say, your sister's little girl didn't look particularly little.'

Ingham's face turned a poppy shade of red. 'It was sis's hen party, guv,' she said. 'Thing is, she's getting married again Sunday.'

'Judging by the state of her, I doubt she will have sobered up by then.' Inspector Obafemi scrunched out his pipe, instructed Ingham to unpadlock the station door and asked, 'where is Sergeant Gummidge?'

'Never works weekends, guv. Never has. Says it's against his religion.'

'Gummidge is religious?'

'No, sir. Not that I know of.'

'I do not believe this sorry excuse for a shambles,'

Obafemi muttered as he followed PC Ingham into the receptionary. 'I am disappointed wth you, constable,' he told her. 'I will forget about your unprofessional behaviour this time, but . . .' he left an ominous *but* hanging in the air. 'Looks like we may have a serial killer on our hands so you better keep your wits about you. And your clothes on,' he added acerbically. 'Thoughts?'

Thankful to still be on the case, Ingham said, 'we need to find out who Dangerfield's visitor was, sir. If she didn't kill him, she was almost certainly the last person to see him alive.'

'Which visitor? The neighbour said he had two.'

'Wouldn't worry about the first girl, guv,' Ingham said with her fingers back in back-crossed mode. 'I mean, Calamity Jane, for pity's sake. Hardly likely, is it? I'm sure Mizz Gomersall was imagining things. Probably busy zooming her gentleman friend,' she said with a smutty smirk. 'In any event, presumably Colonel Dangerfield was still alive when the second woman turned up. If she found him dead, why didn't she call us?'

'My thinking exactly. Short skirt, high heels, brunette, too much makeup, floppy hat, laptop. Know anyone who fits that description?'

'Crikey,' PC Ingham said. 'Elouise Decora.'

'Think I'll pay Miss Decora a visit. Hold the fort while I'm gone.' Inspector Obafemi gave Ingham a stern look. 'And pull your socks up, officer. I won't tell you again.'

Thankful for a breath of fresh air to aerate his muggy head, Inspector Obafemi strolled along Nook Lane with half a mind on the house numbers and the other half on the case. Although smaller than the larger dwellings in the High Street, the houses were similarly half-timbered, thatch-roofed, quarter-paned and stack-chimneyed, each a mirror image of the last - a carbon copy of the next. Being a Saturday, he had high hopes of finding Elouise Decora at home. She would be mowing the lawn, he suspected. If the drone of whirmowers was anything to go by, scalping the lawn was as much a Saturday routine in these parts as him sardining a tube to the Emirates Football Stadium to watch his beloved Arsenal lose in the final minute of injury time.

'I say, you there. What's your game?' a toffee voice shouted. 'Off with you or I'll call the police.'

Shaken from home thoughts, Inspector Obafemi looked round and saw a tallish brunette in a shortish dress, highish heels, brightish red lipstick and a fakeish suntan shaking a fist at him.

'I mean it,' she said at the top of her voice. 'Your sort aren't welcome here.'

Stricken with a wearisome sense of déjà vu, Inspector Obafemi introduced himself and showed the woman his warrant card. 'I would like to ask you a few questions if you can spare a minute,' he said with a laboured smile.

'Certainly not,' said she. 'If the neighbours see me

talking to a black man, I will never hear the end of it. I may have to emigrate.'

Obafemi leant against a gatepost and packed his pipe. 'Nice weather for the time of year,' he said as he lit up. 'I'm sure the sunset will look spectacular from here.' He crossed his arms to make cryptic clear that he intended to stay for the duration . . . and back again if need be.

Taken aback, the woman looked nervously over both shoulders. 'Well, if you are going to be like that, you had better come in before Gladys and Jimbo see you. But make it quick. I have a newspaper column to write.' Scowling like a dromedary with the hump, she ushered Obafemi into her sitting room and bade him take a seat on the settee. After peeking through the curtains to make quite sure that the neighbours couldn't see her hobnobbing with an *unspeakable*, she shuffled an armchair as far away as it would go and sat down with her hands folded in her lap.

'Is there a problem?' Inspector Obafemi asked.

'Of course there's a bloody problem,' Elouise Decora - for it could hardly be another - snapped. 'You are black.'

'Only on the outside.' Obafemi gave her a reassuring smile.

'This is no joking matter, Inspector. Far from it,' Decora said with a righteous toss of the head. 'You mark my words, positive discrimination will be the end of us. As I intend to tell my readers, liberties are taken for the sake of political correctness.' She nodded at her laptop to indicate an article she was concocting for The Sunday Rant. 'In this day and age, all sorts of riffraff are encouraged to join the constabulary. It is a well-known fact that they would not have a hope of being employed if they were English.'

'Well I never,' Inspector Obafemi said. 'I never knew that. Just as well I'm Welsh.'

'You know perfectly well what I mean.' Decora arched her back and looked down her nose at Obafemi as if he was a stain on the carpet. 'I take it you are here about that dreadful Mathers' business. Well, before you ask, I didn't see a thing. I was writing my column and the next thing I knew, Monty Locke-Mortice was kneeling over Mathers' body holding a knife. He told me he pulled it out of Mathers' back when he tried to save him.'

'Most interesting,' Inspector Obafemi said and pocketbooked a note.

'Great Scott, you do shorthand.' Elouise Decora threw up her hands in astonishment. 'Well, who would have thought it? I assumed you would use a Dictaphone and have an educated girl transcribe it at the office.'

'Not a bit of it. I translate my hieroglyphics into jungle-drums myself when I get back to the hut,' Inspector Obafemi said. 'Now, according to Sergeant Gummidge, you recently filed a complaint against Mister Mathers. I understand you claim he was stalking you.'

'Indeed he was. The man wouldn't leave me alone.'

'Might I ask why?'

'Isn't it obvious?' Decora said with an intemperate scowl. 'I am an internationally renowned newspaper columnist and he was some kind of jumped-up hack. He wanted me to use my influence to get him a job in Fleet Street.'

Inspector Obafemi knew that Decora was bending the truth to creaking point. A famed judge of character, he could tell by the shift of the eyes that she was being economical with her lies, so changed tack with, 'mind me asking when you last saw Colonel Dangerfield?'

'Hamilton? Not since I bumped into him in St. Mary Nook tea rooms a few weeks ago - apart from on the train, of course. I remember because he complimented me on a piece I had just written about the collapse of law and order.' Decora sat back with a pious look on her face. 'We must face the fact that our poor country has gone to the dogs since capital punishment was abolished,' she said with a toss of the head. 'For heaven's sake, it is common knowledge that one can't walk the streets these days without being raped by a transsexual.'

'Shocking, isn't it? I hardly dare go out on my own,' Obafemi said, his voice rife with synthetic sympathy. 'Thank you, Miss Decora. If I have any more questions, I will be in touch.' He started to get up but paused midstretch with a feign of woolly-mindedness. 'Oh, almost forgot,' he said. 'Mind telling me where you were yesterday afternoon?'

'Here, of course. Working on an article about immigrants scrounging off the National Health Service.'

'Can anyone verify that?'

'I would have thought it was obvious. Our hospitals are full of people like you.'

'Your whereabouts, I mean.'

'Of course not, but you have my word, and we English are trustworthy people.'

'If you don't mind, I'll see if your neighbours can assist with my enquiries.'

'I most certainly do mind, Inspector. If you are not prepared to take my word, may I suggest that you send a proper officer to interview Gladys and Jimbo? They are respectable people.'

'Yes, ma'am.' Inspector Obafemi made a play of docking his non-existent forelock. 'By the way, is that yours?' He pointed to a floppy felt sunhat on a coat hook by the door. When Decora gave him a blank look, he smiled and said, 'please don't get up. I'll see myself out.'

21

Leaving her wrap with the feather boa attendant, Heather Prendergast launched into a saturnalia of bedevilled revelry. For one enchanted evening she was Miss Daisy Buchanan, the glittermost star in Long Island's social firmament – the Belle of the Gatsby Mansion Ball.

The first of her many dancefloor partners was a cleanshaven young man in dinner jacket, rufflebuttoned shirt and bootlace tie. He hugged her to his pillowy chest with his slender arms and whispered a husky, 'who are you, old sport?' into her ear. 'Daisy,' she giggled as he romanced his delicate fingers through her bob and kissed her blushered cheeks with his full, soft lips.

Fuelled by adrenaline and an injudicitude of alcohol, Heather cast her inhibitions to the wind with gaye abandon. She flirted with Jay Gatsbys of every age, size, shape and inclination; short, tall, willowy, petite, slim, plump, elfin, foppish, effete . . . Prince Charmings, one and all.

Glorying at being the center of attention and proud as punch to be an honorary member of Sammy Ingham's gang, Heather was plied with delicious cocktails by a queue of delectable admirers. As the clock struck midnight, Sammy pressed a glass of absinthe into her hand replete with wormwood, green anise, sweet fennel, sugar lumps, flaming lips and all. Finding it much to her liking, she downed another and then another of what Sammy mischievously called hang-up suppressants.

The upshot was that three sails to the wind, egged on by hooting, clapping, whistling scantily-clad flappers and their tuxedoed escorts, Heather clambered onto the cocktail bar and shimmied the Charleston with the gusto of the rip-roaring twenties. The last thing she remembered before passing out was throwing up in the ladies restroom in front of a goggle-eyed gaggle of fresh faced young men - a delusional hallucination, she assumed.

An indeterminate time later, she woke up on the backseat of Cassie's car. How she got home was a mystery, but one thing was for sure - it had been a night to remember. Which is not to say that she remembered a great deal about the finer or, not to put too blunt a point on it, the vulgar details when she came to the following morning.

As Lady Elizabeth Trevelyan would have it, the greater the pleasure, the greater the hangover, and Heather was to pay the wages of fun in spades. She was burying her head in the pillows when she heard a knock on the door. Moments later Guan-Yin padded in carrying a silver tray. As was tradition at Mooncake Festival, she was clad from tasselled earrings to embroidered cotton slippers in shimmering white silk – lotus patterned high-collared wrapover smock and ankle-length cheongsam skirt gathered at her slender waist in a knotted sash.

Ponytailed as always, her hair was pinned into a high bun with decorative chan-hua hairgrips - delicate silk flowers with jade leaves and beaded berries. She handed Heather a glass and bowed her head. 'Special morning-after cure, Miss Heather. Foolish cannot make new past but wise can make new beginning.'

Heather took a sip and choked as the viscous gloop assaulted her tastebuds. 'It's vile,' she groaned as she scoured her lips with a cornerflip of nighty. 'What is it?'

'Raw egg, Korean pear juice and ginseng.'

'Think I'll settle for a hangover, thank you very much.' Heather set the glass down on the bedside table with her Illustrated Sherlock Holmes Omnibus. As Guan-Yin turned to leave, she asked, 'would you mind keeping me company, Guany? I'm desperate for someone to talk to, but Naff is in London and Aunt Elizabeth never lets me get a word in edgeways.'

'Of course, Miss Heather,' Guan-Yin said with a reticence markedly at odds with the willing sentiment. 'But remember, to talk much and arrive nowhere is the same as climbing a tree to catch a fish.'

Heather patted the side of her bed in an invitation for Guan-Yin to sit down. 'I had such a good time last night. The best,' she said, 'but I'm afraid I might have embarrassed myself.'

'If you don't want anyone to know it, don't do it,' Guan-Yin said as she fussed her pigtail over a shoulder, hitched up her skirt and shunted Heather's legs aside to make sufficient bumspace to sit down.

'I know it sounds silly, but I drank so much I wasn't sure who I was dancing with,' Heather said with a bashful blush. 'Everyone was in costume and it was all a bit of a blur.'

'Only a fish stays sober if it drinks too much,' Guan-Yin reminded her.

'Suppose so,' Heather said. 'But I'm worried I might have made a fool of myself.'

Guan-Yin reassured her with, 'ah, but a fall into a ditch makes you wiser

'Thanks, Guany, but I hope the gang don't think I'm flirty. I'm normally the opposite. Keep it to yourself, but I was voted the girl least likely to at boarding school, or rather the girl least likely to like it.' Heather chewed her bottom lip and gave Guan-Yin a guilty look. 'Promise you won't tell Naff, but I got blotto and passed out. When I came round, Sammy – you know, my new best friend – was cuddling me on the backseat of Cassie's car. She told me that she wanted to take me to bed and tuck me up. At least, that's what I think she said. I was very groggy.' She clasped her hands and sighed. 'She is so caring. Like the big sister I've always wanted. I'm not surprised the gang love her so much.'

Guan-Yin ventured an inscrutable smile. 'Chinese say friend to everybody is friend to nobody.'

'I say, that's a bit harsh. Sammy is a real sweetheart. And so good looking. Every man's fantasy.'

Guan-Yin gazed into the middle distance and sighed. 'When a finger is pointing at the moon, Miss Heather, the fool looks at the finger.'

'Not sure I follow,' Heather said. 'But please, Guany, whatever you do, don't tell Naff. To be honest, I'm having kittens that he'll fancy Sammy to death. She is so pretty.'

Guan-Yin gave her a reassuring pat on the hand. 'Do not worry, Miss Heather. Good name is better than good face,' she said. 'Pearls do not lie on the seashore. If you want one, you must dive for it.'

'Thanks ever-so for listening, Guany. I needed someone to talk to,' Heather said, very much none the wiser.

Her agony-aunt duties done, Guan-Yin rose effortlessly to her feet, clasped her hands and said, 'a bird does not sing because it needs an answer. It sings because it has a song.' Then she picked up the tray, padded out and left Heather to her hangover.

After an ice-cold shower, Heather joined her aunt in the breakfast room. 'How is Uncle Monty bearing up?' she asked.

'Hardly seen him,' Lady Elizabeth said as she ladled dollops of vegan kedgeree onto two monogrammed plates. 'He mopes about the gazebo all day like a wet rag. Complains he has been hard done by. Would you believe, he won't even take the minister's phone calls? Most unlike him.' She waved her fork in the air and said, 'let's hope you find the real culprit soon. Any news?'

Heather risked a taste of veganitarian kedgeree, smothered a belch and pushed the plate away in favour of a jugful of black coffee. 'Remember Officer Ingham?' she asked between sips of headache relief. 'She's offered to keep me posted on developments with the investigation.'

'Correct me if I am barking up the wrong tree, my dear,' Lady Elizabeth said as she tucked into a side plate of tofutarian mash brownies with lashings of Beth's Fairtrade dandelion leaf chutney and fricasseed frognuts. 'Isn't Miss Ingham your new friend?'

Heather nodded. 'She promised to drop by later and brief me.'

'I say, why not invite her to dinner this evening and have her brief us all? Haven't had a good briefing since I played Cleopatra in that ghastly movie with Hugh Grant. Mind you, that was more of a debriefing,' Lady Elizabeth said with a twinkle in her eye. 'Splendid,' she said with a purposeful clap of the hands. 'That is settled then.'

Heather knew full well that she had no need to ask Sammy if she wanted to attend her aunt's soirée. It was an immutable law of nature that only the brave, the rude, the foolhardy or the recently deceased would dare rebuff a dinner invitation from Lady Elizabeth Trevelyan. Nevertheless, she was alarmed at the prospect. 'I'm not sure Sammy and Naff will hit it off,' she told her aunt, fearing that nothing would be further from the truth.

Lady Elizabeth's eyebrows shot up so far they almost hit the candelabra. 'Good grief, Spriggy. I am sure they will get on like a house on fire,' she said. 'Tell you what, I'll have your uncle join us and try out a new recipe.' Ignoring Heather's broody scowl, she folded her monogrammed napkin, rose from the table and withdrew to the kitchen garden to harvest a few homegrown ingredients for her latest culinary extravaganza.

Exhausted after foxtrotting the night away, Heather retired to her bedroom to appease her hangover. After power-napping for much of the day, she was roused from her slumbers by the roar of Naff's Triumph Bonneville speeding down the drive. When she saw the bedside clock, she panicked like a manic-stricken marsupial and hopped out of bed. She threw on a pair of jeans and the first crêpe de chine designer blouse that came to hand and ran to meet him.

When Naff saw her skipping down the stairs, he blew her a kiss and shouted, 'hiya, gorgeous. Fancy that spin on the Bonneville you was on about? Maybe grab us a bevy in a quiet pub, just the two of us. A candlelit meal even, if you're up for it.' He whipped off his shades and took a closer look. 'Heather?' His jaw dropped. 'What you done to your hair? Didn't recognise you there for a minute.'

Heather patted her new pageboy bob, said, 'like it?' and fibbed, 'did it just for you.' Then she frowned as a seedling of doubt grew into a rainforest of suspicion. 'Hang on,' she said, 'if you didn't know it was me, who did you think you were inviting out for a candlelit schmooze?'

'Thought you were me kid sister. Honest,' Naff bluffed through his lying teeth.

'You don't have a sister,' Heather reminded him in unequivocally equivocal terms.

'Well if I did, bet she'd do her hair just like that. Awe, come on, babe. Don't give me that look. I missed you like crazy.' Naff slipped an arm around Heather's waist, cajoled her upstairs, chivvied her into the Blue Room and manhandled her onto the four-poster bed. 'Come on, honey, don't play hard to get,' he said as she turned her head to avoid his probing lips. 'I were pulling your leg when I said I thought you was your aunt. Honest.'

Heather wriggled out of Naff's arms and pummelled his chest with her fists. 'What? You thought you were inviting Aunt Elizabeth out for a date? You are beneath contempt, you disgusting man.'

'Awe, do me a favour. I'm winding you up. Can't you tell?' Naff gave his girlfriend a look of perjured innocence then loosened his collar and mopped his brow when she looked away, not entirely - that is to say, not in the least - convinced.

Reluctantly prepared to give her *unspeakable* boyfriend the benefit of her relative doubts, Heather excused what Naff dismissed as her unfounded paranoia on the grounds that she was feeling insecure. So much had happened lately, she said. She didn't know whether she was coming or going or standing still - where to turn or what to think or when.

'Trust me,' Naff whispered in her ear between nibbles. 'I ain't looked at no one else since I met you.'

'Scout's honour?' Heather asked.

'Hey, wonder who that is.' Naff rolled off the bed as he heard a car pull up outside. 'Well, stone me. If it ain't that busybody copper,' he said as he looked out of the window.

Heather jumped up, clapped her hands and squealed, 'it's Sammy. Constable Ingham, I mean. Aunt Elizabeth has invited her to dinner.' Biting her bottom lip, she ran downstairs to let Sammy in. Any fears she might have had that her new best friend would be unduly friendly to Naff were appeased when, rather than eyefluttering a coy hello, Sammy took out her pocketbook. 'I warned you about that bald tyre, Detective Robinson,' she said. 'And I am not in the habit of repeating myself.'

Naff stared at her, all but lost for words. 'Hang about,' he said. 'Thought you was here for a social night out.'

Sammy nodded at the Panda car. 'My shift doesn't end for five minutes,' she said. 'Until then, I am on duty.' She wrote out a ticket, handed it to Naff, picked up her holdall, turned to Heather, asked, 'would you mind showing me where I can change out of my uniform please, Miss

Prendergast?' and tipped her a wink.

Freshenupped in casual-smart attire, the guests began to assemble in the dining room at seven. Locke-Mortice was already there when Heather arrived. He straightened his dickybow and nodded a curt greeting. 'Well, well, my child,' he said in a humourless voice, 'may I say what a charming young woman you have become.'

Heather curtsied a bashful thank you. 'Most kind, Uncle Montague. Have you met my boyfriend, Simon?' she asked as Naff walked through the door looking awkward in a suit and tie. 'He is also a detective.'

'Ah yes. Your aunt told me about your promotion to New Scotland Yard. Let me say how proud we both are,' Locke-Mortice announced with the driest of smiles. 'I am profoundly grateful that you could spare the time to assist me with this dreadful misunderstanding. If it was left to the local constabulary, I have no doubt that I would already be in The Tower awaiting the hangman's noose.'

Heather was about to fake a belly laugh when they were joined by a late arrivee. Now, it is said that there are entrances and there are entrances, and Samantha Ingham's entrance rocked the room back on its heels. Sporting a simple pastel pink cotton shift and a minimum of makeup, her honeysuckle locks were ribboned in a flowing ponytail tied with a black velvet bow to compliment her sporty white bobby-socks and trainers. As if to prove the age-old adage that true beauty defies the fads of time and fashion, her smooth legs, shapely curves and radiant smile would have turned heads had she been wearing sackcloth and ashes . . . and turned them through seven hundred and twenty degrees had she been wearing nothing at all.

'Like the frock, pet?' Sammy sidled up to Heather to grant her a mate's-eye view. 'Picked it up on the internet. I'll say it don't fit when I've worn it a few times and send it back for a refund. Once you get the hang of online shopping, it's a doddle.'

Before Heather could say, 'really, Sammy, that is just not on.' Lady Elizabeth swished through the door. Modelling an elegant figure hogging little black dress, she stopped in her tracks when she saw Sammy. 'Good grief, Miss Ingham,' she said. 'I do declare that this is the first time I have been upstaged by a guest at one of my dinner parties. I must try harder in future.' She sat down at the head of the table and flicked a wrist at a chair. 'Do take a seat and update us on the latest developments in Monty's case, my dear. And Simon, you must sit beside me and tell me all about your fascinating life.'

Much to Heather's surprise, Naff seemed reticent, if not reluctant, if not both. Of course, she was not to know that her boyfriend's multistorey ego was in freefall. You see, what so confused him was that having spent much of his adolescence obsessing about being in the same room as Veronika Vivendi, even for a minute, to now be but a thigh-rub from her unchained sensuality scared the living daylights out of him. In his energetic under-the-covers fantasies, she had been a submissive supplicant at the altar of his testosterone. But in the here and now of stark reality, she was in control and he was just a poppet on a string. What made matters worse was that whereas his masturbatory urges had been private . . . personal . . . behind closed eyes . . . now his every stilted breath, his every licentious twitch, his every lustful itch were in full view of her family and friends. And so, when she demanded that he tell her all about himself and leave nothing to the imagination, he merely shrugged and said, 'not much to tell, Lady Elizabeth.'

'Oh, come now. Don't be so modest.' Lady Elizabeth gave him an overfamiliar pat on the thigh. 'Tell you what,' she said. 'Why don't we get together later? Just the two of us.' Pretending not to see him break into a cold sweat, she turned to Sammy and clapped her hands. 'Righty-ho,' she announced. 'I am sure that Miss Ingham is itching to tell us all about the latest developments in Monty's case.'

Sammy drained her glass, propped her elbows on the table and looked slowly around the room. 'Get this,' she said in a breathless whisper. 'Colonel Dangerfield has been murdered.'

After a stunned silence, Locke-Mortice stuttered, 'don't believe it,' Lady Elizabeth gasped, 'good grief,' and Heather stared at Sammy in disbelief. 'Golly,' she said. 'But he was our prime suspect.'

Interrupted by the creak of the door, as one they looked round when Guan-Yin padded into the room carrying a lacquer fan in one hand and a cut glass decanter in the other. Resplendent in her dinner-duty worktogs of a billowing emerald green Hanfu gown gathered at the breastline in an extravagant red bow, her locks were coiled into bunches fastened with pendulous tasselled clasps that brushed her shoulders as she padded round the table fluttering her fan and refreshing glasses. 'Wine make many problems and cure many others,' she said with a sophical smile.

'Now tell me something I don't know,' Sammy muttered. She held out her glass and said, 'when,' when wine dribbled over the brim. She took a few sips, dabbed her lips with a monogrammed napkin, lowered her voice and broke into a conspiratorial whisper. 'That bossy DI Kent Constabulary sent to head up the investigation is pointing fingers at Elouise Decora,' she said. 'She fits the description of the last person to see Colonel Dangerfield alive.'

'Thought as much,' Locke-Mortice muttered, visibly relieved. 'Word has it they were having an affair. And in my book there is no smoke without fire.'

'What else,' Heather asked, then scowled when Sammy drained her glass in a few gut-gurgling gulps and gestured to Guan-Yin to top it up again.

'The new DI reckons your Uncle's not the perp.' Sammy shot Locke-Mortice a chin-up wink. 'You'll never believe, but he's black,' she said. 'Sergeant Gummidge sent a strongly worded letter of complaint to his MP. When the Right Honourable Whoever said he'd look into it but that Gummidge shouldn't hold his breath, sarge went spare. Came out with all this guff about Brexit and taking back control and sending Johnny Foreigner back where he belongs. Says he's got a good mind to lodge a formal complaint with the European Court of Justice.'

'You know, the best detective at New Scotland Yard is black. He's a legend at the Met,' Heather told her fellow dinner-partiers. 'I would do anything to work a case with him.' As always when left to its own devices, her mind freewheeled into daydreams of an apprenticeship that would take her one bootstrap closer to becoming Prendergast of The Yard. Sucked back into the realms of reality by the gurgle of Sammy's glass, she turned to her aunt. 'Must say, this hors d'oeuvre is scrumptious. What is it?'

'Araignées Frits et Perce-oreille Marinées. One of the recipes from my new Bethany Baker cookbook - Planet Friendly Meals for Millennials. Fancy some more?'

'Ra-ther. It's heavenly,' Heather yummed as she tucked into a second helping as large if not a small bit larger than her first. After mopping up the last few dribs and drabs with a glutenless breadslice, she pushed back her chair and gave her tummy a gluttonous pat. 'Must say, you really have excelled yourself this time, aunty,' she said with a smack of the lips. 'So what is it called in English?'

'Fried Spiders and Marinated Earwigs with Slugslime Garnish.' Lady Elizabeth told her with a culinary glow. 'So pleased you like it. Must make it more often.'

As she was staggering back from the toilet, Heather bumped into Naff staggering the other way, dabbing a bloody nose. 'Don't ask,' he grunted as he headed for the washroom. So she didn't. When she rejoined her fellow diners, she found Sammy slumped in her chair, legs akimbo, doing her tipsy best to balance a glass of Calvados in one hand and a tumblerful of Armagnac in the other.

'I do so hope that Simon will be alright, Miss Ingham,' Lady Elizabeth said with a note of concern in her voice. 'I saw him make that playful pass at you, but didn't catch what happened next.'

'He stumbled into my fist.' Sammy blew on her knuckles and polished them on her bodice. Looking for all the world like the cat that dreamed the cream, she drained both glasses and held them out for Guan-Yin to refresh. 'Don't worry, pet,' she told Heather with a lopsided grin. 'Who's going to bust me for drunk driving? Gummidge don't work weekends.'

Before Heather could caution a stern reply, Naff poked his head around the door and crookfingered her. 'Remember me mate, Brian the computer boffin?' he whispered. 'Well, he found something on Mathers' memory stick. He just sent it me.' He raised a hand to attract Lady Elizabeth's attention. 'Mind me using one of your computers to download some pictures?'

'Not pornography, I hope, young man,' Lady Elizabeth said with a culpatory scowl. 'Very well, if you must. Let me give you a hand.'

'Some other time, eh?' Naff said with a nod and a wink. 'This is official business.'

So it was that, barely no time later, Heather pulled a chair up to a Regency computer desk in the smaller of her aunt's various studies. With Naff on one side and Sammy to the other, she trackballed the bootup with a double-quick click of a wrist. One by one her eyebrows rose as she felt Naff's arm sidle round her from one side and Sammy's slither round her from the other. She said nothing, as discretion was in her DNA, and in any event her mind was focused on the screen.

As promised, there was indeed an email lurking in Naff's inbox. Heather sat on the edge of her seat, breath bated, and opened the attachment. Too preoccupied to pay attention to Sammy's drunken japes - for example, when Naff tried to grope her behind behind Heather's back, Sammy dug a thumbnail into his wrist, stamped on his foot and blew smoke in his eyes - Heather nodded at the monitor. 'Well, well,' she said. 'The plot thickens.'

'You a church goer, pet?' Sammy slurred. 'See, tomorrow is Saint Mary of Our Nook Festival. Get yourself togged up in your Sunday best and check out that bloke.' She pointed to a grainy picture on the screen. 'If he's not dodgy, I'm the Flying Dutchman.'

22

Resigned to another day in the backneck of beyond, Detective Inspector Obafemi nodded a curt good-morning to PC Ingham. 'You are late,' he said. 'Might I suggest that you invest in a new alarm clock?'

Ingham propped an elbow on the front desk and lowered her voice. 'Women's problems, sir,' she croaked. 'My time of the month.'

Inspector Obafemi took a quick step back as a blast of morning-after breath invaded his personal space. He pinched his nose and suggested, 'try a hair of the dog. Usually works for me. By the way, any idea what happened to the Panda car?'

PC Ingham flinched as a ray of sunshine strayed through the window. 'Haven't the foggiest, guv,' she said unconvincingly. 'I parked up by the pig farm after my shift, like usual.'

'So you have no idea how it came to be on its roof in a field out by Trevelyan Hall?'

'Don't say?' Ingham tried to raise an eyebrow but settled for a half-baked twitch. 'Joyriders, guv. Must be.'

'Must be.' Inspector Obafemi gave Ingham a *look* and tapped his chin. 'Call Bishop's Garage and have them collect it.'

'Right you are, sir.' Ingham rooted through the clutterbish on the front counter in search of the telephone. When Obafemi nodded at the complaints box and suggested that she look in there, she braved a smile and did. 'So what should I tell them, guv?' she asked as she detangled the phone from a rat's nest and sprayed it with multipurpose luminol-hand-sanitiser.

'Say that according to a witness, the car lost control on a hairpin bend, shot through a hedge, somersaulted twice and landed on its roof. It's a miracle the driver got out in one piece.'

PC Ingham avoided Obafemi's eyes and gulped. 'This witness you're on about. Get a description, did he?'

Inspector Obafemi stared at Ingham unblinking – unblinkable, it might be said. 'It was dark and he was much the worse for wear after a night out at the bowls club,' he said. 'Seemed to think the driver was a well-built blond girl in a pink mini-dress. He said she crawled out of the car, kicked it several times, screamed *bastard* and staggered off in the direction of the village cursing and blinding at the top of her voice.' He gave her another *look*. 'Know any joyriders fit that description? By the way, that's a nasty graze you've got on your cheek.'

'Oh, it's nothing, guv. Had a run-in with the neighbour's cat when I shooed him off my bed this morning. The cat, I mean, not my neighbour. He's a manky flee-bitten pest. My neighbour, that is, not the cat.' Ingham forced a feeble smile and fingered a bandaplast under an eye.

'Glad I've got parrot,' Inspector Obafemi joked – or was it a joke? He took off his jacket and, in the absence of a functioning coat hook, folded it neatly on the receptionary bench. 'I've been thinking,' he said thoughtfully. 'We're looking for a brunette who visited Colonel Dangerfield on the afternoon of his murder, but Decora wasn't the only woman on the train, was she? What about the ticket collector? And wasn't a girl with black hair seen running along the platform?'

Ingham squelched an unladylike belch and clamped a hand to her mouth. 'Excuse me, guv,' she mumbled through her fingers as she queezied out to the toilet. Looking a good deal less the worse for wear, she returned clutching a glass of volcanic alkabubble. 'Hot flushes,' she said unconvincingly.

'You should see a doctor.' Obafemi tapped his head and gave her another *look*. 'So, what can you tell me about the ticket collector?'

'Jaimie Smith? Can't say I really know her, guv. Seems a nice enough sort. Didn't Locke-Mortice say she had an argument with Mathers? I assume that was because he was travelling first class on a second class ticket.'

'If we are to work together, constable, you had better learn not to assume anything,' Inspector Obafemi said, then muttered, 'joyriders, eh?' without shifting his *look* from Ingham's shifty eyes. As she fidgeted with her tunic buttons, he said, 'anything else?'

PC Ingham took a sip of seltzer, hiccupped and took a longer sip. 'Not really, guv,' she said. 'Lives at Stationmaster's Cottage over by the tracks.

'Married?'

'Not that I know of. A bit of a loner by all accounts. Keeps herself to herself. Late twenties, at a guess. Dark hair. Quite a character.'

'And what exactly do you mean by that?'

'Let's just say she's not Sergeant Gummidge's type. She says what she thinks.'

'So she could be Colonel Dangerfield's mystery visitor,' Inspector Obafemi said, thinking aloud. 'I checked while you were hot-flushing your hangover down the toilet. According to MaidenRail, she wasn't working on the day of Dangerfield's murder. Think I'll pay her a visit.' He unbenched his jacket, slung it over a shoulder, tossed a pair of sunglasses on the front counter, gave his forehead another tap and left the way he came in - deep in thought.

In that it was shirtsleeveless weather, insofar as he was able Inspector Obafemi kept to the shady side of the street. It helped that he knew where he was going. He had caught a glimpse of Stationmaster's Cottage when The Ordinary Express pulled into St. Mary Nook Station on the morning of his arrival. From memory, he would have said that it was two brickstoreys high, ochre-rendered and slateroofed with ivy creeping up the walls and a grey front door with rusty window frames and guttering. It was frontaged by a neat garden with blooming clematis and honeysuckle boughing a decorative arch on an overgrown lawn. A man's bicycle had been propped against a wall. Missing a pump, he remembered that it had a chrome bell and a black leather saddle. He seemed to recall that the rear mudguard was dangling at an angle, suggesting that it had a screw loose.

Isaac Obafemi's photocopier memory was at one and the same time an occupational blessing and a preoccupational curse. No detail went unregistered, with the upshot that his mind was so cluttered with minutiae that it had little space for anything else. For instance, he could hardly remember his age let alone his birthday. He only knew Sandra's because he had felt-tipped it on a photograph of Bukayo Saka on the Superheroes calendar on his desk at New Scotland Yard.

Having no need to seek directions - whether he liked it or he liked it not, a road once travelled was mapped into Inspector Obafemi's psyche evermore – and in no great hurry, he lazed the crooked lanes, jacket over a shoulder, pipe in mouth, hands in pockets. On days such as this, he could well appreciate why PC Ingham should have chosen to forsake the hurly-burly of Brighton for the pastoral tranquility of St. Mary Nook. To borrow an earlier turn of phrase, she was quite a character. At times, she reminded him of his younger self.

Inspector Obafemi shook his head and chuckled as he recalled how, when he first joined the Met, he regularly used to be late for duty, more often than not hungover after a night out on the lash. His career - and his life - was turned around by Bill Wheeler, then a lowly detective sergeant. While most of his colleagues were taking bets about how long it would be before 'the black bastard' was kicked out of the force, not caring whether he was pink, brown, blue or black, Bill gave him a kick up the parson's nose and took him under a wing. So, maybe he should do the same with PC Ingham? He was looking for a junior detective to augment his team - someone he could mentor as Bill Wheeler had done with him. Of course, it would be a challenge but if nothing else, working with Miss Ingham would brighten his day. The young officer was intelligent, personable and extremely pretty. Not that her looks were here or there. Well, not much, anyway.

Many speculations, ruminations, reflections, cogitations and contemplations later, Inspector Obafemi crossed a level crossing and turned into Station Approach, a tractorwide lane stretching off towards the nether fringes of the parish. The last house on the skirt-tails of the village, Stationmaster's Cottage stuck out like a thumb on a sore hand. He put on his jacket, straightened his tie and knocked on the front door. But rather than being opened by person or persons within, it creaked open of its own accord.

'Hello there?' he called. 'Anybody home?' In the absence of reply, he was about to leave when he smelt burning. Concerned, he followed his nose to a small kitchen-dinerette at the rear, removed a pan of acrid vegatibley *something* from the stove and turned off the hotplate.

Having entered Smith's cottage in the line of duty, Inspector Obafemi felt duty bound to poke around. He was, to say the least, perplexed to find that lights had been left on, doors were ajar and condiment jars unstoppered. It was, he thought, as if Jaimie Smith had Marie-Celested the cottage forewarned that he was on his way. On further nose-pockery, he found a man's jacket hanging in the hall, a selection of men's and women's shoes in the front parlour and several well-thumbed copies of salacious laddish magazines in the living room. When he ventured upstairs, he noticed a bottle of Old Mank male deodorant amongst the perfumery in a bathroom cabinet and men's shirts, briefs, socks and pyjamas with the nighties, knickers and summery blouses in a chest of drawers in the bedroom. For the avoidance of doubt, should he still have any, a nightdress and a pair of pyjamas lay on the double bed. The reading matter on the bedside tables – Vogue and Playboy – spoke, or rather read, for itself.

Deep in thought, Obafemi returned to the garden, sat down on a tree stump and took out his pipe. He would wait, he decided, on the presumption that Miss Smith would return sooner rather than later to attend to her oversimmered dinner. After what seemed an age but might have been more, he was refuelling his pipe for the umptenth time when his cellphone rang. He took the call and listened with a deepening frown. 'Calm down, Ingham,' he said. 'I'll be right over.'

Detective Inspector Obafemi slung his jacket over a shoulder, muttered an enigmatic, 'then there were two,' and set off for Saint Mary of Our Nook Church.

23

The small parish church was packed to overflowing. Although a stalwart member of the congregation maintained that the villagers were there for pious contemplation, the reality was altogether different, as realities all too often are. It was Saint Mary of Our Nook Day, an obligatory tick in the local social calendar.

As Heather Prendergast explained to her *unknowledgably* ignorant boyfriend, in the darkest whenevers at the height of the black-death thingummy, Kent was visited by a viral plague of deleterious drunkenness. Salvation appeared in the unlikely form of a young goatmaid who performed an astonishing miracle that was to return sobriety to the county. Watched on by the great and the good in Canterborough Cathedral, little Mary Nook removed her pinafore, draped it over a vat of wine, sang a song of sixpence and turned the wine into water. The upshot was the restoration of good-tempered temperance to the county. In the words of a contemporary chronicler, Abbot Mabbot of Dinglenook, 'forsooth it was indeed a blessed relief.' And as academics the world over would have it, the rest - so say we all - is history. It need hardly be said that Mary Nook was canonised, a village named after her and a church built in her honour. Legend has it that Saint Mary of Our Nook is buried in the shadows of ye olde touriste boothe.

Were that the villagers were so devotionally minded. The pragmatic truth of the matter was that attendance at the annual Saint Mary of Our Nook Day service was due to a wholly different, albeit a related, tradition.

It had long been customary for the local burghers to donate copious imbibements of locally brewed beverages to fortify the congregation after listening to the vicar extol the virtues of sobriety. Even by the alcoholic standards of the past, this year promised to be notable in its bountitude. For Lady Elizabeth Trevelyan had generously donated some of the liquid fruits of her internationally renowned vineyard - to wit, a dozen jeroboams of Chateau Trevelyan Beaujolais Tres, Tres Nouveau, a favourite tipple of the liverpickled cosmopolitan elite.

What better opportunity, PC Offduty Heather Prendergast reasoned, to poke around the cloistered cloisters of Saint Mary of Our Nook Church to see what lay afoot? In the knowledge that Prendergast of The Yard would one day be a pending mistress of disguise, she donned the most matronly of her late grandmother's Sunday dresses, a woolly cardigan, a pair of clumpy grannie shoes, a *ghastly* grey wig and a natty straw hat beribboned with a dashing sash. Satisfied that she would meld in with the other crotchety old crones, she draped a pigskin handbag over an arm and joined the gossipy posse milling about the vestibule.

The only notable local notable of note notable by her absence was Lady Trevelyan. She had arrived an hour or so earlier in oodles of time - so she claimed - to overhaul the church organ, primed and prepped to perform the odd Bach fugue. In a take-no-prisoners full-frontal assault, she had hectored her husband into attending. A social outing would do the old misery-guts a world of good, she declared.

Once the congregation had settled on the bumhard wooden pews, the pipe organ thundered to its lowest stop and an unkempt dog-collared figure limped to the pulpit. Reverend William Bragg - for it was he - looked slowly around the jampacked nave and cleared a righteous frog from his throat. 'A little while ago,' he said, 'I was asked to explain what prayer is. This is what I said. We are creatures. We are not self-made beings, but the handiwork of a loving creator. Mortal, fallible, limited and fragile. But much of the joy of believing lies in a more positive understanding of being wanted, crafted, loved and cherished. Prayer is perhaps the most human thing we do, because it is the moment above all others when we recognise that we are creatures.' Unsteady on his feet, he propped an elbow on the pulpit, took a hipflask from his surplice and stared at the congregation. Smiling. Smiling. Smiling. After a breathless pause, he blinked, took a sip of *something*, shuddered and wiped his mouth on a sleeve. 'Listening?' he asked. 'Right you are, then. For Deuteronomy teaches, you are the sons of the Lord your God, and the Lord has chosen you to be a people for his treasured possession out of all the creatures who are on the face of the earth, but you shall not eat any abomination.' Taken by the spirit, he raised his arms to the heavens and launched his voice to the rafters. 'And The Lord sayeth, Behold, I have given you every plant yielding seed that is on the face of all the earth, and every tree with seed in its fruit. You shall have them for food.'

As the congregation shuffled in their pews, Reverend Bragg smiled at each and every one in turn before resuming his sermon in a slurred voice. 'The Festival of Saint Mary of Our Nook marks the passage from the scorched earth of summer to the intimate embrace of winter. It is a time for man to propagate his seed and regenerate our creature species. So ask yourselves, what better symbol of this act of sacred union than a bunny,' he pronounced with a certitude that brooked no sense. 'Consider ye this - rabbits are made in the image of our creator. They are fashioned by His Almighty Paw to give meaning to our short and miserable hop from the burrow to the grave.' He reached for his hipflask, drained it in one gutshivering gulp, tossed it over a shoulder, picked up a bible and waved it in the air. 'See this?' he said and hiccupped. 'Well, it says here that for every soul that enters the Kingdom of Heaven, a baby bunny shall be born.' As he stared unblinking at the baffled congregation, a fierce anger came upon his face, markedly at odds with his meek appearance. 'But there are those among us who scorn God's word. Sinners, take heed,' he roared, all of a sudden a manic street preacher rather than a kindly pastoral shepherd. 'For divine retribution shall be visited upon all who stray. The harlot; the usurer; the adulterer;

the bunny-abuser.' Fighting to control a righteous fury in his voice, he boomed, 'oh, hear ye, heathens, oh, hear ye. For it is written in the Old Testament that transgressors shall suffer the divine vengeance of His Almighty Claw.' His hands shook as he raised his arms to the firmament and screamed, 'so sort yesselves out, sinners, or ye shall be consumed by Hellfire and brimstone and stuff.' Clutching the lectern for support, he took a deep breath to calm his troubled soul and said – nay, jabbered, 'all together now, give it up for bobtailed kind. And then we shall partake of the fruit of the vine, the traditional symbol of insobriety that Saint Mary of Our Nook miraculously banished from our Kentish soil.'

After what was, in Heather's humble opinion, a baffling pomposity of ponderous pontification, the most revered Reverend Bragg staggered from the pulpit to a stirring rendition of Elizabeth Trevelyan's famed Syncopated Improvisations on a Messiaenic Organ Fugue. The moment he turned his back, the congregation wandered out to the Garden of Remembrance. Or better said, they stampeded out to a table creaking to the trestles with a superfluidity of bottles, glasses, bottles, glasses, raw carrot and dandelion-leaf nibbles and more bottles, more bottles, more bottles.

Naff nudged Heather in the girdle as they joined the snaking queue. 'Ain't that Elouise Decora, the Sunday Rant columnist?' He nodded at a molasses-haired woman wearing a flowery dress, preposterous high heels and a ridiculous ostrich-feather hat. 'Wonder what she's talking to Guan-Yin about?'

'Your guess is as good as mine. I'd be surprised if she understands a word Guany says. I'm blowed if I do,' Heather quipped, then stumbled as a tall girl with a growly face barged into her. 'Watch where you're going, you clumsy oaf,' she snapped.

'Go fuck yourself, grannie,' the woman said by way of an apology and hurried off to queue-jump the bar.

Locke-Mortice strolled over to join them. 'Unless my eyes deceive me, that was Jaimie Smith, the ticket collector on The Ordinary Express,' he said on the assumption that someone might be listening and if they were, that they might be interested. 'Saw her running down the lane in a bit of a tizz. Common little oik.'

'Bother, I have mislaid my handbag,' Heather fibbed in her crotchiest old-maid's voice. 'Get me a small ginger ale would you, deary. I'll be back in a jiffy,' she told Naff in a prearranged code for him to alert her should anybody enter the church while she was snooping about. Leaving him to keep Locke-Mortice company - cornered by a satrap in a rat-trap, it might be said - she tootled off to investigate Reverend Bragg's private fiefdom, her keen forensic mind masked behind a spinsterish veneer.

The most noteworthy feature of Saint Mary of Our Nook church was the magnificent stained glass window. A kaleidoscopic tableau of shimmering colour – psychedelic some might say if they were stoned – it featured a haloed

Saint Mary of Our Nook kneeling at the feet of Our Lord offering him a bottle of sparkling mineral water. Most biblical scholars maintained that it dated from the early fourteen hundreds, but a few radical upstarts claimed that it was Elizabethan. This was vociferously rebutted by the trustees of Canterborough Cathedral, or The Perrier-Minster as the pile of medieval rubble had been rebranded following a lucrative sponsorship deal with the patron saint of Mammon. The jury is still out. Idiots.

After hitching up her skirts and hatpinning the straw hat to her wig, Heather knelt down to retrieve her *ghastly* pigskin handbag from the flagstones a few feet from where she had been sitting. She draped it over an arm, old crone stylee, and - like a dowager duchess stalking a stableboy - crouched on all fours, peeking about the tiny nave, trying to determine where to nose-poke first. After due deliberation and no little hesitation, she decided to brave the narrow stairway to the belfry. She reasoned that she might as well start at the top and unwind her way down.

Had she known that she would be called upon to crawl up a twisty flight of dust-encrusted stairs on her hands and knees - she suffered from a dizzying dreadhightedness - Heather would have worn something less impractical than an ankle-length dress, a virginal white cardigan, calfskin gloves, an *unspeakably* itchy wig and a straw hat. But as her aunt would say, needs be as needs must when duty calls - itchiness notwithstanding. And so she ventured up and up, one step at a time, fussing and cussing as she scuffed her shoes, snagged her cotton stockings and dragged her skirts through age-old grime.

Her relief as she emerged into the belfry turned to disbelief when she took her bearings. For rather than homing homing-pigeons, bats and earwigs – she shuddered at the thought – she found herself in the bunny shrine to trump all bunny shrines. The flaking plaster was papered from floor to ceiling with lithographed likenesses of flop-eared lagomorphs by the likes of Albrecht Durer, John Tenniel, Andre Gill, Horatio Henry Couldery and that most obsessive of all bunny-painters, John Frederick Herring Senior. She was photosnapping the evidence with Grandmamma Trevelyan's Box Brownie camera when her cellphone rang.

'Better split pronto, gran,' Naff – for it was he on the other end of the ether – cautioned. 'Bragg and Decora are heading your way.'

Trapped eighty winding steps above the nave, Heather's police training dictated that she should keep her grey-wigged head down. But riven by an insatiable - some might say an irascible - precocity, she tiptoed down the stairway from heaven to within eavesdropping distance of the transept where a bad-tempered exchange was taking place.

'He deserved everything he got,' she overheard Bragg say, to which Decora snapped, 'you hypocrite. You have been swapping the communion wine for water and selling it to The Crossed Arms ever since you arrived. Admit it.'

'Hallelujah, it's a miracle,' Bragg mocked and then his voice gnarled to a snarl. 'It is the same stunt our saintly little goatmaid pulled. I'm just following tradition. Anyway, you're a fine one to talk. Does Sergeant Gummidge know what you and Dangerfield were up to? Mathers knew, didn't he? And so do I. Now get out. I need a stiff drink before I wave my drunken congregation goodbye.'

A moment later, Heather heard the church door slam. Believing the coast to be clear, she tipstepped down the remaining stairs and emerged blinking into the light. As she was shuffling for the exit, she heard bootsteps behind her and swung around to see Reverend Bragg brandishing a clenched fist. Plucking every ounce of courage she could muster, she fixed him in the eye and let him have it with an expertly executed scream. Ignoring his intoxicated cackle, she flung her straw hat at him Oddjob stylee, hitched up her skirt and sprinted out of the church to the sunny uplawns of the graveyard, flopped into her boyfriend's arms and buried her wig in his chest. 'Come on, darling. Let's get out of here,' she said. And then she pulled away and took an assured, a very certain, breath. 'Reverend Bragg is our man,' she said with nary a flicker of a quiver of a doubt. 'I'll stake my reputation on it.'

24

'So, Constable Ingham. Thoughts?'

'Blunt force trauma, guv. My guess is the perp sneaked up on him from behind and caved in his skull with that brass cross. He didn't stand a chance.'

'Must say, I'm inclined to agree. But let's see what the pathologist has to say before jumping to conclusions. The sooner you learn that this job is about legwork, not guesswork, the better.'

'Sorry, guv. I'll bear that in mind.'

'Sure you feel up to it? You don't look too good.'

'A bit queasy to be honest, guv. Don't know how you can carry on like it's just another day at the office.'

'I've seen worse. Any witnesses?'

'No, guv. The verger found him after the congregation left and called us straight off.'

'Very well. Ask him for a list of everyone who was here.'

'Already have, sir. He reckons they were all local apart from a young bloke and an old woman he saw kissing in the graveyard.'

'She was probably his grandmother.'

'Doubt it, guv. Who nibbles their gran's ear?'

'Takes all sorts. Talking of which, any idea who the small oriental lady is? I passed her in the lane on my way over. At first I thought she was a refugee from The Inn of The Seventh Happiness as she was wearing a wrapover smock, baggy linen trousers and wooden clogs. She had a flowerpot on her head - at least, that's what it looked like. When I said good day, she tucked her hands into her sleeves, bowed her head and said, goodness is a result of conscious activity; man's nature is evil. I wasn't sure whether she was on hallucinogens or if I was.'

'Oh, you must mean Miss Guan Yin, Lady Trevelyan's secretary. I met her when I drove Locke-Mortice back to Trevelyan Hall. She don't speak a lot of English. If you want my opinion, sir, she's teapot.'

'Teapot?'

'Barking, guv. Off her trolley.'

'I did wonder. Good work, Ingham. Stay here and wait for the pathologist while I take a look around. Oh, and Ingham . . .'

'Yes, guv?'

'We better arrange protection for Locke-Mortice and Decora. I have no idea what's going on, but it's possible their lives might also be in danger.'

'Locke-Mortice is taken care of, guv. There's a couple of coppers staying out at Trevelyan Hall.'

'Know their names?'

'Not off the top of my head, but I believe one of them is from London. Pretty high powered by all accounts. The other is a Northerner. Huddshire judging by his accent. Looks like he knows how to take care of himself. I gave him a speeding ticket the other night so his details will be in the draw at the station.'

'Which drawer?'

'Not drawer, guv. Draw. Sarge runs a raffle to decide who gets charged with what.'

'Unbelievable.'

'With you there, guv. And that's not the half of it.'

'I shudder to think. By the way, did you notice a musky smell on the body?'

'Whisky, guv. I found an empty bottle in Reverend Bragg's surplice.'

'No, not that. I'm talking about perfume. I'm pretty sure it's the same brand we found on Colonel Dangerfield's body at Bishop's Farm.'

'Now you come to mention it, guv, I did. Chanel Number Ten, if I'm not mistaken. A member of the congregation?'

'Could be, but I don't like coincidences. And I have a hunch that forensics will confirm that the bloody footprint we found by the body was made by the same size shoe as some of those at the Dangerfield crime scene. Seems we might be looking for a female killer.'

'No doubt about it, guv. Our perp is definitely a woman. Think forensics can lift any DNA from the straw hat?'

'They'll give it a go, but judging by the grey hairs in the headband, I suspect they'll say we're looking for a yak or a woman in a cheap wig. What about our old lady with the young boyfriend? Did the verger give you a description?'

'Typical old biddy. Frumpy dress, white cardigan, costume broach . . . Cripes - he said she was wearing a straw hat when she arrived.'

'Cowgirls, pantomime dames, phantom mystery girls jumping off trains, drunken flappers raising merry hell in the middle of the night . . . I thought you came here for a quiet life, constable? Compared to St. Mary Nook, Brighton must seem like an old folk's home.'

Hardly had Inspector Obafemi finished speaking than a woman marched into the church brandishing a rolled umbrella like a sheleighly. 'I say, you there . . . yes, you.' She snapped her fingers at Obafemi. 'Are you in charge?' Elouise Decora – for it was she – demanded. 'I hear that Locke-Mortice has murdered Reverend Bragg. Why haven't you arrested him?'

Obafemi turned to Ingham. 'Escort Miss Decora out and instruct the verger to lock the doors until forensics get here. This is a crime scene, not a public spectacle.'

'Get orff.' Decora shook PC Ingham's hand off her arm. 'I demand protection, or must I wait for your superiors to send a competent officer to replace you?' She narrowed her eyes at Obafemi.

'I'll post Sergeant Gummidge to stand guard outside your house, Miss Decora,' Inspector Obafemi assured her, all the while struggling to keep a straight face at the juxtaposition of the words post, stand, guard and Gummidge. 'But in that you are here, would you mind telling me when you last saw Reverend Bragg?'

'Are you deliberately trying to get under my skin or are you just thick-headed? At the service, of course.' Decora tossed her head, affronted – nay, offended – by the implied impertinence. 'Poor, dear William.' She made a pretence of dabbing a tear from her eye. 'We were such good friends. He was most supportive of my moral crusade, you know. Of course, he had worked in Africa so knew all about your sort.' She gave Inspector Obafemi the kind of look that made him wish that he had never been born. Or rather, she gave him the kind of look that made him wish that she had never been born. 'No pulling the wool over poor William's eyes when it came to human nature,' she said, ignorant, oblivious or wilfully careless that her insults cut no slick with Inspector Obafemi, PC Ingham or the spirit of a saintly little goatmaid looking down from her windowperch with her hands miraculously pressed to her ears . . . praise be! 'I will miss dear William dreadfully,' Decora blathered. 'I only hope they don't appoint a woman vicar to replace him. If they do, I will just have to become a Catholic.'

Having ejected Decora as politely as possible, bearing in mind her howls of police brutality, racial discrimination, sexual harassment and every other offence in the A to Zee of inappropriate improprieties, Inspector Obafemi instructed Ingham to keep a watchful eye on the crime scene while he ventured up to the belfry. His nerves were, to say the least, a little fraught lest there be spiders webbing in wait. Arachnids were not, never had been and in all due likelihood never would be, his favourite creepy crawlies.

Expecting a must of dust and a crust of fust, a shiver scuttled down Obafemi's spine when he emerged into the belfried gloom. For in plain sight stood a table laid out with wiresnips, a balaclava, vandalised CCTV cameras, a fountain pen, blood-red ink and paper. The conclusion went without a great deal of saying – Bragg's had been the hand of bunny-vengeance.

Noticing footprints in the flagstoned grime, Obafemi squatted down to take a closer look. Although faint, he assumed the hobnailed boots must belong to the victim but had no idea who could have left the clumpheeled shoeprints. Preoccupied, he sat down on the only chair and reached for his pipe but not his tobacco; he knew better than to pollute a psychopath's shrine. He cupped the bowl in a hand like a miniature cup or a tiny bowl and engaged his deductive processes.

It was a fair assumption, Obafemi assumed, that Bragg's

was the deranged mind behind the Bunny Liberation Front. And unless he was mistaken - unlikely to within a fraction of a decimal point - the other footprints had been made by old-fangled shoes typical of those worn by an old biddy in a frumpy dress and a straw hat. So who was she, he wondered - a bunny-accomplice or the hand of retribution? Deep in thought, he lined the caseducks up in his mind.

A newcomer to the village, Trevor Mathers had been audaciously murdered in broad daylight on the Ordinary Express. However, according to the statements that his fellow-travellers gave to Sergeant Gummidge, it would seem that none of them had seen a sausage. It was therefore fair to assume that someone must be lying, unless the killer was the ticket collector or the mysterious girl seen leaving the train at St. Mary Nook. But why? That was the ten-dollar question. If Mathers was indeed a journalist, as his passport stated, why travel all the way from Canada to the backnooks of beyond? He must have been investigating something altogether more salacious than a petfood swindle or a deranged vicar with a funny-bunny obsession. Whatever Mathers had been poking his nose into had cost him his life and almost certainly those of Colonel Hamilton Dangerfield and Reverend Bragg.

By an elementary process of elimination, Inspector Obafemi narrowed down the suspects to Montague Locke-Mortice, Elouise Decora, Jaimie Smith and the girl seen leaving the train at St. Mary Nook. In that the finger of guilt pointed to a woman - bearing in mind Dangerfield's last visitor, a common crime scene whiff of Chanel Number Ten, the straw hat and now these footprints - he surmised that Locke-Mortice could not possibly be responsible. Unless, of course, he had a female accomplice.

His mind a good mind clearer, Inspector Obafemi plotted a plan of action. In that motive was the missing link, he decided to beg a telephonic favour from an acquaintance in the Royal Canadian Mounted Police. He would have him dig up everything he could on Mathers – family, friends, newspapers he worked for and articles he was researching. But first he would visit Jaimie Smith to hear what she had to say for herself. Then he would hail a cab to Trevelyan Hall to check that the security arrangements passed muster.

Decidedly determined, Obafemi returned to the nave where he found PC Ingham throwing up in the baptismal. He put an arm around her broad shoulders, not unduly surprised when she gave him the brush off; he knew that she wished to be treated as one of the lads. 'I've asked Tunbridge Wells to send backup. Ever come across Inspector Turner?' he asked as Ingham scoured the vomit out of her mouth with an antique lace christening gown requisitioned from a nearby display case.

'Not half,' Ingham said between sips of holy water. 'If you don't mind me saying, guv, she's got a reputation as a bit of a stickler.'

'Sounds just what we need. She'll have a couple of uniformed officers with her. Show them the ropes and say I'll see her back at the station after I've interviewed Smith and Locke-Mortice. When forensics get here, drag Sergeant Gummidge out of the Bowls Club and tell him to stand guard outside Decora's house until I can find a competent officer to relieve him.'

'What'll I do if he refuses, guv? He's not in the habit of taking orders.'

'Say I'll have him transferred to Blackheath. That should do the trick.'

Leaving PC Ingham to man the crime scene - in a gender-neutral manner of speaking – Inspector Obafemi made tracks to Stationmaster's Cottage where he found Jaimie Smith chopping wood in the front garden. Although wearing civvies, he straightway recognised her as the girl who had punched his ticket on the Ordinary Express. Isaac Obafemi never forgot a face, a mixed blessing he often thought when looking in a mirror.

'Piss off, scumbag,' Jaimie Smith said. To reinforce the chummy greeting, she raised her woodchopper to a threatening angle.

Undeterred, albeit unamused, Inspector Obafemi showed Miss Smith his warrant card. 'Mind if I ask you a few questions?' he asked rhetorically. 'Or we can talk at the station if you prefer,' he suggested unrhetorically.

Smith put down the axe and planted her hands on her hips. 'Need a solicitor, do I?'

'You tell me.'

'Get on with it, then. I've not got all day.'

Inspector Obafemi took out his pocketbook and licked the tip of his pencil. 'Mind telling me where you were between midday and two this afternoon?'

'Here,' Smith said. 'Minding my own business. Not like some.'

'If I were you, I'd think carefully,' Obafemi suggested. 'You were seen at the Saint Mary of Our Nook Service.'

'Oh, yeah. That's right. Went to see a man about a dog. Had a quick bevvy and came straight back.'

'Can anyone verify that? Your boyfriend, perhaps.' Inspector Obafemi cast an exaggerated glance at the man's bicycle propped against a wall.

'Here, you been snooping about?' Jaimie Smith picked up the axe and brandished it in Obafemi's direction. 'Unless you got a warrant, you can fuck off.'

'Rest assured, I'll be back with one, Miss Smith,' the Inspector rest-assured her. 'You can count on it. Meanwhile, I suggest you keep your doors and windows locked until I can arrange for an officer to stand guard outside your house.'

'Oh, don't you worry about me.' Smith middle-fingered Obafemi an ungentlewomanly fare thee ill. 'I'm well took care of,' she said. 'It's that snotty cow, Decora, you need to keep a beady eye on. She's not all she makes out to be, that one. Not by a long chalk. I don't trust her an inch. And if you got any sense, nor should you.'

25

Heather Prendergast paced Trevelyan Hall's drawing room anxiously wringing her hands. Every second second, so it seemed, she checked her smartphone and in between, she checked it again. At a loss what to do, she scrolled through the function doodah to make sure that the whatsit was properly thingied. When the little green blip in the corner of the display-saver - a saucy photosnap of a chocolate orange - blinked to confirm that it was fully juice-apped, she was tempted to reprogram the oojamaflip so that it ringtoned more annoyingly. With thoughts of the last time she attempted a change of something – on that occasion a tweak of the brightness gizmo - she threw in the flannel. She knew from first-hand experience that the process would be so complicated, so convoluted and so rocket-scienceable that she would need the assistance of a quantum physicist, a professor of applied metamechanics or a twelve-year-old child. Unconvinced by the cellular phone's claim to be functionally correct – to her way of thinking, technology was a silicon snake in the valley - she gave it a vigorous shake to make sure the invisible wire was still attached. Then off she went again, restlessly pacing to and fro like a peripatetic perambulator, glancing, checking, listening, sweating, fretting.

'My phone is broken,' she told Naff for the umpteenth time in as many minutes. 'Maybe the network is down.'

'Relax, babe. She'll bell you soon as she's got a minute.'

'Something's happened. I know it. She could have . . . what's that?'

Naff rolled his eyes in a show of anatomical exasperation. 'Ain't you gonna answer it?'

'What if it's a wrong number or a cold-caller or someone I don't want to speak to, like my stepsister or daddy?' Heather shuddered at the unthinkable thought. 'Don't want to tie up the line.'

Life getting shorter by the ringtone, Naff took the call, said, 'hang about,' and passed the phone over.

Heather pressed the cellphone to her listening ear and unleashed a garbled, 'Sammy, where have you been? I've been worried half to death. Didn't you get my messages? I left half a dozen.' She laughed out loud and said, 'come on, don't exaggerate. There were nowhere near that many,' then raised an eyebrow. 'Oh, you counted them.' She tried not to smirk, lest Sammy detect a note of triumphalism in her voice. 'Guess what. I know who the killer is. You'll never believe . . . it's Reverend Bragg. And I can prove it.' Of an instant, her cocksure smile transmuted to a muted gasp. 'Oh my gosh. Was it suicide? I suppose when I fought off his attack, he must have realised the game was up and . . . murder?' Her second gasp was louder than the first by a factor of degrees. 'He was what with a what? But he was our killer. Had to be.' The blood drained from her freckled cheeks until, 'Sammy, wait. Hello? Hello?'

'So what did your mate say?' Naff asked as Heather slumped down in an armchair staring at the phone with her mouth opening and closing like a winded fish.

'Can't believe it. Sammy says Reverend Bragg has been murdered,' Heather said when she had gathered sufficient wits to string ten words together. 'She had to go because the pathologist needs a hand. She's been told to wait for backup from Tunbridge Wells so we can't meet up until this evening.' She nodded a tacit thankyou as Naff poured her a glass of brandy. She took a sip and shuddered, in part with the shock of unfolding events but largely because she abhorred the taste of neat brandy when she was sober. She held her nose and grimaced as the afterburn reminded her why she never drank spirits when there was a bottle of chilled Chardonnay to hand.

Despite her alcoholic anathema, Heather braved another sip of nerve medicine, as she was to wittily refer to Cognac when, years later, it became her staple after-dinner tipple. 'Sammy says her new guv'nor is on the way over to interview Uncle Monty,' she said with a note of guarded hysteria in her voice. 'She told him about us, Naff. She didn't give him my name, thank goodness, but he's bound to ask all sorts of questions.' Trembling like a gimbal in the wind, she reached for Naff's hand. 'How am I going to explain what I was doing at the church in disguise? I can't fib. I'm a police officer. And when he finds out I was one of the last people to see Colonel Dangerfield alive, he's bound to put me in the frame. Oh, Naff, this could scupper my career.'

'Make yesself scarce, babe. Leave Inspector Plod to me.' Naff gave her a reassuring smile. 'I'm an undercover detective, right? I'm allowed to lie through me teeth. Goes with the turf.' He nuzzled her ear, whispered, 'I'll sort it,' then looked at her askance and broke into a foxy grin. 'That new hairstyle is real cute. Turns me on like nobody's business. Hey, I know - why don't we just forget about your dumbarsed uncle and go to bed?' he said as he slipped a probing hand into his girlfriend's jeans.

Heather shimmied her hips and wriggled free - practice had perfected the slithery manoeuvre - and slapped Naff's straying hand with the first slaphandable object that came to hand – a decorative china figurine of a tiny parakeet perched on an egg-shaped globe, in all probability deeply symbolic to those interested in airy-fairy piffle. 'Decora must be the murderer. She's the only suspect left,' said she with a certitude that brooked no possible debate . . . as if Naff cared. His mind was still in verboten territory. 'Tell you what,' she said. 'Why don't I make a citizen's arrest?'

'Awe, come on, babe. Give it a rest,' Naff groaned punnily as his passion parade was rained upon by Heather's obsessional preoccupation. 'We're on leave, remember? We only got a few days left.'

'I know . . .' Heather ignored him as if he was wasting his breath, which of course he was. 'Why don't I pay Decora a visit and see what I can dig up? If I can pin the murders on her, it'll get me off the hook.'

Wondering what more he could do to hitch his

girlfriend's wagon to his rampant stallion, Naff sat down on the arm of her armchair and rolled a one-handed cigarette. 'Not sure that's the best idea you had all day,' he said as he struck a match on his bootzip and lit up. 'Come to think, the last one weren't exactly a winner.'

But Heather was beyond persuasion – undisuadable it might be said. 'Must you always be such a wet rag, darling? Trust me. I know what I'm doing.'

'Yeah, right. Ain't that what you said when you put sugar in your mate's petrol tank to soup up the engine? The old banger sure went with a bang after that.' Naff frowned and smiled at the same time as only a true-blue rogue knows how. 'OK, babe. You do what you want. Guess I'll just have to spend the afternoon kicking me heels with your aunt. What a drag.' He managed to mask a wolfish grin behind a gaping yawn. Or was it a yawning gape? To be frank, he didn't give a sausage.

'Never mind, sweetheart. I'll make it up to you tonight. Promise.' Heather blew Naff a kiss and headed for the attics to rummage through one or two of her aunt's castoff wardrobes.

And so it was that an hour or so later – it may have been a little more – Heather Prendergast ratatatatted her shooting stick on Elouise Decora's door. Sporting dapper huntin`, fishin`, snootin` garb of baggy corduroy trousers, brown leather brogues, white collarbuttoned shirt, tweed blazer and a natty flat cap, she asked herself, am I nervous? Not on your life, she replied. Because the fact of the matter was that she lived for undercover sleuthing. It stimulated her juices, it floated her boat, it pumped up her phagocytes and countless other ass-about-mule clichés. She was in her element. For longer than she cared to remember, her burning ambition had been to fight the good fight by any subterfugical means at her disposal. Like Sherlock Holmes before her, she lived, breathed and ate any opportunity, no matter how dietetic, to bring a villain to book. By so doing, she hoped to help forge a better future for her brothers, her sisters and their children, relatives and pets. If she became a national treasure in the process, so be it; she was resigned to suffering in the cause of righteousness. And of course, disguises were as much a tool of her chosen trade as her trusty magnifying glass, deerstalker hat, wigs, moustaches and false eyelashes.

After what seemed an age, Elouise Decora answered the door. Dark shadows under her eyes suggested that she had been snatching a catchup catnap. 'May I help you, young lady?' she asked with a note of reserve in her nasal twang.

'I jolly-well hope so,' Heather said in the bumptious whineglass accent she had honed to a tee in Undercover Subterfuge class; she was immensely proud of her merit in poshspeak. 'I'm after the Master of Hounds. One of the stable lads tells me he lives in Nook Lane.' Having doorstepped Decora's attention, she pretended to take a second take. 'By jingo,' she gasped with a look of spontaneous surprise. 'Tick me orf if I'm being a complete ass, but aren't you Elouise Decora, the newspaper columnist?'

'One and the same.' Decora volunteered a celebrity smile and gave her hair a perfunctory pat. 'Can't tell you what a bind it is to be famous, but there you are,' she said with a sigh of weary longsufferance. 'We all have our crosses to bear.'

'Well I'll be jiggered. I was only saying to Rollo the other day that if it wasn't for good-old Elouise, there would be no one to speak up for the silent majority now the BBC has been hijacked by the loony left. Your column has been a beacon of light in the Findlay household since . . . oh, since the year dot, I dare say.' Heather pretended to capture a fleeting thought. 'I say,' she said, 'I know this might sound a frightful cheek, but I couldn't take a snapshot of you holding the flag, could I?' She dug into her shoulder basket for Guany's gran-tourismo Union Jack tea towel.

'Well, I'm really not sure.' Decora hesitated, caught in two minds.

'Oh, go on, Miss Decora. Be a sport. Mind if I call you Elouise? I've been lapping up your words of wisdom for so long I feel as if I've known you yonks.'

'Well in that case, it would be a pleasure, Miss . . .'

'Bunty. Bunty Findlay. And for my sins, it is Missus Findlay,' Heather said, sticking to her oven-ready script. 'Got swept off me feet by one of daddy's Rotarian chums at Henley Regatta last year. Twice my age, but what the heck. He owns property all over the shop. Warehouses mainly, but he has the odd arcade.' Having slotted seamlessly into Bunty guise, Heather ratcheted the deception up another notch. 'I say,' she said, 'you couldn't spare a mo for a natter? I've been gasping to meet you ever since reading your spiffing article about how the dimwits running the show ought to make badger-baiting and hare-coursing official Olympic sports. Top hole idea, what? That'll show Johnny Foreigner that Britannia rules the bloodsports roost.'

'Most kind, Bunty, but I'm really not sure. The constabulary say I'm not to allow strangers into the house.'

'What a ruddy cheek,' Heather snorted. 'Since when did Elouise Decora cow-tow to the nanny state? And really - do I look like a stranger? For Gawd's sake, it's hardly as if I'm wearing a hijab.' She hee-hawed a whinny and gave her thigh a what-ho slap. 'If you ask me, it's political correctness gawn mad.'

'How right you are, Bunty.' Persuaded, Decora invited Heather into her bijou abode and asked, 'have you time for a cup of tea? A scone, perhaps?'

'Ra-ther. Wait till I tell Rollo I've had a cuppa and a chinwag with Elouise Decora. Bet he'll be jealous as heck,' Heather aka Bunty gushed as Decora ushered her into the front room, told her to make herself at home and excused herself to the kitchen to rustle up a pot of Earl Grey tea and some oven-baked scones.

The moment Decora closed the door behind her, Heather leapt into action. Keeping an ear on the door - metaphearically speaking - she applied her trainee forensic skills to casing the joint, to use a technical term picked up in college Copperslang class. Her first, second and third impression was that the decor was a *ghastly* assemblage of shoddy reproduction crappery. Other than a regency-stripe settee and two matching rickenbackered recliners, the furnishings comprised a veneertop table, four dining chairs, a pouffe and a prissy display of knicknackered bric-a-brac cluttering the mantelplace. But the primary focus of interest was a reproduction sit-up-and-brag writing bureau.

Deeming this to be as good a place to rummage as any, Heather dug through a pile of correspondence waiting to be filed. A dozen or so fan-mails down, she chanced upon two very different letters penned by two distinctly different hands. The topmost was addressed to Colonel Hamilton Dangerfield at Bishop's Farm in what she took to be Elouise Decora's cultured hand. It read . . .

Hamilton,

If it is not enough that you have embezzled my inheritance, to now learn you are still conducting a squalid affair with that grotesque travesty behind my back is beyond the pale. After all I have invested in our personal and business relationships, I shall expect an explanation when I return my engagement ring. Have no doubt, I intend to make sure that you regret ever having met me.

And there the letter ended, as if Decora had abandoned it midscribe in favour of a face-to-face confrontation. Or maybe her course of mind had been injuncted by the contents of the second letter? Brief and to the point, it pulled no punches.

My Dear Miss Decora,

I trust you are in good health.

If you do not want me to go public about what Hamilton and your good self have been up to, meet me in the nave after the St. Mary of Our Nook service and I will tell you what is required to buy my silence. It is high time that you got a taste of your own medicine.

Kind Regards,

William Bragg.

As trained at police college, Heather phonesnapped the letters for evidence safekeeping. On hearing footscuffs in the hall, she dashed back to her chair and made a pretence of reading the first magazine that came to hand.

'Here we are, Bunty.' Elouise Decora set a tray down on the dropleafed table. 'I'll be mother. Milk?'

'I should coco,' Heather said with a beaming Bunty smile.

'Sugar?'

When Heather shook her head, Decora passed her a cup of fragrant Earl Grey tea and offered, 'scone? I make them myself, you know. Goodness only knows where I find the time. Oh, I see you are interested in the environment,' she said when she noticed an open copy of Science Denier Monthly on Heather's lap. 'Of course, there is no such thing as global warming,' she said. 'As I made clear in a recent Daily Rant column, it is solar warming that we need to worry about. Anyway, who cares if the polar icecaps melt and the odd species goes extinct, as long as we get warmer summers? Never did the dodo any harm.' She sat up on the sofa with her pinkie crooked, sipping tea and nibbling a scone. 'So what is it you do, Bunty, if you don't mind me asking?'

'For my sins, I'm a homemaker. Every gal's dream, I know, but it can be a frightful bore. Rollo is out all day - as I mentioned, he's in commercial property - so I have my hands full with the family.'

'Children?'

'Not bally likely. Ghastly little blighters. I prefer dawgs. I have three toy poodles - Itsy, Bitsy and Lochtaymore Chevalier de Pompidou of Tillycorthie.'

Decora leant forward and gave Heather a pat on the knee. 'Promise not to tell a soul,' she said with a cosmetic smile, 'but I couldn't agree more.'

'Spiffing place you have here, Elouise,' Heather fibbed as she looked around. 'Must have cost a packet. I'll wager The Sunday Rant pays you oodles, and quite right too. Where would they be without you, eh? Up the jolly-old creek without a paddle.'

'Strictly between the two of us, Bunty, they pay me next to nothing but my column provides a platform for my moral crusade,' Decora confided. 'As luck would have it, I came into a sizeable inheritance some time back. After buying this modest house, I invested the rest in a friend's business. He assured me that the venture couldn't fail, but I'm afraid it has. Looks like I've lost the lot.'

'The cad,' Heather said, and was about to move on to, 'the bounder,' and possibly 'the scallywag,' when the door burst open and an unshaven man in an ill-fitting uniform strolled in.

'Good day, ladies.' Sergeant Gummidge tipped his cap. 'Front door was on the latch so I let mesself in. Hope you don't mind.'

'Actually I do,' Decora said. 'As far as I am concerned, this is most inconvenient.'

'Couldn't agree more, but there you have it. I've been sent to keep an eye on you, but not to worry - you'll hardly know I'm here. I'll kip on the sofa if you've not got a spare room.' To Decora's undisguised disgust, Gummidge sat down beside her on the settee and looked around with the air of a travelling salesman inspecting a doss house. 'Breakfast at eight, is it?' he asked. 'Bacon and eggs for me. Sunny side up. And just the three slices of toast. No need to bother with black pudding, unless it's no trouble. Don't put yourself out on my account.' He kicked off his boots, undid his trousers, stretched his legs and sat back twiddling his thumbs. 'If you don't mind me saying, Miss Decora, you're looking your age,' he said. 'If you ask me, cut-price facelifts aren't worth diddly-squat.' He looked her over as if she was a scruff of rough, and shook his head. 'Pardon me for saying, but that skirt is far too short for a woman your age, especially with such skinny legs. Let's face it, no one's got time for mutton dressed as lamb.' He tipped her a wink and said, 'just saying, that's all. No offence.' Then he leant forward with his hands on his knees and squinted at Heather. 'Hello, hello, hello,' he said. 'And who have we here?'

'Bunty Findlay.' Heather reached out to shake hands but drew back when she saw that Gummidge's hands were already shaking.

'Got any means of identification, Miss Findlay?' Gummidge asked.

'Great Scott. What do you take me for?' Heather expressed outrage at his impertinence. 'In the circles I move in, a gal's word is her bond. And if you please, it is Missus Findlay.'

'I'll believe you, thousands wouldn't.' Sergeant Gummidge jotted a note on the back of his hand in felt-tipped pen. 'Mind if I ask you some questions?' he said. 'Can't be too careful with a killer on the loose.'

'Jolly inconvenient,' Heather said, 'but if you must.'

'Age?'

'Well I say. You've got a ruddy nerve. We gals treasure our little secrets, don't we Elouise?'

'Fair enough.' Gummidge said. 'Address?'

'Of course. Several.'

'Mind me asking where you were born?'

'What do you take me for, you pleb? England's green and pleasant land, of course. Do I look like a scrounger?'

'Very well, everything seems in order. Carry on, ladies. Don't mind me.' Gummidge settled back on the sofa, said, 'oh, don't mind if I do,' and helped himself to the last scone. He stuffed it in his mouth, screwed up his face and spat it out on the rug. He reached across Decora for her teacup, drained it in one swallow, said, 'ah, that's better. Thought you'd poisoned me there for a minute,' belched and wiped his mouth with the back of a hand. He nudged Decora aside to make more space, unleashed a mighty yawn, propped a cushion behind his head and lapsed into a snore.

'I'll be pootling off then, Elouise,' Heather said. 'Can't tell you how chuffed I am to have had this little chinwag. Wait till I tell the pooches I've had a good old natter with Elouise Decora. They'll be yappy as heck. Little tails wagging all over the place, I wouldn't wonder.'

'Must you go so soon?' Decora cast a despairing look at Sergeant Gummidge. 'What about that photograph you wanted of me holding the Union Jack?'

'Gawd, I'll be forgetting my own name next. Tell you what, why don't I pop back after the St. Mary of Our Nook Day hunt for a glass of sherry and another chinwag?' Heather said with one eye on her watch and the other on the door. 'I'll drag Rollo along and bring the dawgies, bless their little cotton socks. They're spiffing fun.'

'My pleasure.' Crestfallen though she was, Decora managed a half-hearted smile. 'Oh, nearly forgot,' she said, 'the Master of Hounds lives two doors down. Number eight.'

'So?'

'I thought that's who you were after.'

'Not likely. You must be thinking of someone else,' Heather said as she retrieved her shooting stick from the umbrella stand and made a beeline for the door. 'Must be orf, old girl. I'm late for something. Toodle pip,' she said as, with more haste than decorum, she waved goodbye.

Bubbly with excitement, Heather rushed out of Decora's *ghastly* house and hotfooted it round the corner. Making sure that no one was looking, she liberated her cellphone from her shoulder basket and autodialled the primary number. 'Naff, you'll never believe . . . Elouise Decora was engaged to Colonel Dangerfield,' she gushed down the invisible line. 'She was livid when she found out he'd swindled her and was having an affair with another woman behind her back. And get this - she arranged to meet Bragg after the service for some kind of showdown.'

Heather Prendergast took a deep, deep breath. 'Elouise Decora is our murderer,' said she with a certainty of purpose that brooked not one shred of ambiguity. 'No doubt about it. I'd stake my reputation on it.' Her eyes glazed over as she rang off, her head aswim with dreams of cracking the case of the decade. Confident that she was but a hop and a skip from being promoted to Prendergast of The Yard, she tucked her shooting stick under an arm and whistled her merry way along the yellowstone road to Trevelyan Hall. Half way there, she suddenly remembered that she was on a promise . . . unless - please God - Naff had forgotten.

The second leg of Heather's trudge home was a good deal less supercalifragilisticexpialidocious than the first.

Time is like a river. It flows by and does not return.

26

'Good of you to give me a lift, lift, Lady Trevelyan, but you really didn't have to. I could have called a cab.'

'Think nothing of it, Inspector. I always take the Porsche for a spin on Sundays. Gets me out of the house.'

'I saw you perform Shostakovich's Third Cello Concerto at the Royal Albert Hall a few years ago. If I may say, it was one of the most unforgettable evenings of my life.'

'Too kind. I must confess that I was rather rusty, but the orchestra was top notch. Better tighten your seat belt. These bends can get a bit hairy.'

'Don't you think you should slow down a little?'

'Not a bit of it. The old jalopy holds the road better at eighty-five than thirty. Safety first, I always say. Anyway, I am reliably informed that Constable Ingham is at the church doing whatever it is she does and Sergeant Gummidge doesn't work at weekends so it is not as if there are any officers on duty - present company excepted. So, Inspector, am I to take it that you are a music lover?'

'Passionate. Always have been. I used to be a leading light of the Metropolitan Police Choir. As it happens, that's where I met my wife.'

'I say, do you like Bach? Tell you what, why don't

I dust off one of my Stradivariuses and rattle you off a few tunes after you have spoken to my husband. You do know that he is innocent, don't you? He wouldn't hurt a fly - more's the pity. Ghastly things.'

'I would be delighted, Lady Trevelyan. Can't tell you how honoured I'd be.'

'Fiddlesticks. My pleasure. And do please call me Lady Elizabeth. No need to stand on ceremony. Now hold tight. This is where Miss Ingham came unstuck the other night. My, my, what a fondness for a tipple that young lady has. And the constitution of a trooper. It was all I could do to keep up with her.'

Five hair-raking minutes later, Lady Elizabeth swerved the Porsche to a juddery standstill outside Trevelyan Hall in a screech of squealing brakes and a hail of flying gravel. She jumped out of the car, took off her headscarf and sunglasses and brushed the creases out of her Broderie Anglaise culottes and Anglaise Broderie gilet. 'Guany,' she shouted, 'be a treasure and let Monty know the Inspector is here. And if you can spare a mo after you have done the alpacas, give me a hand in the kitchen. Chop, chop.' She slung her faux-mink coat over a shoulder and led Inspector Obafemi up the steps to her ancestral home. Having swapped her everyday heels for a pair of designer loungeabouts, she ushered him into the drawing room and introduced him to Naff. Leaving the menfolk to chat about kickabouts and wiff-waff, she disappeared to the kitchen to rustle up a quick snack for all and sundry.

Inspector Obafemi came straight to the point. 'Detective Robinson,' he said. 'I'm hoping you can provide protection for Mister Locke-Mortice until backup arrives from Maidstone. Tunbridge Wells have offered to help, but I'll be honest – they're not up to a job like this.'

'Consider it done, boss.' Naff mockeyed a cockeyed salute. 'I got to shoot up to Town to see a boffin mate tonight, but I'll be back in the morning. After that, I ain't going nowhere in a hurry. Too busy getting to know Lady Trevelyan, know how I mean?' Before he had time to elucidate, elaborate or gesticulate, Guan-Yin showed Locke-Mortice into the room. 'I'll leave you to it, boss. Give me a shout when you're done,' he said over a shoulder as he followed Guan-Yin to the kitchen.

'You again.' Locke-Mortice made no bones about his contempt for Obafemi. 'Should you not be out catching murderers instead of harassing innocent citizens in the sanctity of their own homes?'

'Please take a seat,' Inspector Obafemi said, unruffled by Locke-Mortice's gratuitous display of inhospitality. 'I would like to clarify a few points, if I may.'

'Well be quick about it,' Locke-Mortice said as he sat down in his favoured armchair by the Adam firegrate. 'I have an in-tray of pressing train timetables to attend to.'

Patience sorely tested, Inspector Obafemi balanced a well-thumbed pocketbook on a well-bent knee and asked, 'mind telling me where you were on Thursday afternoon?'

'Good grief, are you suggesting that I had something to do with Hamilton Dangerfield's murder?' Locke-Mortice huffed like one his precious puffers. 'My good man, if you know what's good for you, you will watch your tongue. I am not Jack the Ripper, if that is what you are implying,' he quipped. 'If you must know, I was in the gazebo catching up on official correspondence. The Department Without Any Portfolios doesn't run itself, you know. We have eels to deal with, a new air corridor over the Shetlands to delay, the Crumpet Cornflour Legislation to guide through the House, that cockup with daylight saving time to rectify and a host of other matters to attend to. Can't let the country go to the dogs just because I'm being victimised by you lot.' He scowled at Obafemi, leaving him in no doubt that he was scowling. 'Fact is, apart from attending church this afternoon, I have been too busy to leave the house since you last interviewed me, if your catalogue of fallacious allegations and slurs can be so described. I suggest that you ask Miss Guan-Yin if you are not prepared to take my word.' He waved a hand in the vague direction of the ornamental pond. 'And if I may make so bold, Inspector, I do not like your tone of voice,' he said. 'Mark my words, you will find yourself assigned to traffic duties if you do not drop these ludicrous charges forthwith.'

Having made due note of Locke-Mortice's slanders, Inspector Obafemi asked, 'what about today? Did you come straight home after the service?'

'By Jove, you've got a bally nerve,' Locke-Mortice

fumed. 'What is this – the Gestapo?'

'I vud ask zat you answer ze qvestion, Herr Locke-Mortice,' Obafemi quipped, then bit his tongue. If the steam coming out of Locke-Mortice's ears was anything to go by, he was less than amused by his lingua franca.

'I hardly see that it is any business of yours,' Locke-Mortice said, 'but since you ask, I was in the graveyard counting headstones while Elizabeth tuned the church organ. There are fourteen hundred and twenty-seven, not including the mausoleum, but you are welcome to count them yourself should you doubt my word.' He paused and gave his chin a thoughtful tap. 'Now I come to think,' he said, 'I seem to recall seeing Reverend Bragg enter the church with a woman, but can't say that I paid much attention. I can assure you that he was very much alive when I tired of waiting for Elizabeth and returned home. Now if that is all, I am sure that you have more important matters to attend to. I most certainly do.'

'I won't detain you much longer.' Obafemi raised a hand to bid Locke-Mortice remain seated. 'Now, I gather you stay in Westminster during the week and spend the weekends at Trevelyan Hall. Might I ask if you bring work home?'

'Might I ask you the same question, Inspector?' Locke-Mortice said abrasively. 'Of course you do. As do I.'

'Does that include classified documents? I understand you chair the National Security Council.'

'Good grief, man. What are you suggesting?' Mortally offended, Locke-Mortice erupted in a ferocity of pomposity. 'Had you been doing your job, Inspector, you would know that my security clearance goes as high as it gets. Even the Prime Minister is denied access to much of the classified information that crosses my desk. Needless to say, on the rare occasion I bring sensitive documents home, I keep them in my safe, so I suggest you keep your misplaced innuendos to yourself.'

Unflustered by Locke-Mortice's bluff and bluster, Obafemi persisted with, 'does anyone else have access to this safe?'

'I should say not.' Locke-Mortice snorted. 'Well, apart from my good lady wife and her secretary, Miss Guan-Yin, of course.' He went on to explain that when Lady Elizabeth was mentoring Salman Rushdie, Mister Rushdie urged her to keep her draft manuscripts under lock and key. It had never crossed her mind, but he pointed out that upward of a dozen unpublished Mellissa Moncrieff novels could be worth a King's ransom to any number of discerning bibliophiles, libraries or collectors. And of course, if her diaries fell into the wrong hands it would in all likelihood bring down the government. 'Better safe than sorry,' he said stuffily, blissfully unaware that he had been scripted such an amusing pun.

With headbangers and brick walls in mind, Inspector Obafemi pocketed his pen. 'Thank you, Mister Locke-Mortice. That will be all for the time being,' he said as he showed Locke-Mortice to the door. 'I must ask that you stay within the grounds until further notice. Detective Robinson has agreed to stand guard until Kent County Constabulary can provide a suitably qualified officer to relieve him.'

'If that is all, Inspector, good day. I trust that you catch this lunatic soon so that I can get on with my life.' Lock-Mortice said, and with one last look back in anger, strode off in the direction of the gazebo to deal with his troublesome eels.

After taking some time to mull over Locke-Mortice's testy-moany, Inspector Obafemi joined Lady Trevelyan and Naff in the kitchen. Gracing the table was a mouthwatersome feast of vegan-buttered muffets, four different varieties of vegancake, a bounty of homegrown stookberries aswim with vegan cream and a platter of glutenless chocnutties, all whipped up in a jiff by Lady Trevelyan with a helping whip from Guan-Yin.

In that it was the worst part of a week since he last indulged his gluttony, Obafemi made the most of what was, in truth, a veritable humdinger of a tummy-zinger. After wiping the last few crumbs and dribbles from his mouth with a well-dabbed serviette, he asked Naff, 'am I right in thinking that you were at the Saint Mary of Our Nook Festival this afternoon?'

'Sure. Nothing like a bit of local colour to put a smile on me face.'

'Would you mind telling me who the elderly lady in a straw hat was?'

'Beats me,' Naff said with a shrug. 'Some old biddy tending her old man's grave.'

'Really? A witness claims he saw you kissing.'

'Oh yeah. Right. See, it were the anniversary of her hubby's death and she needed comforting.'

'Comforting. Ah, yes. And are you in the habit of poking your tongue into the ears of strangers to comfort them?'

'All the time,' Naff said. 'Usually does the trick.'

'I see. Must give it a go next time I'm called upon to comfort a victim of domestic abuse.'

Overhearing Obafemi's tasteless quip, Lady Elizabeth butted in with, 'I say, there is no call for that, Inspector.' She nodded at the wallclock. 'Simon and I have a pressing matter to attend to, so if it is all right with you, I'll drive you back to the village when we are done. Feel free to look around the grounds while you wait. The Cypripedium, Bletilla, Calanthe and Cymbidium are spectacular at this time of year. Orchids are a little hobby of mine, don't you know?' she said with a heliotropic smile. 'I have one named after me. Stumbled across it in the Himalayas on my last Everest ascent.'

Thankful for some peace and quiet to juggle his thoughts, Inspector Obafemi packed his pipe with

Virginia shag and puffed a leisurely way across the upper lawn. And yes - the landscaped gardens were indeed spectacular. To think that Lady Elizabeth managed this sprawling estate all on her own. Apart from Guan-Yin, of course. And five gardeners. And three stable hands. And a team of maintenance staff. And a couple of groundspersons. And a gamekeeper. And a housekeeper. And three cleaners. But apart from that, she got by single-handed. What a remarkable woman. Quite remarkable. The more he saw of her, the more impressed he was with her intelligence, her beauty, her impeccable taste and her multifarious talents. But more than anything, her probity and unimpeachable integrity were beacons of moral virtue in a world of sinners, fallen angels and reprobates . . . there but for the grace of Lady Elizabeth Trevelyan go I, he thought with a ponderous shake of the head.

As he neared the ornamental pond, Obafemi saw Guan-Yin kneeling on the balustrade cooing to the Koi carp. 'Hello there,' he called. 'Miss Guan-Yin, isn't it?'

Like a picture-perfect portrait of chaste maidenhood in a floaty blue silk chang dress and red mandarin-collared frog-buttoned jacket, Guan-Yin pressed her hands together in a gesture of suppliance and bowed her head. 'Nǐ hǎo.'

Obafemi strolled over to join her and asked, 'spare a minute?'

'Time is like a river,' Guan-Yin replied with a serene smile. 'It flows by and does not return.'

'Indeed.' Obafemi cleared his throat. 'As I'm sure you are aware, I am investigating the murders in the village. I wonder if you can help me.'

'Ah-so, Inspector,' Guan-Yin said and proceeded to impart some pearls of oriental wisdom. 'Going into country first time, ask what is forbidden. On entering village, ask what are customs and on entering private house, ask what should not be mentioned.'

'Quite.' Struggling to strike a balance between an enlightened smile and a baffled frown, Inspector Obafemi asked, 'have you worked for Lady Trevelyan long?'

Guan-Yin nodded. 'Do everything at its time,' she said, 'and one day will seem like three.'

'So I suppose you must have a pretty good idea what goes on round here?'

'Always ears on the other side of a wall,' Guan-Yin said with an enigmatic smile.

'So I gather. Now, Mister Locke-Mortice tells me that until today he hadn't left the grounds for a week. Can you confirm that?'

Guan-Yin turned to look at the gazebo. 'Only wisest and stupidest of men never go out,' she sighed.

'I see,' Obafemi said, although if truth be told, he didn't. 'Tell me, Miss Guan-Yin, do you think the killer will strike again?'

'Coming events cast their shadow before them.'

Profoundly unenlightened, Obafemi gave Guan-Yin his card. 'I would be grateful if you could let me know if you see anything suspicious.'

'Tell me, I will forget; show me, I will remember; involve me, I will understand.' Guan-Yin tucked the card into a sleeve, bowed her head and padded off to the house.

Wondering where the last few minutes of his life had gone, Inspector Obafemi watched Guan-Yin fade into the distance. Then of their own accord, his eyes strayed up to a first-floor window where he glimpsed a naked woman staring down at him. He was about to look away when a man appeared behind her. The muscular studivarious kissed her on the nape of her neck, nibbled her ear and fondled her breasts. As she sank back into his arms with a haughty look on her handsome face, he winked at Obafemi and zipped across the curtains.

Detective Inspector Isaac Obafemi had always prided himself on being the most open-mindedness of men. Nevertheless, he could scarcely bring himself to imagine the orgy of ribald passion, blighted troths and ungentlemanly relish playing out behind the brocade tucks and damask pleats of those bedroom curtains. Despondent, disillusioned and disheartened, he sat down on the marble balustrade and, with the heaviest of hearts, sighed, 'and so are life's illusions shattered.'

27

Samantha Ingham reported for duty at Trevelyan Hall in her plainest plain-clothes hipster jeans, t-shirt, baseball cap and trainers. A little late, she was bearing a bottle of premium Crossed Arms' screwtop wine as a modest token of her appreciation; Lady Trevelyan had graciously invited her to stay as a houseguest rather than freeze her bones to the numb guarding the front door.

In a last scrape of the dice, Inspector Obafemi had assigned Ingham to Locke-Mortice protection duties while Naff was in London. Not to poke too large a point at it, he was - to put it dyslexically - down to the brae boones of his maigret resauces. To his frustration, he was desktied coordinating the investigation while Sergeant Gummidge was on Decora-watch and Inspector Turner's Tunbridge Wells contingent were conducting house to cottage enquiries.

Lady Trevelyan greeted Sammy with a flurry of airkisses and socially-distanced mmmwah-hugs. 'For me? How kind,' she said in a sham of delight when Sammy presented her with the giftbottle. She glanced at the label, raised an arched eyebrow, said, 'how very quaint,' and handed it to Guan-Yin with instruction to use it variously as vinegar, toilet deinfectant and sink unblocker. Although initially concerned that Sammy might not be able to cope unaided by . . . *ahem* . . . a male officer, she was reassured when Sammy assured her that she had passed a bruising Police Academy course in martial arts and thuggery with flying collars.

Unnoticed by Sammy, Naff was lurking nearby doing his burly best to block her line of vision to his motorbike's bald tyre. When he overheard her bragging about her pugilistic prowess, he scoffed, 'so you reckon you can look after yesself, do you, babe?' and made a playful lunge.

'Steady on, Sammy. He's got a long drive ahead of him.' Heather said as she helped Naff to his feet and dabbed his bloody nose with her standby hanky.

'Sorry, Miss Prendergast,' Sammy said with a disingenuous expression of concern. 'Seems I don't know my own strength.'

Although Sammy's role was ostensibly to provide protection for Montague Locke-Mortice, behind the rear she and Heather had cooked up a crusty plan to set a cunning spidertrap with which to web a murderess fly.

After much one-sided debate, Heather had convinced a sceptical Sammy that her audacious strategy could not possibly probably fail. Accordingly, earlier that evening Step One was sprung when Sammy phoned Sergeant Gummidge to inform him in the strictest sworn confidence that Naff would be spending the night in London. Of course, she knew that as sure as eggs is eggs Gummidge would flap his blabby tongue and tell Decora that Locke-Mortice's guard was temporarily downtown. And as sure as those aforementioned eggs remained eggs, it stood to reason that once Decora had been tipped the wink, she would grasp the narrow escutcheon of opportunity to eliminate the last upstanding witness left standing - Montague Locke-Mortice.

With legendary Holmsian cunning and a dash of Prendergast of The Yard derring-do, Step Two would see the sleuthsome twosome sneak out of the house at midnight to stake out the gazebo. With eggsian inevitability, they would intercept Decora redhanded, all tooled-up for murder. The rest, as some mothers say, would be child's play. Heather would confront Decora with evidence of her murderspree and in a high-tech twist, secretly record her sobbing confession on the miniature digiblah recorder that she had 'borrowed' from work – borrowed being a euphemism for half-inched.

And so to Step Three . . . in a final bish-bash-bosh finale, Decora would be bang to rights, Locke-Mortice would be exonerated, Sammy would be a local hero and Heather would be one boot further up the slithery ladder of promotion, a mere strut or two from achieving her life's goal as Prendergast of The Yard. After all, as she confidently assured Sammy, it always worked in the movies, so why not in real life?

Needless to say, Heather knew it was a risky gambit, but as her unofficial motto had it, *qui somnium vidisse se, vincit*, which online transgarbles as 'she who dreams, pork chop.' After all, Sammy's martial arts credentials were as plain as the broken nose on Naff's face and Heather all but had a brown-belt in Jujitsu, bar the buckle. What could possibly go wrong?

Not privy to the plan, Lady Elizabeth was delighted to have Sammy stay the night. Indeed, she offered to rustle up a light five course meal in her honour. 'I will have my husband join us,' she said. 'And after dinner we can play a hand or two of bridge.'

'Most kind, Lady Elizabeth, but I haven't brought a thing to wear,' a downcast Sammy said.

'Good grief, young lady. This is not the Ritz. There are no jumped-up nouveau riche plebs here. Jeans and a t-shirt will do just fine. For heaven's sake, a handsome gal like you would cut a dash in a plastic mac and a shower cap.'

'Who let the cat out of the bag?' Sammy said with a teasing grin.

It went without much saying that the meal was utterly feastacious. With Guan-Yin's able assistance, Lady Elizabeth rustled up a consummate melon-grass consommé and a mouthwettening starter of pondnuts and delicatised beansprouts. This was followed by a delectatious h'ors d'oeuvre of sweet and sour vegan eatmeats with fingerlicking sake sauce. By far the main course was a Bethany Baker Veganitarian Puffin Pie. Not least but last came a choice of almondnut mousse or treefruit flimflam. Copious glasses of Chateau Trevelyan

Beaujolais Tres, Tres Nouveau were enjoyed by all, and even Uncle Monty joined in with the dinner table conversation.

'Did you know that Great Western Railways used to run an overnight mail train from Crewe to Inverness?' he announced above the yawns. 'I have high hopes of persuading my minister to reintroduce the service, although the treasury maintains that no one of any consequence lives in Inverness. Of course, the Scottish Nationalists dispute this but have yet to provide any evidence to the contrary. As far the opposition is concerned, they claim that in this day and age everyone uses email. Bit rich coming from a rabble of unreconstructed Stalinist Luddites, wouldn't you say?' He clutched his sides and roared with laughter. 'In any event,' he said as he dabbed the whimsy from his eyes. 'They are all missing the point. It has nothing to do with fulfilling a need. It is tradition like King and Empire, The Playing Fields of Eton and The House of Lords. And as we all know, tradition is what makes Great Britain so great. Where would our proud nation be without it, eh? You tell me that. Like as not, we would be an insignificant little island off the coast of Europe populated by troglodytes and spivs, like Ireland.'

In an effort to stay awake, Lady Elizabeth drew her chair to within thigh-rubbing distance of Sammy. She shielded her mouth with a hand and whispered, 'Miss Ingham, I have a confession to make.' For reasons best known to herself, she cast a furtive glance over a shoulder. 'I took the liberty of emailing a few snapshots of you to my dear, dear friend, Jean-Paul Gautier and he has just called me back. We conversed in French with a smattering of American, but to tell the truth, I found it impossible get a word in edgeways. You know what JP is like. Garrulous isn't the word.' She squeezed Sammy's knee and chuckled. 'So here's the thing,' she confided. 'He is desperate to have you model his new collection of unisex lingerie at Milan fashion week. As long as you are agreeable, he intends it to be the launchpad for a glittering career. You are to be known as Artemis, become a famous film actor, marry a pop star, get divorced, enjoy an overnight career as a social media influencer and have your own reality television show.' She clapped her hands, delighted with the sequence of events. 'He has already booked a venue for the wedding and can offer you a choice of Justin Bieber or Harry Styles as a groom. Unless, of course, you would prefer someone more mature. Paul McCartney perhaps, or Elton John - divorce courts willing.'

After a brief hiatus to top up her glass, drain it and top it up again, Lady Elizabeth drew her chair closer. She was hardly able to contain herself. After all, it was common knowledge in society circles that organising other people's lives was a little hobby of hers. An obsession, some maintained. 'Anyway,' she said, 'you will no doubt be thrilled to hear that Ridley Scott has agreed to direct the home movie of your whirlwind romance in the tropics, your wedding in Westminster Cathedral, the reception in St. Moritz, your wedding night in the foothills of Mount Kilimanjaro and honeymoon in Tahiti. Jean-Paul has given the Kardashians' personal plastic surgeon a whopping deposit to make you deliciously gorgeous. But remember - after the surgery you must on no account attempt any facial expressions other than glassy disdain or haughty aloof.' She raised a cautionary finger. 'Whatever you do, do not smile. If you are tempted, think of poor Donatella.' Stricken by a vision of one of her closest casual acquaintances, she stared into an imagined distance, shook her head and sighed. 'Be that as it may,' she continued, 'Jean-Paul has retained a top team of celebrity lawyers to handle your divorce. I am terribly afraid that it will be one of those ghastly tell-all headline-grabbing affairs. But not to worry. You will be awarded oodles of alimony and custody of the chihuahua. So, my dear, what do you say?' When Sammy's jaw dropped, she gave her a playful slap on the thigh and said, 'just my little joke, dear,' with a mischievous twinkle in her eye. 'Let's face it, Miss Ingham - you hardly need a plastic surgeon.'

Chocked up to the gills with after-dinner nutmints and lip-tingling liqueurs, the hostess, her sullen husband and their house-guestesses left Guan-Yin to clear the table, stack the dishwasher and feed the leftovers to the alpacas. Wonderfully relaxed, they retired to the drawing room to digest dinner, ingest alcohol and digress with a few après le dinner hands of contract bridge. Lady Elizabeth threw another choplog on the fire, primed the Blam and Olufsen ambiosonic stereo-fi with her chart-topping Veronika Vivendi Sings Bjork vinyl long player and arranged four chairs around the Chippendale card table.

'I will partner Monty and you two can be a pair,' Lady Elizabeth told the girls. Set fair, she rolled up her sleeves, lit a cigar and shuffled the cards with a deft sleight of hand. 'I once had a holiday job as a croupier in one of daddy's Knightsbridge casinos,' she told Sammy. 'I had just completed the induction course in slut-slang when the Feds busted the joint. Well, when the beak twigged I was just a patsy, the chips really hit the fan. Papa had to splash backhanders all over the shop to beat the rap.' She broke into the smile of a hardened cardsharp. 'If I have time, I will show you how to deal off the bottom of a deck and rig a roulette wheel before we tootle off to bed. Me oh my, what a little tearaway I was at finishing school.' Riddled with nostalgia, she shook her head as she dealt from the top of the deck – or so she claimed. 'Righty-ho, Spriggy,' she said. 'You are sitting on the dealer's left, so you can start the bidding.'

Heather sat back and fanned her cards in descending order of ascending importance. As she examined her hand, a subtle smile crept across her face. Fighting a smirk, she opened the bidding with, 'six no trumps.' When her aunt gave her a startled look, her uncle-in-law scowled, and Sammy said, 'nice one,' she clapped her hands and squealed, 'I win. Let's play another hand.'

'Spriggy, dear, we haven't actually started yet,' Lady Elizabeth pointed out, much to Heather's dismay. She turned to Sammy and said, 'righty-ho, cards on the table. Let's see what you've got. You're the dummy.'

'Who blabbed?' Sammy said under her breath as she laid her cards down face up. And so began a devilish game of bluff and counter bluff.

After Lady Elizabeth led with a king of spades. Heather examined her cards, stroked her chin, nodded and played a six of spades from dummy. When Locke-Mortice gave her a sceptical look and put down a ten of spades, Heather clicked her tongue, said, 'think I'll trump that, thank you very much,' tossed down a four of diamonds and scooped up the cards.

Lady Elizabeth intercepted Heather's hand midscoop. 'You can't do that, Spriggy. You bid no trumps, remember?'

'Doesn't that mean I get to decide what trumps are when I want?'

'I am afraid not, my dear. It means there aren't any.'

Heather reviewed her hand, frowned and said, 'mind if I change my bid to no no-trumps?'

Having decided to play snap, a high-spirited time was had by all, fuelled by plentiful strong spirits, much jocular badinage and a jiggy lilt of smoochy background music. Even Montague Locke-Mortice's mood lifted, albeit from dour to droll. Every now and then, Guan-Yin appeared with another bottle of vintage conversation uninhibitant from Lady Trevelyan's legendary wine cellar. These were accompanied by plates of fortune cookies containing such thought-provoking mottos as, *a bird in the hand is worth plenty feathers*, or, *late to bed, early to rise, always tired.*

As the smaller of the hands on the mantel-ledge clock nudged eleven, Guan-Yin poked her head through the door. Looking for all the world like a diminutive moon-nymph in a virginal white nighty with her pigtail tucked into a beekeeper's hairnet embellished with bobbles, pompoms and doodads, she said, 'I go bed. Toodleypips.'

'Think I'll join you,' Locke-Mortice said, then quickly added, 'merely a figure of speech, my dear,' when his wife glared at him. As he strode off to the gazebo, Heather took Sammy to one side and whispered, 'time for our stakeout. Got your night vision binoculars?'

'Chill, pet.' Sammy topped up Heather's glass and then her own. 'Plenty of time.'

'Don't you think you should go easy on the wine? You're on duty,' Heather said, concerned when Sammy downed another measure of tonsil lubricant in double quick time.

'Who's going to grass me up, sweetie? Come on, live a little. Try a taster of this.' Sammy poured a brimfull of Bacardi into Heather's glass, said, 'bottoms up,' and winked.

As the evening wore on, Heather grew ever more bored as she watched Sammy and Lady Elizabeth huddle on the larger of the Chesterfield sofas giggling like fourth-formers at the back of a no holds barred sex-education class. By her later admission, she probably drank a little too much. In actual fact, she lost count of how little too much she drank. 'Sammy,' she whispered loudly as the tick of time tocked towards the watching hour. 'We really ought to be making a move.'

Eyes riveted like tintacks on a glossy magazine on her lap, Sammy muttered, 'what? Oh, yeah. Sure. Be with you in a tick. Just taking a look at one of your aunt's Playboy centrefolds.' Her eyes opened ever wider as she studied the photospread from a variety of angles. 'I'm amazed she wasn't arrested,' she muttered as she turned the page. Shocked, she caught her breath, gave Lady Elizabeth a startled look and, in response to Lady Elizabeth's who-me? vestal eyelash flutter, collapsed in ribald hoots of thighslapping lipsmacking eyewatering kneejerking ribtickling shoekickoffing fingergesticulating hysterics.

And so Heather fretted and she brooded and she brooded and she fretted. For the want of something to do, she kicked off her shoes and counted her toes. Fed up with cataloguing her tootsies, she opened another bottle of Bacardi, filled her glass, drank it in a few gutshivering gulps and then downed another two or three large measures. To say that she found an overindulgence of numb-relief relaxing would be a gross miscarriage of the facts. Well, as is so often the case, two glasses of Bacardi led to another. And another. She seemed to remember getting tipsy and she vaguely remembered getting woozy and she definitely didn't remember a thing after that.

Heather woke up some time later in front of the dying embers of the fire. Flat on her back like a flatpack hatrack, she was hugging an empty Bacardi bottle to her chest like a drunken sailor in the scuppers with a blah, blah, blah. Her vision was blurred, her head throbbed like a punchbag, her breath stank like a brewer's sewer. As she lay on the rug watching the walls circulate the ceiling, she glimpsed the little hand on the carriage clock. Five, it read, or rather, it pointed to the Roman numeral V.

Wishing that she was dead and not entirely sure that she wasn't, Heather crawled across the floor in search of her shoes. Duty did not call, it screamed. Wishing it would keep its voice down, she staggered to the coat-hall, found her smartphone in her blouson pocket and dialled Sammy's number. After an interminable wait, a breathless voice answered, 'what?'

'Sorry I'm late for our stake-out, Sammy. I came down with a migraine,' Heather fibbed, doing her best to disguise a froggy croak in her voice. 'I'll be there quick as I can.'

'No mad rush, pet,' Sammy whispered down the invisible line. 'I'm a bit tied up just at the minute. I'll come get you soon as I'm free.'

And then the strangest thing happened. Heather heard a loud binaural mutterance of, 'who is it, dear?' followed by, 'do keep still,' echoing like a duckquack on her cellphone. As she looked up at the first floor landing, she saw two shadowy figures in skintight latex jumpsuits, platform thigh boots and faceless rubber masks sneaking out of her aunt's bedroom. Assuming she was hallucinating, she slumped down on a stairstep and buried her head in her hands. She was still nursing her insobriety when she felt a tap on the shoulder.

'Sorry. Must have nodded off.' Sammy avoided Heather's eyes as she belted up her jeans and tucked in her t-shirt.

'I say, everything all right?' Lady Elizabeth appeared at the top of the stairs in a diaphanous negligee and mule-heeled slippers. She brushed a sweaty tangle of hair out of her eyes and stretched her arms in an unconvincing yawn. 'Pardon me,' she said and yawned again. 'You girls woke me up. I have been asleep for ages.'

Deeming now not to be the time to press this or any other point, marginally more awake than not, Heather followed Sammy out to the garden. She slumped down in a clump of bushes overlooking the gazebo, rested her head on Sammy's shoulder, said, 'wake me up if you see anything,' and nodded off.

Sometime later, Sammy shook her awake. 'Look. He's off for breakfast.' She pointed to Locke-Mortice, who was strolling up to the house whistling *Rule Britannia*. 'Guess we can thank our lucky stars he's still alive,' she said as she heard the beep of her walkie-talkie.

'Wonder why Decora didn't murder him while our guard was down?' Heather wondered.

'Because she's dead.' Sammy stared at her two-way radio in disbelief. 'Her body has just been found in

Poacher's Wood.'

28

Elouise Decora's body lay in a coppiced glade - hazel, hawthorn and hornbeam in the main with a noble oak or two and a few proud elms. Half buried in a thicket replete with corngrass, tree-marrow, maiden royal and pennypinks, it was not a pretty sight.

According to Detective Inspector Obafemi's contemporaneous notes, Decora had been strangled with a pair of fishnet tights. The victim of a frenzied attack, her face was contorted into a grotesque death mask. Her eyes had been gouged out, her cheeks were slashed to the bone - quite possibly by razored fingernails - and hanks of hair ripped out at the roots. Concealed in an overgrowth of undergrowth, she lay face down in a pool of congealed blood. She showed no sign of rigor-mortis, leading Inspector Obafemi to surmise that she had died shortly before sunrise. In a macabre twist of the knife, the killer had sliced out her tongue and left it beside the body as a tasty peckadillo for an early bird in search of worms.

As he surveyed the gruesome scene of mutilation, Inspector Obafemi asked himself, was Elouise Decora's severed tongue indicative of the fact that she had been telling tales out of school – a schoolpigeon, so to speak – or merely symptomatic of the killer's deranged mind? He had no idea, and upon reflection, had even less.

He was deeply troubled. In all his years of investigating homicides, he had never before witnessed such a ruthless killing spree. Ruthless? Sadistic might be a better way of putting it, although that is open to debate. For goodness' sake, even the notorious Hammersmith Hammerer had taken longer victim-breaks between hack-attacks. But The Butcher of St. Mary Nook, as the killer would surely be known to posterity, seemed missioned to murder without mercy. This was her fourth victim in ten days.

Decora's body had been stumbled across - figuratively and literally speaking - by a Mister Larry Huckstep of no permanently fixed abode. Although keen to make a move, he was happy, or better said he was advised under caution, to assist Inspector Obafemi with his enquires.

'Mind me asking what you were doing in Poacher's Wood at five this morning, Mister Huckstep?' Obafemi asked.

'Walking the dog.'

'And what do you have in the sack?'

'Funny you should ask,' Huckstep said, not noticeably amused. 'See, Rover caught a hare. Two, as it happens.' He scowled at the lurcher and wagged a finger. 'Bad dog,' he said. 'Bad, bad, dog.' Worried that Inspector Obafemi might probe a little deeper, he pointed to the sack and said, 'there's a couple of pheasants in there. Fell out of a hedge. Dead as a stone. Old age, I reckon. And that salmon jumped out of a stream into Rover's mouth. I was taking it back to my mobile home to give it the kiss of life.'

'Thank you, Mister Huckstep. If I have any more questions, I will be in touch.' Having bade Huckstep au revoir, adieu and bon appetit, Inspector Obafemi made a mental note to book a table at The Crossed Arms' restaurant. He had a gut hunch that poached salmon, roast pheasant and jugged hare might be back on the menu. For one fanciful moment, he was minded to invite PC Ingham to join him, but his mind soon came to its senses.

Although professionally as thick-skinned as they come, Isaac Obafemi was as naked as the new born hay when it came to personal rejection, so it was a risk he never took. After all, why invite humiliation to dinner? Anyway, when all was said and done, who needs friends when you only have one season ticket to The Emirates, the hallowed home of The Arsenal Football Club?

Speaking of which . . . at that very moment PC Ingham came sprinting into view. She stumbled to a stop, took one look at Decora's body, clamped a hand to her mouth and ducked behind a tree. She reappeared several minutes later looking much the worse for wear. 'Sorry, guv,' she said with a bilious burp. 'Must be something I ate.'

'No need to apologise, Ingham. I have lost count of the number of murder victims I've seen, but this one takes the biscuit.'

At the mention of biscuits, PC Ingham clutched her stomach and disappeared behind her favourite tree.

When she returned, Inspector Obafemi shepherded her a discreet distance from the crime scene. He thought it best. 'Did Locke-Mortice leave Trevelyan Hall at any time last night?' he asked.

PC Ingham furrowed her brow in a concerted effort to avoid the question. 'No, guv,' she misremembered. 'I kept a close eye on him. He went to bed around eleven and got up at seven. I watched him like a hawk,' she said.

Inspector Obafemi stroked his chin and gazed into the clichéd middle distance. 'What about the Chinese lady?'

'Miss Guan-Yin? Went to bed same time as Locke-Mortice. I remember `cause he said he'd join her.' In response to Inspector Obafemi's raised eyebrows, Ingham hurriedly explained, 'it's not what you think, guv. That's how posh people talk. No idea what she did after that. I was busy watching Locke-Mortice. Didn't let him out of my sight.'

'You're a woman, Officer Ingham,' Inspector Obafemi said, or rather he stated the bleeding obvious. 'Stilettos?' He pointed to footprints in the clay.

'I'd say kitten heels, guv. Decora's?'

'No. She's wearing Wellington boots. And did you notice, she isn't wearing any makeup.'

'Can't say I looked that close, guv,' PC Ingham said with a queasy belch.

'Take it from me, she isn't. I gather that is most unusual

for her. My guess is, she left home in a hurry. Looks like she put up a fight. She was clutching a few strands of black hair. They stink of perfume, but I'm pretty sure it's not hers.'

'Chanel Number Ten?' PC Ingham asked and nodded when Inspector Obafemi nodded. 'So we're definitely looking for a female perp,' she said. 'Narrows down the field.'

'It does indeed. I'll wait for the forensic report, but I'll be surprised if the footprints and hair don't match those we found at Bishop's Farm.' Alerted by a jaunty whistle, Obafemi looked round and gave his watch a tetchy tap. 'Explain yourself, Sergeant,' he demanded. 'What time do you call this?'

'You're the one with a watch,' Sergeant Gummidge said with all due irreverence. 'Had to pop home for some shuteye. Me back was killing me. I'm too old for kipping on sofas.' He stretched his arms in a vesuvial yawn. 'The missus give me a right old bollocking, I can tell you. Said I'd woke her up and asked where me trousers were. Moan, moan, moan.' He caught his breath when he saw Decora's mangulated body stretched out on the grass like a prop from a macabre corps and robbers movie. 'Blimey. Wondered where she'd got to.' He stuck out his tongue and gurned his face into a curdle of critical disgust. 'Don't look too well, does she?'

'I gave you strict instructions not to let her out of your sight, Sergeant,' Obafemi said. 'Make no mistake, I will be reporting your dereliction of duty to my superiors.'

Gummidge hung his head like a miscreant puppy without a bone to pick. 'Sorry, sir,' he mumbled. 'Promise I'll keep a close eye on her in future.' Then he rallied to the defence of his threadworn credentials with, 'but weren't my fault. Honest, guv. Someone must have slipped a Mickey Finn in me cider `cause I went out like a light after the tenth pint.'

'You haven't heard the last of this, Sergeant.' Inspector Obafemi glared at Gummidge and clenched his fists. Not wishing to squander more breath than needs must, he turned to PC Ingham. 'Wait here and make sure Gummidge doesn't piss all over the crime scene,' he told her. 'I need to clear my head.'

Insofar as he was able, Inspector Obafemi kept to a footpath which for no circuitous reason meandered from here to there by way of nowhere in particular. No matter how he racked his brains, they hit a brick wall. After exhausting all his options, he was forced to admit that he lacked a prime suspect. Having said that, an overwhelming body of evidence pointed to a female perp . . . strands of silky black hair; that perfume; those footprints; the straw hat. But who? Unless he was barking up a mad tree, the only candidates left in his sights were Jaimie Smith and the mystery girl seen leaving the Ordinary Express at St. Mary Nook Station. He cursed MaidenRail for refusing to hand over the surveillance footage and made a mental note to ask Chief Inspector Wheeler to find out what the devil was going on. Someone, he assumed, must have something to hide. But who? And what? More to the point, why? But the who, the what and the why of the matter were only part of the puzzle. The missing piece of the jigsaw was motive.

Inspector Obafemi could only speculate, but let's say, he said to himself, that Mathers' murder was a crime of passion. If so, presumably the killer was hellbent on silencing potential witnesses. That was the only explanation he could come up with to explain why Mathers' fellow-travellers were being eliminated one by two by three.

The footpath led to a fallow field circumferenced by a sturdy fence. Having reached a dead end in more ways than one, Inspector Obafemi leant against a fencepost puffing his pipe and watched an infestation of bunnies hopping, skipping and humping for all their negligible worth. Having settled on a theory that added up, tied up loose ends and held water – albeit after a mixed-metaphorical fashion – a picture began to slot into place.

He recalled that Stationmaster's Cottage had been cluttered with personal effects of a masculine gender so sneaked a suspicion that Jaimie Smith must have, or have had, a live-in lover. Could that have been Trevor Mathers? If so, perhaps she killed him in a rage of passion. Alternatively, he deemed it not beyond the bounds of posthumability that the mysterious trainjump woman was a jilted lover hellbent on revenge. Of the two possibilities, both were equally plausible. And both were equally implausible.

As the risen sun broke through the cottonwool clouds and bathed the near horizon in a gentle butterpat melt, Obafemi took off his jacket, unbuttoned his waistcoat, slackened his tie, uncufflinked his shirt and rolled up his sleeves. Albeit much against his city nature, he had to admit that found the view enchanting. On mornings like this, he could well understand why a bright young spark like PC Ingham should have chosen to settle in such a godforsaken backwater. Nevertheless, he thought it a shame that such a talented young officer should let her life pass by. From what he had seen, given a guiding hand and some fatherly advice, she had the ability to rise quickly through the ranks.

Although Obafemi knew that it was none of his business, he wondered whether Samantha Ingham was engaged. He was sure that she must have a queue of handsome admirers eager to beaver her up the aisle, plight their troth and carry her across the threshold to a life of domestic drudgery. Still, if that was what she wanted, good luck to her. After all, it was her career. Her life. If he was fifteen years younger and forty pounds lighter, he would be sorely tempted to join the queue.

Isaac Obafemi's spirits slumped like a lumbered puncture as his thoughts turned to Sandra and his shipwreck of a marriage. For a man regarded by his colleagues as decisive and authoritative, he was a chicken-livered ostrich when it came to his private life. Never do today what you can put off till tomorrow was how Sandra dismissed his easygo attitude towards their relationship. And to be brutally frank, he knew that she had a point. But time pressed on as only time can press. He scrunched out his pipe, stowed it in his pipe pocket and relegated thoughts of his fractured marriage to the drifts of his mind. He had work to do.

But no, damn it . . . that was typical of his abject spinelessness, was it not? In a rare moment of marital decisiveness, Obafemi determined to have a serious heart to heart with his long-suffering wife the moment he returned to London, not so much for his sake as for hers. She deserved better than an obsessive workaholic who stank of pipe tobacco and ate like a fish. Ate like a fish? He puzzled at the peculiarly piscine turn of phrase he had been dealt.

When he and Sandra separated, as he knew they would, and sold their flat, as he supposed they must, how better to invest his share of the process than in a small cottage on the outskirts of St. Mary Nook? Bachelorhood and early retirement would be his Nirvana. He could roll out of bed when he woke up, smoke his pipe whenever he liked and write or paint or maybe learn another language should the fancy take him. In other words, to cut a long sentence short, he would be able to relax until the heifers came home. Then he broke into a resigned smile. For the fact was, he knew himself too well. A life of leisure would send him as barmy as a barnyard bunny. He shuddered as he remembered how bored and depressed he became during Coronavirus lockdowns one, two, three . . . pick a number. Any number.

But enough of idle speculation. Duty called and he had a crazed killeress to bring to book. He slung his jacket over a shoulder and returned to the crime scene where he found PC Ingham marshalling a squadron of new arrivals. A platoon of overalled forensticians were dusting, photosnapping, tweasering and plastercasting everything in sight, or so it seemed. Nearby, a pathologist was poking and prodding the mutilated corpse with an occasional nod, a sporadic uhm and an intermittent ahh.

'Sorry to drag you out at such an ungodly hour,' Obafemi said with all due deference; last night, DI Turner informed him that Kent County Constabulary had enlisted the services of the distinguished Professor of Pathology at Canterborough University to make quite sure that no bones remained unturned. However, Obafemi had not expected such an attractive woman. Tall and slim with a trim figure, she was a natural blond with intelligent blue eyes.

The pathologist got to her feet and shook her head. 'Don't quote me, Inspector,' she said, 'but looks like we've got a homicidal maniac on our hands.'

Inspector Obafemi returned the pathologist's frown with an equally severe one of his own. 'That's what I was afraid of,' he said. 'Still, thanks for coming out so quickly. I appreciate it.'

'Don't mention it.' The pathologist took off her rubber gloves and tucked them into her coveralls. 'My lab is in Canterborough but I live in St. Mary Nook, so it wasn't far to come. Anyway, I was awake when you phoned. My husband was out all night and woke me up when he came in.'

Inspector Obafemi gave his chin a thoughtful scratch. 'Correct me if I'm wrong, but do I detect a slight German accent?'

'Well spotted.' The pathologist's smile was a ray of sunshine in an otherwise dismal day. 'I met my husband when I came to Canterborough on holiday twenty years ago.' She looked warily about and lowered her voice. 'Between you and me,' she said, 'it feels like a lifetime.'

'Das Herz regiert also deinen Kopf, oder?' Inspector Obafemi asked with a polyglotitudinous smile.

The pathologist chuckled. 'Yes, I suppose my heart has always ruled my head. I must say, Isaac, your German is excellent.'

'A little rusty, but I get by. By the way, how do you know my name?'

'My husband has told me all about you.' The pathologist took off her spectacles and examined Obafemi with her head to one side. 'Have you left your horns at home? You're not at all what I was expecting.' Amused by Obafemi's puzzled frown, she reached out a hand to cement what was to become a lasting friendship.

'Delighted to meet you at last, Inspector,' she said. 'I'm Professor Gummidge, but do please call me Heidi.'

'Am I glad to see you, darling. You'll never guess what happened while you were in London.'

'You got laid?' A picture of roguish impudence, Naff grinned as Heather sputtered for words. In sequential order of petting, he wrapped his arms around her, ran his fingers through her hair and blew in her ear. 'Hows about we make up for lost time,' he whispered in the deepthroat voice that victims of his amorous intentions found fiendishly flattering, irresistibly seductive, highly hilarious or grossly offensive, depending on their age, disposition and degree of desperation.

Heather fended off her boyfriend's advances with a push and a shove. 'Elouise Decora was murdered,' she told him. 'And we have proof that Uncle Monty couldn't have done it. Isn't it wonderful?'

'Not for Decora, it ain't. So how come your uncle's in the clear?'

'Me and Sammy were staking him out. We didn't see him set foot outside the gazebo.'

'Bet Veronika's chuffed - I mean Lady Elizabeth.' Naff hid his blushes behind a lean and thirsty gulp. 'I'm parched,' he said. 'Any chance of a cuppa?'

As they locked arms and headed for the house, Heather

asked, 'darling, can I pick your brains?'

'Not sure I got any left,' Naff said. 'The roads were choc-a-bloc with dozy tourists. Caravans all over the shop.'

'Thank goodness you changed that bald tyre.' Heather tried to catch his eye. 'Oh, Naff,' she said when he looked away. 'If Sammy finds out, I'll lose all credibility.'

'No problemo. I'll do it tomorrow,' Naff assured her with a confidence that brooked all and every possible doubt.

Heather let go of Naff's arm and planted her hands on her hips. 'Simon Robinson, you are the absolute limit. That is what you said yesterday.'

'Yeah, but it ain't tomorrow yet,' Naff said and hastily shunted his girlfriend's train of thought back off track. 'So what's this brain pick you was on about?'

'I need to bluff my way into Stationmaster's Cottage,' Heather told him. 'Can you think of a disguise that won't make Jaimie Smith suspicious?'

Naff gave her one of his trademark cockeyed looks. 'Ain't you caused enough trouble already?' he asked rhetorically. Ironically might be a better way of putting it. Or pissedoffedly. 'Like I said,' he said. 'Leave it to the cops.'

'Please, Naff,' Heather protested. 'I know what I'm doing.'

'Yeah, right. Like you knew what you was doing when you put black pepper on the rice pudding in the staff canteen. Said it was today's special. Weren't kidding, were you?'

'Not that again.' Heather rolled her eyes. 'If I've told you once, I've told you a thousand times,' she told him for the thousand and oneth time. 'I thought it was nutmeg. It was an honest mistake. Anyone could have done it.'

'Yeah, like anyone could have used salt instead of sugar in the apple crumble, put prunes in the lamb curry and added Senokot to the pilau rice thinking it were cardamom.'

'It's easily done,' Heather said with an expression of insouciant esculence. 'I know – how about a nurse?'

'No need. Inspector Dobson's already back at work.'

'No, I mean as a disguise. We've worshipped nurses ever since the pandemic. Not even Jaimie Smith would turn away a ministering angel.' Before Naff could catalogue his top ten doubts, Heather shouted up the stairs to summon her aunt.

A waft and a flutter later, Lady Trevelyan glided down the bannisters in a tutu, ballet shoes and a silk headscarf. 'You called, my dear?'

'You're a doctor, aunty. Have you got a nurse's uniform?' Heather asked with her fingers crossed.

'I am hardly a doctor,' Lady Elizabeth said with a self-effacing smile. 'Merely a consultant neurosurgeon. And I don't practice these days unless a member of the royal family requires brain surgery.' Struck by a thought, she raised a finger. 'Now I come to think, I believe I may have a nurse's uniform. I wore it in that ghastly medical drama George Clooney bullied me into starring in a few years ago. At first I said no because shooting clashed with Harry and Meg's wedding. Needless to say, they agreed to postpone the ceremony until I had a free slot in my diary, but I wouldn't hear of it. Plenty more maids of honour in the sea, I told them.' She broke into a diffident smile then looked around and lowered her voice. 'I will let you into a little secret, my dear. I was always going take the role. You know what Loony-Cloons is like. Such a charmer. I could hardly say no, could I? But I played hard to get until he agreed to make whoopee.' Much against her better nature, she allowed herself a smutty smirk. 'Darling Cloono was adamant that my performance deserved at least two Oscars – my performance in the film, that is, not my performance in bed. Although . . . ' Eyes atwinkle, she cleared an imaginary tickle from her throat. 'Well, let's just say, George swears that it was the most unforgettable thirty seconds of his life. But far be it from me to kiss and tell.' Her eyes glazed over, then her face fell. 'But really - can you believe that I was only nominated for just the one Academy Award? Shameful,' she sighed with the heaviest of hearts. 'But enough about me,' she announced with a purposeful clap of the hands. 'Let me pop upstairs and have a look through a few of my old wardrobes.' With an elegance of grace befitting a swan, she pirouetted back upstairs to take a pas de deux through the starbangled costumery in her dressing room.

With a heady cocktail of excitement and nervous apprehension flooding through her veins, Heather hurried Naff to the servant's pantry, boiled a kettle and dunked a Fairtrade teabag in two mugs – first one, then the other, then the first, then the other . . .

'Thanks, honey. No sugar or salt,' Naff said cuttingly as Heather handed him a lukeweak mug of tea. 'So what's this all about?'

'I've worked out that the murderer must be the ticket collector, Jaimie Smith. Has to be.'

'Stake your reputation on it, would you?'

Heather ignored him. 'My bet is, Mathers was blackmailing Smith about some kind of murky secret. A murder she committed years ago or something. So she silenced him.'

'Guess anything's possible,' Naff said, hardly convinced. No, let's get real. He thought it a complete and utter cockamamie of a flopwitted idea. Nevertheless, he humoured her - a good night's sleep depended on it. 'Hows about that other bird,' he suggested. 'The one seen leaving the train?'

'We only have Uncle Monty's and Reverend Bragg's word that she exists. They both say they saw a woman with black hair getting off the train, but that could be anyone. So how did your clever computer friend get on?'

'Not good.' Naff shook his head. 'He reckons you trolleyed Mathers' memory-stick big-time. Says it was a stroke of luck he recovered that stuff about Bragg.' He gave his girlfriend the kind of look that suggested she ought to limit her digiblah activities to buying impractical frivolities from online shopperies or downloading recipes for – say – lamb curry, apple crumble or rice pudding. 'But get this,' he said, 'he reckons the CCTV footage from St. Mary Nook Station ought to be backed up in the datacloud. Says it's par for the course these days. He's gonna take a look and email me anything he comes up with. If we're in luck, it'll show us who the mystery girl was.'

'But surely the police will have checked that ages ago?' Heather said. Her blind faith in the grasping arm of the law was tantamount to zealotry.

'Got any idea the paperwork required to access data in the cloud . . . unless you're MI5 or a dodgy hacker.' Naff tapped both sides of his nose. 'Doubt the local force would know where to start. Let's face it, from what I been told, it's all Sergeant Gummidge can do to hold a pen.'

Naff was trying to inveigle Heather into bed and she was trying to chivvy him into a cold shower when they were joined by Lady Elizabeth carrying a costume unrummaged from one of her Hollywood wardoberies. 'You are in luck, Spriggy,' she said. 'I knew I had a nurse's uniform somewhere. I never throw anything away, you know. As I always say, waste not, never want for waste.'

'I can't wear this,' Heather gasped, shocked to the gingertips of her hair by the ankle-length highcollared puff-shouldered pinafore dress with whalebone corset, feathery pantaloons and taffeta petticoats. 'What was the film called - Little Women?'

'The Secret Life of Florence Nightingale,' her aunt explained. 'Needless to say, I played the title role.'

'But I'll look ridiculous.'

'Fiddlesticks,' Lady Elizabeth scoffed. 'Take it from me, all the nurses in this neck of the woods wear uniforms like this. To say that St. Mary Nook is behind the times would be doing the village a kindness.'

'Well, if you're sure . . .' Heather tried not to sound too sceptical. She had, after all, been raised never to question her aunt.

'Of course I am sure, my dear,' Lady Elizabeth said. Avoiding Heather's eyes, she shooed Naff out of the maid's pantry with a flick of a wrist and stuffed a napkin in the keyhole to stop him tom-peeping her niece's change of gear. 'Now then, my dear,' she said with a purposeful clap of the hands. 'Let me help you on with the costume and dab some rouge on your cheeks. Trust me, by the time I have finished, you will look more like a nurse than I did in that ghastly movie.' She tossed her head in a show of petulant pride. 'Would you believe, the critics said I wore too much makeup?' she humphed with the take-no-prisoners righteousness of a critical victim. 'And not one of the illiterate halfwits mentioned my deathbed soliloquy. Oh, except the mental defective who said that when I burst into tears as Lord Kitchener proposed to me while I lay dying of a broken heart, so much mascara trickled down my cheeks that I looked like Freddie Kreuger.' She fought back a choke in her voice and mumbled, 'heartless,' a number of times.

Many squeezes, grunts and groans later, Lady Elizabeth announced that Heather was a perfect picture of nurseyness. She summoned Naff with a shrill shout, instructed him to keep a watchful eye on her niece and waved them off on what all agreed was a mission that might - just might - finally unriddle The Curious Case of The Butcher of St. Mary Nook and The Wiped Out Witnesses.

After a corset busting motorbike ride through the village, Naff negotiated the level crossing at the end of Nook Lane, turned left into Station Approach and skewwhiffed to a stop outside Stationmaster's Cottage.

Battling an acute attack of tummy-flutters, Heather dismounted, hitched up her underskirts, took a deep breath and rang the doorbell. To be honest - which she went to great pains to be - she was suspicious that Aunt Elizabeth might have had her tongue in both cheeks when she ribboned a lace bonnet over her bunned hair and draped a red cape over her shoulders. But as her aunt would say, needs be as needs must in the line of undercover duty - corset and starched petticoats notwithstanding. So she stiffed her upper lip and put her best pantaloon forward. Nevertheless she felt uneasy, in no small part because the whalebone stays pinched like tummycramps, the buttonup boots were a toenail too small and the *ghastly* lace bonnet just *would not* stay ribboned.

A moment later the door was opened by a tall girl in a MaidenRail uniform – short-sleeved cotton shirt, navy waistcoat and canvass slacks. When she saw Heather, she rubbed her eyes and said, 'who you collecting for - Save the Panto?'

Heather beamed a wunderbar hello. 'I wonder if you could possibly assist me, young lady.'

'Bit late for that,' Jaimie Smith said with the rib-tickling jocularity of a slipped disc.

Heather pretended not to notice a tsunami of sarcasm in Smith's gruff voice and laboured on with, 'I am awfully afraid that my automobile has broken down.'

'The bloke with the red flag knackered, is he?'

Hard though she was finding it, Heather maintained an angel of mercy unflappability. 'The trouble is,' she said, 'I am due back at the hospital within the hour.'

Smith looked her over from bonnet to boot and shook her head. 'I'm amazed they let you out.'

Her smile now more a fixgnashed grin than a pearly ray of nursey virtue, Heather said, 'might I possibly use your telephone to call a colleague and have him collect me?'

'Doctor Livingstone, I presume,' Smith said. 'Suppose so. As long as he leaves his Penny Farthing outside.' She showed Heather into the hall and pointed to an old-fashioned Bakelite telephone on a nest of tables.

'You are a true saint,' Heather gushed before pretending to dial a number and conversation an emergency friend. 'How terribly bothersome,' she sighed as she replaced the receiver. 'He is going to collect me on his Daisy Bell tandem.' She hitched up her skirts and showed Smith a pantalooned leg. 'I doubt I will be able to mount the stoker's seat in my uniform. I couldn't possibly beg a favour and ask you to lend me something more appropriate?'

Smith gave her a wary look, quipped, 'might have an old ball gown or a deep-sea diver's outfit knocking about. I'll see what I can find,' and headed up the narrow staircase to her bedroom.

The moment Jaimie Smith was soundly out of sight, Heather sprang into action like starched lightening. Ears pricked for returning footsteps, she bustled to the living room and set to sleuth. After adjusting the bonnet to unrestrict her vision and loosening her apron strings to unconstrict her bladder, she cast a forensic eye around the trappings of Smith's life. At a glance, she thought the living room an everyday mishmash of marital domesticity – top shelf laddish mags, bottom shelf glossy fashion magazines, men's workboots and women's shoes on the hearthrug. Airing on the two-seater sofa was a tumbledry of washing - men's briefs and girly undies, denim jeans and summery dresses, woollen shirts and floaty blouses. She caught her breath when she spotted a framed photograph of Trevor Mathers on the dresser. It was scribed . . . *To the Love of My Life, Jaimie. Forever yours, Trev.* She was covertly phonesnapping evidence of the secret tryst when she heard approaching bootsteps behind her.

'Here, what's your game?' Jaime Smith placed a heavy hand on Heather's puffed-sleeved shoulder. 'Thought you said you'd not got a phone?'

Thinking quickly in her lace-up boots, Heather donned a buttermelt smile. She held out her smartphone and fluttered a sigh of nursey exasperation. 'This? Oh my goodness, the battery is as flat as a catheter. It is as useless as a punctured fibrillator,' she said then bit her lip when the ringtone buzzed with the unmutable urgency of a hazard siren.

Jaimie Smith snatched the phone from Heather's hand and flung it on the floor. As Heather backed away, hands raised to fend off an attack, she growled, 'my mate reckons there's a nutter on the loose. Can't be two of you,' and let fly with a left hook fit to deck a prizeweight pugilist. As Heather collapsed in a crumpled heap of pinafored crinoline, Smith buried a hobnailed boot in her corset and stood over her with her fists clenched.

'You were having an affair with Trevor Mathers, weren't you?' Heather gasped between snatches of breath and pointed to the blokey jackets, boots and magazines.

'Keep your fucking nose out of my business, Florence.' Smith picked up a poker from the firegrate. Ignoring Heather's valiant screams, she raised it like a cast-iron cutloose poised to strike the living daylights out of the angel of chicanery.

As Heather lay on her back bravely covering her eyes, a knight in a leather biker jacket kicked open the door and raced to her aid. Naff - for it was he - grappled Jaimie Smith to the quarry tiles and wrestled the poker from her grasp.

Ignoring Heather's anguished pleas to cease and desist, Smith fought like a Tasmanian She-devil. She bit Naff's nose and scratched at his eyes with her sharp nails and, as he doubled up in pain, grabbed his testicles in both hands and squeezed with all her might. As he reeled back howling in agony, she picked up the poker and lashed out like a barbwire fencer creosoting a post.

Having recovered his balance, if not his cool, Naff sprang to his feet like a jack-out-of-a-box. Crouching side on like a karmic tiger, he said, 'you asked for it, babe,' and lunged.

Much like a matador toreadoring a rampaging bull, Smith sidestepped Naff's charge and helped him through the door with a well-aimed boot to the butt. As he lay on the path outside nursing his ego, she turned to Heather and said, 'right. You're next, Flo.'

Propelled by her pantalooned legs, Heather scuffled backwards on her bustle until her cape was pressed against a wall. Legs trembling beneath her crinolined skirt, lungs heaving in her corset, sweat pouring from her bonneted brow, she stared up into Jaimie Smith's crazed eyes and mouthed a silent prayer. But just as Smith was about to plunge the poker into her whoknowswhere or whocareswhat, the telephone rang.

Smith lowered the lethal poker, narrowed her eyes, pointed at Heather, said, 'don't move, Florrie,' and took the call. Her frown deepened as she listened. With a groan of, 'fucking cops,' she slammed down the phone, turned to Heather, flicked her head at the door and said, 'piss off back to the asylum. I got to pack.'

Saved by the bell in the nick of time, Heather grabbed her cellphone and stumbled out into Naff's waiting arms. 'The evil witch saw through my disguise,' she sobbed as she buried her bonnet in his chest. 'Mathers was her lover. He must have jilted her, so she . . . gosh. It's too horrible. The woman is a monster.' She closed her eyes and hugged Naff tight.

As Naff was strapping the traumatised Nightingale-alike to the Bonneville's pillion with his lovehandles, his cellphone pinged to announce an incoming email. Although tempted to ignore it, curiosity got the better of the cat so he sneaked a peak. 'It's from Brian, me boffin mate,' he told Heather as he downloaded several stills hacked from St. Mary Nook railstation's datacloud. 'Well

I'll be . . .' he said. 'You ain't never gonna believe who our mystery woman is.'

30

Inspector Obafemi gazed out of the box room window at the pig farm. If asked, he would have probably said that he could imagine a more inspiring view. If pressed, in all probability he would have said that he could not imagine anything less inspiring. To describe the pigs as disgruntling would be an appalling play on words.

Not normally one to whistle his own praises, Obafemi was nevertheless pleased to have made good progress. After an inordinate amount of to-ing and fro-ing, haggling and headshaking, browmopping and teabreaking, drilling and screwdrivering, DI Turner's electrician husband had replaced a fire hazard of rotting cables and the police station's electrics were now as good as old. And then there was the cleaner suggested by the waitress at The Crossed Arms - a relative of her sister's boyfriend's cousin once divorced by marriage. Overalled, she had proved efficient and industrious, if a little flighty. In a final whip of the leash, Larry Huckstep's gnarly lurcher had dispatched the remaining territorial rodents in a few short shrifts. The breezeblock eyesore had then been fumigated with fulminous pipeblasts of noxious Virginia shag.

Much against his better judgement, Inspector Obafemi turned a blind eye to Sergeant Gummidge's unorthodox method of back-of-a-stuffed envelope accounting. Having said that, he did have a quiet word in Gummidge's deaf ear to make clear that he took a dim view of selling confiscated game to The Crossed Arms for cashpoundnotes, but left it at that. He was pressed for time and Gummidge's free market enterprisisms meant that the bills were promptly paid without undue paperwork . . . without any paperwork at all, in fact. And the upside of the downside was that this sidestepped the never-and-a-day delay for dribs and drabs of petty cash to dribble into the station coffers from Kent County Constabulary's Payment Vacillation department.

Would that The Curious Case of The Butcher of St. Mary Nook would make such progress.

Not for the first time, Obafemi weighed the evidence between two minds. For the want of an alternative, he asked himself, what if he was looking for a number of killers rather than a lone boar? He draped a fire blanket over the pigside window to blot out the view, though sadly not the stench, then, brow furrowed in concentration, paced his tiny office, ticking off potential scenarios on the fingers of one hand.

What if Colonel Dangerfield had planted that knife in Trevor Mathers' back because Mathers was about to expose his petfood fraud? Reverend Bragg could have shotgunned Dangerfield to venge his sacred bunnies. Elouise Decora might have bludgeoned Bragg to a pulp in retribution for him killing her lover and . . . and there Inspector Obafemi drew a blank. His fingers might add up were it not for the fact that a *someone else* had strangled

Decora. And what of the evidence that trussed the crimes together like turpentwine? Those strands of hair, the footprints, that distinctive scent.

In need of a pipe break, Inspector Obafemi wandered out to the receptionary to check the time - the station clock was now working like clockwork thanks to an intemperate thump. One o'clock. All being well, DI Turner should be at the railway station and her Tunbridge Wells contingent squadcarring the roads in case Jaimie Smith tried to slip the knot like a slithery eel on the lam.

One poser above all others puzzled Obafemi. Who, he asked himself, could the mysterious trainjump woman be? He had a gut hunch that she might be the missing link in this mind-fuddling affair. Mind-fuddling? More like a bafflement of bazaar bemusement. For the waters were muddying by the day. Thanks to a phone call from Montreal that morning, he now knew that the victim had not been a journalist after all. Far from it. And nor had he been Canadian.

A bout of coughing and wheezing announced the arrival of Sergeant Gummidge. Inspector Obafemi gave him a cursory nod and, to make conversation, said, 'I met your wife this morning, Sergeant. Charming woman.'

'The Sourkraut – charming?' Gummidge stared at Obafemi as if he had just announced that the world wasn't flat. 'Wouldn't be my choice of words.'

Obafemi was unamused and told Gummidge so in no

uncertain terms. 'I have had just about enough of your racist xenophobia and misogyny, Sergeant,' he said.

Gummidge arched his back and glared at Inspector Obafemi with all the considerable contempt at his command. 'I will have you know, I am hardly a racist,' he had Obafemi know. 'I got time for everyone, even the likes of you. And as for Miss Jenny, don't believe a word nobody tells you. We're just good friends.'

'Neanderthal,' Inspector Obafemi muttered acerbically.

'For your information,' Gummidge said with a righteousness that brooked all wrongfulness. 'Some of the finest cheese in Kent is made in the Vale of Neander.'

Their cosy clenched-fist eyeball-to-eyeball chat was interrupted by the arrival of a breathless PC Ingham. 'Sorry I'm late, guv,' she panted as she slumped against the front desk mopping her brow. 'Left my whatsit at thingummies so had to go fetch it. Have I missed anything?'

'There was almost another murder.' Inspector Obafemi laboured the words *almost*, *another*, and - for the avoidance of doubt - *murder*. 'Man the station while I go for a walk. Something round here stinks.' He glared at Gummidge and stormed out.

Simmering like a milk pan off the boil - his brain a fuddle of nonsensical puzzles and conflicting contradictions – Inspector Obafemi took a circuitous route to anywhere but there by way of Nook Lane. Distracted, he paused outside Elouise Decora's house to mull over the events of the past few days.

If ever a building could said to be morose, Chez Decora was morosity personified. The curtains were drawn, the lights were off and a simple wreath was pinned to the front door. A lump grew in Obafemi's throat as he read a card from a well-wisher tucked into to the figured hollied ivy, pinecones and eucalyptus. *Forever Missed but Ne`er Forgot.*

It was at moments like this that Isaac Obafemi was minded why he was so missioned to crusade for the lost, the vulnerable, the possessed, the dispossessed, the disadvantaged and the disenfranchised. No matter how they might have erred in life, all were equally innocent in death. Wrestling his emotions, he closed his eyes, clasped his hands, lowered his head and mouthed a silent prayer . . .

Bring me my bow of burning gold:

Bring me my arrows of desire:

Bring me my spear:

O clouds unfold!

Bring me my chariot of fire.

I will not cease from mental fight,

Nor shall my sword sleep in my hand

Till we have built Jerusalem

In England's green and pleasant land.

Although death was his profession, Detective Inspector Obafemi was finding The Murder on The Ordinary Express uncommonly stressful. But hopefully the end was almost nigh. For now that he knew Trevor Mathers' true identity, he had a pretty good idea of the killer's motive. As yet, however, he was unsure who the killer was. The sooner he found out, the sooner he could escape this golf-forsaken backwoods. He was fed up to the back teeth with the bigotry of Gummidge, the pettiness of the local gossips, the stench of pig shit in his office and the bland food, vinegary wine and cranky plumbing at his hotel. Determined to bring the investigation to a head and draw the case to a timely close, he returned to the police station, jotted down a list of names and instructed PC Ingham to summon them to Trevelyan Hall. 'Make sure they all come, and I do mean all,' he said. 'I'll phone Lady Trevelyan and have her make a room available.'

PC Ingham ran an eye over the castlist and raised an eyebrow. 'Jaimie Smith?' she said. 'I heard she'd gone on holiday.'

'DI Turner collared her at the station as she was about to board the Ordinary Express,' Inspector Obafemi told her. 'She had a one-way ticket to London and if her luggage was anything to go by, she wasn't planning to come back in a hurry.' Then he broached a subject that had been playing on his mind all week. 'Mind if I call you Samantha?' he said and when Ingham smiled, asked, 'ever thought of putting in for a transfer to New Scotland Yard?'

PC Ingham fidgeted with her fingers and avoided Obafemi's eyes. 'As it happens, guv, I'm thinking of moving back to Brighton. If you must know, I'm engaged.'

'Congratulations.' Obafemi forced the shallowest of smiles. 'I'm sure you'll make a young man very happy.'

'Wouldn't count on it,' Ingham muttered and reached for the phone.

Leaving PC Ingham to corral the suspects, Inspector Obafemi withdrew to his office to prepare for the meeting. He was about to pop out for a pipe when he heard a knock on the door.

A flustered Ingham showed two men in. Like clotheshorse clones, they were sporting identikit grey suits, white shirts, black shoes, red ties and sunglasses. 'Sorry, guv. Told them you were busy, but they were having none of it,' she said. 'Seemed to think you should be expecting them.'

Inspector Obafemi frowned, or better said he glowered, or best said he glared. 'Thank you, Samantha. Close the door on your way out.' The moment Ingham left, he stood up, planted his hands on the desk, lent forward and narrowed his eyes. 'What is the meaning of this?' he thundered. 'Explain yourselves.'

Unfazed, the suaver of the two greycrashers

fingerflicked a dead cockroach off a packing crate, sat down, crossed his legs and looked around. 'Bit different from your office next to the staff canteen at New Scotland Yard, isn't it, Isaac? Or can I call you Izzy like your mother, Gwendolyn, does?'

To say that Inspector Obafemi was taken aback would be putting it predictably. 'How the devil do you know that?'

Sunglassman said, 'it is our job to know everything.' He glanced at his colleague and smiled. His colleague glanced back and nodded. 'Oh, by the way,' he added casually. 'How is Sandra's sciatica? Has she kicked you out yet, or is she waiting until she's passed her driving test? Oh, didn't she tell you?' he said as Obafemi's jaw dropped. 'Suppose you better decide who gets the parrot. You know, if you supplement her fruit and nuts with hemp seeds, she could live another fifty years. By then you'll be ninety-two - if you don't die of a heart attack when you're fifty-six as your father, Madu, did.' When, lost for words, Obafemi gave him the blankest of blank looks, sunglassman took a grainy photosnap out of his inside pocket and tossed it on the desk. 'She is your killer,' he said. Then he placed a second photograph on top of the first. 'And this is one of ours,' he said. 'So hands off.'

31

It was overcast. Cloudy. Nubilous. Detective Inspector Obafemi had a gut-hunch that it might be coming on to rain and Detective Inspector Obafemi's gut hunches were seldom wrong. Apart from an occasional traction engine and a combine harvester or two, the road was deserted. He smiled when Samantha Ingham told him it was rush hour and raised an eyebrow when she added that it was busy for the time of day.

Despite her foibles - and they were many and they were quirky - Inspector Obafemi suspected that he would miss Miss Ingham. Having said that, he doubted whether he would miss her driving. He gritted his jaw and gripped his seatbelt as she rammed a foot to the floor and overtook a mule and cart on a horsehair bend. Thankful to still be alive, he asked, 'so what are your plans when you move back to Brighton?' hoping that they wouldn't involve anything of a vehicular nature.

'Join the family firm, I suppose. Ingham's Balls. Heard of us? We're all over the place,' Ingham said above the tortured squeal of the Ghia's engine as she accelerated over a humpbacked bridge as if it was a launchpad to oblivion. 'Mum and dad have been pestering me to give it a go for ages. Or I might try my hand at modelling. Play it by ear, I suppose. I'm not cut out for this lark.'

'Any plans to start a family?'

'Not likely, guv. Not the state the planet's in.'

'What did Bishop's Garage say about the Panda car?'

'Looks like it's a write off, sir. Totalled.'

'So how much did you have to drink the other night? You could have done yourself a serious injury.'

'Don't know what you're on about, guv. I'm near as not teetotal,' Ingham said as she screeched round a sharp righthander into Trevelyan Hall's long drive. She parked the Karmann Ghia in a squeal of burning rubber within touching distance of DI Turner's squad car - a pearlmobile beside a swinewaggon. 'You've not met Lady Trevelyan's niece, have you, sir?' she said. 'I'll introduce you. She's smashing.' She helped Obafemi out of the passenger seat and went ahead, leaving him to retrieve his briefcase from the parcel shelf.

Heather was waiting on the steps of Trevelyan Hall, her nerves an elasticated fret of anticipation. When she saw Inspector Obafemi, she grabbed Sammy's arm and gasped, 'cripes - it's Obafemi of the Yard.'

It need hardly go without much saying that Sammy assumed she was joking. 'Obafemi of the Yard, my foot,' she said, expecting Heather to nudge her in the ribs and wink. 'He's that new DI I told about. You know, the one Maidstone sent to head up the enquiry.'

'No, he's from New Scotland Yard. Guide's honour.'

Heather pressed two fingers together and held them up for Sammy to see. 'Golly, he must be undercover. Better make myself scarce.' She looked frantically around for the nearest means of invisibility but sneaked a peek too late.

'This is Heather Prendergast, guv. Lady Trevelyan's niece.' Sammy introduced Heather to Inspector Obafemi with the proud smile of a head prefect presenting a bright young sibling to her headmaster.

Obafemi shook Heather's hand. 'Pleased to meet you, Miss Prendergast,' he said. 'But haven't we met before?' He was about to suggest where, when Lady Elizabeth came striding out of the house and demanded his attention.

While her aunt and the Inspector engaged in a one sided conversation about the *ghastly* weather, the *unsufferable* plight of the unemployed, the *outrageous* cost of caviar, the *preposterous* rate of tax on unearned income, the *scandalous* abomination of benefit scroungers and how the country was going to the dogs because of the *unspeakably* woke government, Heather took Sammy to one side. She whispered, 'I'm in a spot of bother, Sammy,' and cast a nervous glance at Inspector Obafemi. 'Promise not to breathe a word, but it's just possible I might have misled Aunt Elizabeth a tiny bit by mistake.' She mopped her brow and gulped. 'Thing is, I told her I was a CID officer.'

'You mean you're not?' Sammy's eyebrows all but went sputnik.

'Well, almost. Kind of. Bar the shouting.' Before Heather could dig a deeper dungeon, her aunt summoned her with a shrill come-hither shout.

'Inspector, I believe you have already met my niece.' Lady Elizabeth placed a hand on Heather's shoulder and presented her as if showing off a pedigree pooch at Crufts. 'She is a rising star in the Metropolitan Police, don't you know? Future Commissioner material.' She took Inspector Obafemi's arm and escorted him up the steps to her modest little mansion – her description. 'You are welcome to hold your meeting in my drawing room,' she said with an obliging smile, 'but on one condition. My niece came to our rescue when Monty was falsely accused of murder. She has been working round the clock to solve the case so I feel it only right that she be allowed to present her findings. Of course, you are welcome to contribute, although I hardly think that will be necessary. She is a brilliant detective. Highly thought of at The Yard.'

Despite his reservations, or better said, despite an overwhelming urge to collapse in bellyfits of laughter, realising that Lady Trevelyan was not to be dissuaded, Inspector Obafemi said, 'very well. I would be most interested to hear what she has to say.' Then, using the excuse of needing to make a phone call to his wife - yeah, right - he lingered while Lady Elizabeth went ahead to find Guan-Yin.

As soon as they were alone, Obafemi took Heather to task. 'If I may say, young lady, I take an extremely dim view of your deceitful behaviour,' he said as she hung her head wringing her hands. 'I am sure that your aunt would be shocked to learn how you have misled her,' he said, all the while minded that Lady Trevelyan was not without a few shocking secrets of her own. He looked Heather over, tapped his chin and nodded. 'You know, short hair suits you. I'm sure Chef Dibley will approve.' Leaving Heather to discombobulate, he joined the others in the drawing room. After a quick head count, he wandered over to the French windows, leant against the shutters and gazed out at peacocks strutting their feathered stuff on the upper lawn like birdbrained popinjays.

The silence of a pork chop fell over the room as the assembled host awaited Heather's entry. Lady Elizabeth sat on the armrest of her husband's chair smoking a Cuban cigar, enthralled by the thrill of it all. Disinterested to say the least, Jaimie Smith lounged on the smaller of the buttonleather sofas staring at the ceiling with an air of bored indifference. Naff and Sergeant Gummidge sat on one of the other four sofas making sure to keep their distance. DI Turner and her Tunbridge Wells contingent stood at the door with their legs apart and their hands behind their backs. PC Ingham sat at keen attention on the Eames lounger, toying with her cuffs. All the while, Guan-Yin padded in and out, refreshing teacups and ferrying plates of homespun fortune cookies.

In that it was the eve of the annual ancestor tomb sweeping ritual, Guan-Yin was formally attired in a ceremonial red silk Hanfu wedding gown with billowing yi sleeves, mandarin-collar and embroidered dog's-head motifs on the bust – according to her, a family heirloom from the Qing dynasty. Her face was porcelain white from chin to brow apart from a decorative plum-blossom flower on her forehead. In keeping with tradition, she was wearing wormiform earrings and had her hair swept up into a prominent beehive bun secured with a jade tiara adorned with delicate pearl tasselclasps. The finishing touch was a flutter of red ribbons plaited in her pigtail, which hung down her back to a dragon-wing bow behind her tiny waist.

As she explained to Heather over a light lunch of Beth's Fairtrade Lotus Leaf and Grasshopper Nest soup, Guan-Yin could trace her lineage back to Gao Xin, one of the Three Sovereigns and Five Emperors of Chinese mythology. More specifically, she claimed a direct line of descent from Gao Xin's daughter and her husband, Pan Hu. If Heather understood her correctly - by no means a given as Guan-Yin didn't really do pronouns, verbs, adjectives or definite and indefinite articles - Pan Hu started life as a worm in Gao Xin's ear before becoming a dog with five kinds of hair as was not uncommon in China before Confucius brought some rectitude to proceedings. After marrying Goa Xin's daughter - who, as coincidence would have it, also happened to be his sister - Pan Hu carried his confused bride to the Nanshan Mountains where she combed her hair into a servant bun and dressed in red silk from head to sandal, hence Guan-Yin's costume - a tribute to her revered forebear. Anyway, to cut a convoluted story short, it seems that the couple gave birth to a litter of six boys and six girls, one of whom was Guan-Yin's ancestor.

Needless to say, Heather was sceptical. I mean, twelve children for goodness' sake. Twelve? Pretty far-fetched.

But back to the future . . . Guan-Yin topped up Naff's cup with Beth's Fairtrade Dragon-Well and Dandelion-Stem tea and offered him a fortune cookie.

'What's this?' Naff said with a baffled frown as he read the motto. 'A stitch in time saves twine?'

Guan-Yin gave him a disdainful look, tapped her head and said, 'outside noisy, inside empty.'

It is said that on occasion the fabled finger of fortune cards an ace to those sufficiently foolhardy to trump the winds of fate. At least, that is how Heather Prendergast was to describe how she grappled the once in a lifetime opportunity to garnish her tarnished credentials before an illustrious audience including Detective Inspector Isaac Obafemi, legend of the Yard. She whispered, 'wish me luck,' to Sammy before stepping boldly centerstage. Fortitude duly plucked, she tucked her blouse into her slacks, crossed her arms and looked slowly round the room waiting for the buzz of anticipation and cookie-confusion to die down.

'We are gathered here to unmask a manifestation of pure evil that knows no bounds,' she announced. 'One of you has a dark secret.' She cast an eye around the room. 'As you all know, Trevor Mathers was brutally murdered on the Ordinary Express just over a week ago. All the evidence pointed to Uncle Monty. He was found beside the body, he was holding the murder weapon, he had Mathers' blood on his suit and he has no alibi. Coincidence? I think not.' She shook her head and chuckled. 'That is what we were supposed to think. The fact is, he was trying to save Mathers. No – the true culprit is sitting here amongst us. By the time I have finished, the truth will out.'

'Bravo, Spriggy.' Aunt Elizabeth flicked cigar ash on the priceless antique Kerman rug and gave her niece a hearty round of applause.

'Aunty, please.' Heather groaned. After taking a moment to recompos her mentis, she picked up the *a priori* threads with, 'the question I will lay before you is this. Who had motive and opportunity to commit this heinous crime? Let us look at the facts. There were five passengers in the first class compartment of The Ordinary Express that afternoon.' She ticked her fingers one by one, not forgetting her thumb. 'The victim, Uncle Monty, Colonel Hamilton Dangerfield, Reverend William Bragg and Elouise Decora. But let us not forget the ticket collector.' She turned to Jaimie Smith, cupped her chin in a hand and gave her a polysemous look, at one and the same time vague and assured. 'Unless I am mistaken, you were there, were you not? And now I come to think, you were seen arguing with Mathers.'

'Piss off, Agatha,' Smith muttered under her breath.

Not to be thrown off her stride, Heather paced the room with her shoulders hunched, hands clasped behind her back. 'And what about the woman seen getting off the train at St. Mary Nook?' she asked with a rhetoricallity that suggested she was about to reveal a Rumsfeldilogical unknown unknown. 'Let us examine the sequence of events.' She drew to a halt and cast her other eye about the room. 'What do we know about the second victim, Colonel Hamilton Dangerfield? Well, on the face it, he was a reputable farmer and entrepreneur with a successful online petfood business. But dig beneath the surface and a very different picture emerges. The reality is that he was a fraudster, an inveterate gambler and a philanderer. And we now know that he had a partner - in both the business and the personal sense of the word.'

'Elouise Decora,' PC Ingham chipped in chirpily.

'Sammy . . .' Heather rolled her eyes and groaned. 'You've ruined the plot.'

'Sorry, pet . . . I mean, Miss Prendergast.' Sammy chewed her bottom lip and mumbled, 'my bad.'

Dogged in the pursuit of justice, Heather pressed on undeterred. 'Colonel Dangerfield's death appeared to be suicide. Or let me put it another way – the scene was staged to make it look like suicide. Badly staged, if I may say. Strands of black hair were found on the victim's body, there was perfume on his shirt and stiletto footprints were found in the yard.'

Inspector Obafemi looked round from the window, scowled and wandered over to put what, for want of a better insect, might be described as a flea in PC Ingham's ear.

'Me?' Sammy said with an expression of virtual virtue. 'Why would I leak confidential operational information to Miss Prendergast? I hardly know her.' When Inspector Obafemi resumed his window-gazing, she sidled up to Heather and whispered, 'don't grass me up, pet. If the DI asks, say you got Gummidge ratarsed and he spilled the beans.'

But Heather was too far down the road of luminary elucidation to care. 'As PC Ingham has already told you,' she said with a sideways scowl at Sammy, 'we now know that Colonel Dangerfield was secretly engaged to Elouise Decora - was being the operative word. Before she died, Decora told me that she had invested the bulk of a large inheritance in Dangerfield's pet food business and he had swindled her out of every penny. As if that wasn't enough, I found evidence that she knew he was carrying on with a another woman behind her back. Hell hath no fury like a woman scorned, isn't that what they say?'

'Who?' Gummidge asked.

'Winston Churchill,' Heather said with an assuredness that brooked no credibility.

'I believe you may be thinking of William Congreve.' Drawing upon his photocopier memory, Obafemi said, 'heav'n has no rage, like love to hatred turn'd, nor hell a fury, like a woman scorned.' Duly flattered when Lady Trevelyan gave him a hearty round of applause, he said, 'but please continue, Miss Prendergast. I am sure that we are all on tenterhooks.'

'As William Congreve said, hell hath no . . . waffle, waffle, waffle,' Heather said. 'But seriously, it would hardly take a Sherlock Holmes to deduce that Elouise Decora had every reason to want Dangerfield dead. Elementary, one might say.'

'Oh, do me a favour,' Jaimie Smith groaned.

Heather shot Smith a deathwish glare, but not to be deterred, continued. 'You see, that is precisely what our murderer – or should I say, our murderess – wanted people to believe.'

'I say, how terribly exciting.' Lady Elizabeth turned to Obafemi. 'She is rather good, isn't she, Inspector?'

'Two down, two to go,' Heather said by way of a recap. 'Reverend William Bragg was next in line. Again, the finger of guilt pointed to Decora. For we now know that Bragg was the Bunny Terrorist responsible for bankrupting Dangerfield's fraudulent petfood business - a business, don't forget, that she had sunk her life savings into. And in the words of William Congreve, revenge is a dish best served cold.' She gave Obafemi a haughty look. 'But wait . . . was revenge really the motive? Remember, Dangerfield and Decora had confided in Reverend Bragg. What if he was threatening to expose their murky secret?' She took a snapshot out of her pocket. 'I have here evidence that Bragg was blackmailing Elouise Decora.'

'Where did you get that?' Obafemi asked, concerned to say the very least.

'Facebook?' Heather suggested and moved swiftly on. 'But of course, Decora didn't kill Bragg. How could she? She was living on borrowed time. She was the only witness left who could identify the murderess. She had to die.'

Enthralled, Lady Elizabeth sat on the arm of her husband's chair rubbing her hands. 'How thrilling,' she said. 'That's my girl. Go, Spriggy, go.'

'Aunty, don't embarrass me in front of all these people. Please.' Blushing like a beetroot, Heather took a sip of Beth's Fairtrade Synthetic Spring Water. Nerves duly settled, she prepared to ascend to the pinnacle of her probationary career . . . the unmasking of The Butcher of St. Mary Nook.

'But our killer was careless,' she said in the cool, calm, collected manner for which she was - or would one day be - famed. 'Our killer left a string of clues at the crime scenes. Her footprints, those strands of hair, that distinctive perfume. So when we weigh the evidence, we are left with only one possible conclusion.' She swung around and aimed a finger at Jaimie Smith. 'You were Mathers' lover. Don't deny it. His things are all over your house. What did he do - tell you he already had a wife in Canada? Confess that he had another lover?' She tossed her head in a show of tousled contempt. 'You decided that if you couldn't have him, no one could. So you plunged a knife in his back when you were punching his ticket.' She looked slowly around the room, tapped her foot and made a pretence of thinking. 'But then the doubts set in. What if you were seen? The only way to cover your tracks was to eliminate all the other passengers. Love knows no mercy, eh?' She waved a hand at Gummidge. 'Cuff her, Sergeant.'

Gummidge got up from the sofa, stomped across the room and gave Smith a clip around the ear.

'I meant handcuff her.' Heather groaned. 'Take her away and book her for the murders of Mathers, Dangerfield, Bragg and Decora.'

As Gummidge rummaged through his tunic pockets for his missing handcuffs, Obafemi raised a hand. 'Very impressive, Miss Prendergast.' He gave Heather a nod of respect. 'But I'm afraid you have overlooked a rather important detail.'

'Really? I think not.' Heather folded her arms and tossed her head in a game, set and match show of slamdunk confidence.

Inspector Obafemi looked from Heather to Jaimie Smith and back again at Heather. 'Have you considered the possibility that Trevor Mathers was Miss Smith's brother?'

'I think you mean lover.'

'I know what I mean, Miss Prendergast.'

'Oh, come on. I hardly think that's likely,' Heather dismissed the suggestion with an off-hand flick of a wrist. 'It might have escaped your notice, but Smith and Mathers are different surnames. And as far as I am aware, England and Canada are different countries. Or did that change after Brexit?' Her smug smile shrank to a look of horror when Inspector Obafemi showed her a photocopy of Mathers' birth certificate. 'You mean, Trevor Mathers was born in St. Mary Nook and his real name was Trevor Smith?'

'Not that it's none of your business, Columbo, but all that bloke's clobber at my place is mine.' Jaimie Smith disentangled Gummidge's hand from her arm and gave Heather a birdie's-eye view of her middle finger. 'That's why me and Trev had that row on the train. He didn't approve. Anyway, Bragg were alive when I left the church. I had a quick bevvy and went to see a mate.'

'A likely story,' Heather scoffed as she hung onto her vanishing credibility by the skin of a varnished fingernail. 'And I suppose someone can verify that?'

Sammy cleared her throat. 'I can,' she said sheepishly.

'You know her?'

'Could say that.' Sammy closed her eyes, took a deep

breath and swallowed. 'We're engaged.'

'What? You mean . . . Golly.' Heather was not just flabbergasted, she was addled to the pith. Although profoundly shaken and deeply stirred by the salacious revelation - to say nothing of Inspector Obafemi's wry well-I-never headshake - she was not to be denied her moment of triumph. Gathering what few wits she still had, she turned to Guan-Yin. 'Aha,' she said. 'I see my cunning ruse caught you off guard, Guany. Because I have left the most important fact to last.'

As a pregnant hush fell upon the room like a parturient anchorite, Heather folded her arms and looked from one guest to the other to the next. 'What, you may ask,' she asked rhetorically, 'was Trevor Mathers doing in St. Mary Nook - something so dangerous it was to cost him his life?' She gave her chin a pensive tap and looked slowly around the room. 'My guess is that Dangerfield's lavish lifestyle and ruinous gambling habit were funded by a secret lover. And how did she come by so much cash?' For the want of an answer, she suggested, 'I suggest that she was selling state secrets to the Chinese. And that is what Trevor Mathers was investigating.' She straightened her back, crossed her arms and glared at Guan-Yin. 'And you, you despicable swine, were Dangerfield's bitch. His Chinese takeaway. His gutter-geisha. The facts speak for themselves. You have access to classified documents in Uncle Monty's safe, you have jet black hair, I have often seen you in high heels and you have a fondness for expensive perfume,' she said with a certitude that

305

brooked not one atom, not one electron, not one quark of a possible doubt.

Guan-Yin raised an eyebrow, said, 'the woman who claims to know everything, knows nothing,' and gave Heather a pitiable look.

'Don't deny it, Guany.' Heather raised her voice. 'Mathers was onto you, wasn't he?' She took a photograph from her pocket and passed it round. 'This still from one of St. Mary Nook Station CCTV cameras shows you getting off the train. There can be no doubt that you murdered Mathers. Then, terrified that you might have been seen, you ruthlessly eliminated potential witnesses.' Unable or unwilling to look Guany in the eye, she screwed up her nose as if in near proximity to a nauseous obnoxion. 'You disgust me, you vile she-devil. You are beneath contempt. Hanging is too good for you. May you rot in hell.' She snapped her fingers. 'Lock her up and throw away the key, Gummidge. And may God have mercy on her wretched soul.'

Having thus far been little more than a passenger on Heather's runaway train of deductive elucidation, Inspector Obafemi intervened. 'It's possible, I suppose, Miss Prendergast,' he said. 'But I am afraid your theory is flawed. You see, Miss Guan-Yin is a secret service agent planted at Trevelyan Hall to investigate a major security leak. Trevor Mathers was a colleague. Or should I say, agent Smith was her handler. He briefed her on the train that afternoon and believe you me, he was very much alive when she left.' He took a snapshot from his briefcase. 'This is your killer.'

'Gosh. Sorry Guany. Looks like I might have dropped a clanger. No hard feelings, eh?' Blushing like a blooper, Heather avoided Guan-Yin's contemptuous glare wishing that she was somewhere - anywhere - else. 'But I don't understand,' she said with a puzzled frown on her freckled brow as she examined the photograph. 'Who is this woman?'

Inspector Obafemi raised a hand as Lady Elizabeth offered him a cigar. Preferring his own brand of nicotinous poison, he took out his pipe and nodded when Locke-Mortice offered him a light. 'Thank you, Mister Locke-Mortice. By the way,' he said as he cupped his hands around the flame. 'If I may say, you have very attractive legs. How long have you been cross-dressing?'

As Locke-Mortice fumbled to tuck his pinstripes into his tartan socks, Heather flopped down on the sofa, buried her head in her hands and groaned, 'I want to crawl into a hole and die.'

32

Eyes goggled. Minds boggled. A pen could be heard to drop.

Montague Locke-Mortice fixed Inspector Obafemi with a contemptuous glare. 'Preposterous,' he thundered. 'Are you seriously suggesting that I dress in womens' clothing, Inspector? Damn it, man. I would not know where to start.'

'How about Hot Gurls, Winnie's Wigs, Victoria's Whispers, Patsy's Perfumery, Top Totty, Goody You Shoes, Busty Boys?' Obafemi debriefcased a handful of invoices, purchase orders and bank statements salvaged from a trashed Whitehall computer by special branch tech-boffins and held them up for all to see.

'How dare you impugn my integrity?' Locke-Mortice fumed, outraged, contemptuous and offended in joint and several measure. 'You have a filthy mind, Inspector. I will have you know that those were presents for my dear wife.'

Eyes blazing, Lady Trevelyan stormed across the room and snatched the invoices out of Obafemi's hand. Her peaches and cream complexion turned a ruddy shade of apoplexy, and metaphorical steam billowed out of her ears. She unleashed a barrage of swear-balloons including but by no means limited to, 'you have never bought me a stitch of clothing in your miserable life, you little shit.' She narrowed her eyes and waved a bill of salacious sale in her husband's face. 'And if you think for one second that I would be seen in a French Maid's costume except on a movie set, you are even more stupid than I took you for.'

In the face of his wife's ferocious tongue-lashing, Montague Locke-Mortice raised his hands and backed away. 'My dear, it was intended as a surprise for our wedding anniversary.'

'A shock, you mean.' Lady Elizabeth tossed her auburn locks in a show of postured petulance. 'For God's sake, you disgusting little man, I am hardly a size fourteen.'

'You will be after I have taken you out for a slap-up meal to celebrate, my dear,' Locke-Mortice quipped with the feeblest of smiles.

Having heard more than enough, Lady Elizabeth flipped a wrist at Obafemi. 'Take him away, Inspector. I'll throttle him later.'

Whenever Heather Prendergast recounted the events of that fateless afternoon - as she did on unnumerable occasions - she liked to liken what happened next to a scene from The Incredulous Hulk. In the bat of an eyelid, her uncle's expression turned from benign blandishment to raving monsterment and he shrieked, 'enough,' in an earcurdling high-pitched scream.

Before anyone could stop him, Locke-Mortice hauled Heather off the sofa, pinned her to his chest, whipped a flintlock pistol out of his cummerbund and held it to her head. With madness raging in his eyes, he screamed, 'have you any idea what it is like being married to Veronika Vivendi? She is so damned perfect, she makes me feel like a pathetic little worm.'

'Fiddlesticks,' Lady Trevelyan scoffed with an intemperate toss of the head. 'Pull yourself together, you pathetic little worm.'

Locke-Mortice turned to Inspector Obafemi, narrowed his eyes, said, 'want to know a secret?' and in the absence of a reply, told him - told everyone - 'that woman might look like every red-blooded man's wet dream, but take it from me, copulating with her is like trying to pump up a flat tyre with a slow puncture.'

'Humbug,' Lady Elizabeth snorted. She flicked the hair out of her eyes with a feisty toss of the head and turned to Naff. 'Tell him, Simon.'

Heather struggled to unpinion her arms, the better to scratch Naff's eyes out. 'Tell him what, exactly?' she hissed.

'Beats me, babe,' Naff said with a hapless shrug as, innocence exemplified, he examined his fingernails.

Somewhat less than unamused, Lady Elizabeth shot Naff a frosty glare to trump all weathers. 'So glad the age of chivalry is alive and well,' she said with a cutting irony that all but wilted the begonias in the pewter pot stands. Pride royally spurned, she turned to Sammy. 'In which case, Miss Ingham,' she said with a lofty snoot, 'you have my permission to award me marks out of ten for my sexual prowess. Starting at fifteen.'

Jaimie Smith's mouth fell open like an unchained malady but nary a word, nary a gasp, nary a fuckaduck came out.

Sammy glanced at her watch. 'Crickey, is that the time?' she said in a panicky voice. 'Must dash. I'm late for my origami class.'

Her mood fast turning from bad to worst, Lady Elizabeth snapped, 'stay where you are, you wet blanket,' and turned to Guan-Yin. 'Tell them, Guany,' she demanded, 'and don't spare my blushes. Chop, chop.'

Guan-Yin tucked her hands into the sleeves of her high-bodiced gown and bowed her head. 'In the skies we shall be birds flying side by side,' she said with a serene smile, 'and on the earth we shall be twinned trunks flowering sprigs on the same branch. But only in your dreams.'

'Oh, for heaven's sake,' Lady Elizabeth groaned. 'Very well, you lily-livered fly-by-nights, you leave me no alternative. I will just have to phone George Clooney for a reference.'

'The devil you will.' Lock-Mortice tightened his stranglegrip on Heather's epiglottis and cocked his flintlock.

As a deathly silence engulfed the room like a limp

biscuit, Guan-Yin padded to within sophistry distance of Locke-Mortice. 'Confucius say, keep five yards from a carriage, ten yards from a horse and hundred yards from an elephant,' she said, 'but the distance to keep from a wicked man cannot be measured.'

Locke-Mortice stared at her as if she had just announced that the moon was made of cheese. 'Wicked, you say. Wicked?' he raised his voice to fever pitch. 'For pity's sake, I am more sinned against than sinning. Truth is, all I ever wanted was to be happy.'

Guan-Yin sighed and shook her head. 'Wise men know truth uttered before its time is always dangerous and happiness is the absence of the striving for happiness.'

By now, Locke-Mortice was too far gone to give a care. 'I loved Hammy Dangerfield with all my heart and he loved me. Lord only knows, he told me often enough.' He wrestled a tear from his voice and a croak from his eye. 'Apart from my train timetables, he was the only thing that made my life worth living so I surrendered to my basest passions. By Jove, I have been a damned fool,' he sobbed, his voice hoarse with remorse.

The tassels in Guan-Yin's pigtailed bun fluttered as she nodded. 'Ah, but those who realize their folly are not true fools.'

Beyond inconsolable - irreconsolable it might be said by those who know no grammar - Montague Locke-Mortice retched out his wretched emotions like metaphysical vomit, more to purge his tortured soul than to elucidate the tragicomedy of his spurned lovelust. 'I found out that Hamilton and that vile harridan, Elouise Decora, were carrying on behind my back,' he raged. 'They were laughing at me. Laughing at me, for pity's sake - Grace Golightly.' Tears of humiliation welled in his eyes. 'I tried to convince myself that Hammy still loved me and foolishly allowed our tryst to continue in the hope that things would work out.'

Guan-Yin raised a finger and tut-tut-tutted. 'Man who waits for roast duck to fly into his mouth must wait very long time.'

Locke-Mortice ignored her and continued to plough a slough of desolate despond. 'And then the blackmail started,' he said, at one and the same time righteous and confessional, as if his murderous intent was not merely justified, but was to be lauded. 'Hammy threatened to send a photograph of me in a blond wig, corsets, fishnet stockings and stilettos to The Sunday Rant so I paid up. I had no choice,' he said with a plaintive look in his crazed eyes. 'Had my perversion become common knowledge, it might have cost me my knighthood. But the more I gave, the more he demanded.'

Although Guan-Yin showed every empathy, there was a hint of scold in her softly-spoken voice. 'Good will be rewarded with good and evil with evil, Mister Locke-Mortice,' she said. 'Is only matter of time.'

'I became desperate,' Locke-Mortice croaked, every

plea one sob louder than the last, yet one sob quieter than the next. 'Can you not see? I was trapped. I couldn't see a way out.'

At this point, Inspector Obafemi interlocuted the inevitability of Locke-Mortice's fall from Grace, as Locke-Mortice called his alter-egress. 'So that's why you sold classified documents to the highest bidder,' he suggested, or rather he stated. For the great detective already suspected the inevitable denouement.

'What else could I do?' Locke-Mortice sobbed in a plea of beg-forgiveness. 'As Chair of The National Security Council, I had access to state secrets and believe you me, there were plenty of willing buyers.'

'Golly,' Heather said, shocked to the quick by her uncle-in-law's treachery. 'So you betrayed King and Country for a few pieces of silver? Really, Uncle Monty. That is just not on.'

Guan-Yin turned to her, tucked her hands into her billowing sleeves and bowed her head. 'Miss Heather,' she said. 'If you are smartest person in a room, you are in the wrong room. Anyone can find the switch with light on.'

Locke-Mortice tightened his stranglehold to prevent Heather from interrupting again. 'And then Mathers came sniffing around,' he said, remembering aloud. 'By a stroke of good fortune, I intercepted a report that he was planning to submit to MI5. I realised that if I didn't silence him, it would be curtains for my career. Don't you see,' he pleaded, 'it was Mathers or me. So when an opportunity arose, I did what any self-respecting politician would do and stabbed him in the back.'

Inspector Obafemi's slow nod suggested that none of this came as a surprise. Nevertheless, to make quite sure that he hadn't crossed any wires, he said, 'I assume that Colonel Dangerfield saw you kill Mathers.'

'He demanded half a million to keep his mouth shut. I loved him,' Montague Locke-Mortice aka Grace Golightly sobbed. 'But when I discovered that he and Decora had plighted their troth, a red mist descended. Damn it, man. The bounders deserved all they got.'

'And Reverend Bragg?'

Keeping Heather pinioned to his waistcoat with one hand, Locke-Mortice dabbed a tear from his eye with the other. 'When Dangerfield and Decora went to the vicarage to discuss their nuptial arrangements,' he said self-righteously, as if he deemed himself a victim rather than a sinner, 'Elouise drank too much sherry and told Bragg about my little peccadillo. She confided that she and Hammy had been fleecing me for months.'

'So Bragg turned the tables and tried to blackmail her - and you. And that's why he had to die.' Inspector Obafemi stated what was, beyond the realms of a feasible doubt, the inevitable consequence of the lethal spiral. After all, hell hath no fury . . . waffle, waffle, waffle.

'The man was deranged.' The blood vessels in Locke-Mortice's receding brow pumped fit to burst and his eyes bulged like hardboiled eggs. 'He demanded ten million to fund a rabbit sanctuary. Can you believe it?'

'And Decora?' Obafemi asked, at one and the same time, repulsed and fascinated. Of all Locke-Mortice's murders, Elouise Decora's was the one that would keep him awake at night bucketing cold sweat.

'I phoned her just before dawn and told her to meet me in Poacher's Wood. I claimed to have evidence that the Butcher of St. Mary Nook was French so knew she would come straight away.' Locke-Mortice looked about expecting a round of applause. He scowled when all he heard was silence. 'The moment my niece passed out and PC Ingham was safely chained up in my good lady wife's fetish chamber, I changed into a darling little black number and sneaked out to the rendezvous.'

Sammy gave Inspector Obafemi a sheepish look and mumbled, 'told you I wasn't cut out for this lark, guv.' But she need not have feared for her bad name; Inspector Obafemi was too engrossed in Montague Locke-Mortice's dastardly tale of dagger-do to care.

'You have no idea the thrill I felt when I gave the Jezebel her just deserts. It was even more exhilarating than having rumpy-pumpy with Hammy.' Locke-Mortice pressed his knees together and bit his lip so hard it bled. 'I only wish you could have heard her screams and seen her eyes bulge when I strangled her with my tights, Inspector,' he told Obafemi. 'Must say, I had to chuckle when I cut out the blackmailing witch's tongue and left it for the foxes. Poetic justice, don't you think? It gives me a fuzzy feeling here just to think about it.' He placed a hand on his heart and broke into a maniacal cackle.

'That is quite enough, you shitty little pervert,' Lady Elizabeth strode across the room, planted her hands on her hips and confronted her miscreant spouse with, 'I want a divorce.'

'Just because I have been having an affair with a man and murdered a few people? My dear, it is not as if anyone will miss them.' Locke-Mortice sounded shocked. Nay, he sounded offended. 'Whatever happened to stand by your man?'

'Put down the pistol, Locke-Mortice,' Inspector Obafemi said. 'Trevelyan Hall is surrounded by a heavily armed SWAT team. If I take this pipe out of my mouth, you will be dead before you hit the floor.'

As Lock-Mortice cast a panicky look out of the French windows, Guan-Yin hitched up her skirt, screamed, 'ay-eeee,' and launched herself tigerdragonlike into the air. With the elegance of pigtailed tumblefly, she summersaulted twice and kangarooed Locke-Mortice flat in the face. As he dropped the flintlock, let go of his hostage and stumbled back, she felled him like a treepole with two expertly executed karate chops, one to the Adam's apple, the other not. To the sound of breathless gasps from the onlookers, she planted a foot on his chest, flicked her pigtail over a shoulder and brushed her hands together. 'The best time to plant a tree was twenty years ago,' she said. 'The second best time is today.'

'Not sure I follow. I'll have to think about it,' Heather croaked as she slumped down on a sofa feeling her neck.

Leaving Lady Elizabeth to comfort her niece with three-star nerve medicine, Inspector Obafemi instructed DI Turner to have Gummidge book Locke-Mortice - and be sure to double-check the paperwork. Duty duly done, he wandered back to the window, leaned against the shutters, relit his pipe, took a few puffs and gazed out.

Naff poured two tumblerfuls of Trevelyan Special Reserve Doublemalt Kent Whisky and joined him. 'Well, boss,' he said as they clinked glasses, 'got to say, that was a turn up for the books.'

'Not really.' Inspector Obafemi took a sip of whisky and dabbed his lips with his top-pocket handkerchief. 'It's logical if you think about it,' he said. 'All that was missing was a motive. Hard to believe someone married to Lady Trevelyan would take a lover. I would have thought any man worth his salt would give his eye teeth to go to bed with her.'

'Believe me, boss, all that glitters ain't gold.' Naff glanced at Lady Elizabeth, mopped his brow and gulped. 'Hey,' he said, 'shouldn't you call off that SWAT team before someone gets hurt?'

'SWAT team in this godforsaken neck of the woods?

Why bother when I have Miss Guan-Yin?' Inspector Obafemi said as he watched Guan-Yin pad around the drawing room like a teacup courtesan stacking crockery onto a tottery tray almost as big as she was.

'The Chop-Chop cop, eh, boss?' Naff joked as he watched Guan-Yin go about her undercover dishwork.

'Indeed.' Obafemi scrunched out his pipe with his trusty pipescrunch and slipped it into his pipe pocket. 'The Chop-Chop cop.'

'So I guess that's it, then,' Naff said. 'Mind telling me how come you always get a result?'

'Oh, there is no great secret to the art of detection, Detective Robinson,' Obafemi said as if the answer should be self-evident. 'Confucius summed it up in a nutshell over two thousand years ago . . . he who knows all the answers has not been asked all the questions, for if we don't know life, how can we know death?'

Detective Inspector Isaac Obafemi placed a fatherly hand on Naff's shoulder. 'You would do well to remember that, Simon,' he said. 'And so would your ambitious young girlfriend.'

33

Heather Prendergast had never come to terms with her father's rejection. How could she? She had been a flossheaded ten year-old more at home with the fairies than the real world when her mother died.

Having inherited her mother's stoic gene, Heather soldiered through a troubled adolescence without exhibiting a notable talent for anything of note except cracking murder riddles, be they true life crimes or pulp fictions. And so, driven by dreams of future fame and glory, after escaping from finishing school she joined the Metropolitan Police. Although lacking an academic bent, she resat her exams with flying colours and embarked upon a career that she was confident would take her to the shape of things to come. Dogged and persistent, no matter what setbacks she encountered - and they were many and they were bothersome - she was determined to make her late mother proud by becoming the greatest detective the world had ever known.

But dreams are destined to be just that, and *The Curious Case of The Butcher of St. Mary Nook* was to prove a crude awakening. In an unforeseen twist of the knife, the bubble of her ambitions was burst by a miscalculable deductive misstep. What made matters worse was that it rendered her evidentially naked in the eyes of her great hero, the legendary Detective Inspector Obafemi of The Yard.

Although it is said that no man - and in all likelihood, no woman - is an island, Heather was an isthmus of despair. To add perfidy to ignominy, she had been cruelly betrayed by those she held most dear; her new best friend, Samantha Ingham; the love of her life, Simon Robinson; and in the cruellest cut of all, her aunt, Lady Elizabeth Trevelyan, someone she had always placed upon a pedestal of virtue.

And so, lonely as a solitary cloud adrift in a maudlin malaise of misanthropic misery, Heather wandered the grounds of Trevelyan Hall deep in the dumps of despair. She weighed options as she shuffled across the upper lawn with her shoulders hunched and her hands in her frock pockets - become an agnostic nun, a freelance traffic warden, a career waitress or dedicate her remaining days to obsessively plotting the downfall of her backstabbers. But no. Although just twenty-one and counting - albeit only until her twenty-fifth birthday when she intended to stop the clock as her aunt had done - she knew that far from being a dish best served cold, revenge is a maliciously injudicious desert best not served at all. Nevertheless, the wickedest of her many minds urged her to put bromide in Naff's tea, sugar in Sammy's petrol tank and earwigs in Aunt Elizabeth's bed as some squiggly reminders of her parasitic duplicity.

Heather was shaken from her scheming daydreams by the sight of her aunt striding across the lawn. At first she was minded to ignore her but upon further thought, she thought, why should I turn my back and walk away? She had done nothing to be ashamed of. Indeed, to paraphrase her disgraced uncle-in-law, she was more sinned against than sinning. Far more. So she held her head high and stood her ground.

'Ah, there you are, Spriggy. I have been searching high and low,' her aunt said. 'Can you spare a mo for a chat?'

'No,' said Heather. 'We have nothing to discuss.'

'Please, my dear. I swear that nothing happened. When it came to it, I couldn't. Not behind your back.'

'I seem to remember you once telling me, nothing ventured, nothing gained. Well, I only hope your gain was worth my pain.' For perhaps the first time in her life, Heather addressed her aunt with defiance rather than deference - de mujer a mujer one might say, or woman to woman should one prefer. 'Anyway, it's the thought that counts. Isn't that what you told me when daddy sent me a fifty-pence postal order for my eighteenth birthday? Well, correct me if I'm wrong,' she said, 'but you have been trying to get my boyfriend into bed ever since you first set eyes on him. Well, for your information, he is now my ex-boyfriend. I have given him his marching orders. Told him to pack his bags and leave. I never want to set eyes on him again. Satisfied?'

Lady Trevelyan raised a scheming eyebrow. 'So does that mean Simon is now a free agent?'

'Aunty, you are beneath contempt,' Heather said. 'Oh, forget it. I'm sure he'll come running if you whistle. I'm not surprised Uncle Monty went off the rails.'

'You have every right to be disappointed, my dear.'

'Disappointed. Is that what you call it?'

'Very well, if you must. Betrayed. But I promise I didn't mean any harm.' Lady Trevelyan wrung her hands in a plaintive plea of sufferance. For rejection was not merely anathema to her, it was the cruellest athema of all. Unable to bear her niece's frosty silence a moment longer, she asked, 'do you know the fable of the scorpion and the fox?'

Adopting the pose that never failed to elicit a standing ovation whenever she strode onstage - head back, arms outstretched, legs apart like a latterway Joan of Arc – Dame Elizabeth Trevelyan, as she must surely one day be, swept an arm towards a distant flock of deer as if they were a fawning audience. In the melodramatic voice that she had perfected for her critically-acclaimed roles as Lady Macbeth, Juliet Capulet and Princess Tzara of Zog, she launched into a moral tale of mortal woe.

'Once upon a time in a far-off land, a fire raged in the forest,' she said as if narrating a Greek tragedy. 'The only means of escape for the woodland animals was to swim across a river. A fox was about to take the plunge when he heard a tiny voice. He looked down and saw a scorpion.' Lady Elizabeth sank to her knees and cupped a hand to an ear. 'Carry me across the river, the scorpion begged,' she squeaked in a tiny falsetto voice, 'to which the fox replied, if I do, you will sting me and I will die. Grrrrr . . .' She crouched on all fours with her long red hair bunched into a foxtail growling like a pantomime mutt.

Warming to her duopolous roles, Lady Elizabeth squeaked, 'of course I won't,' as she fancied a loquacious scorpion might. 'Because if I do, we will both drown.' She rose nimbly her feet, opened her eyes as wide as they would go, turned to Heather and hammed into the role of bedtime fairyteller. 'Well, my dear,' she said with an infantile smile upon her handsome face. 'Persuaded by the scorpion's logic, Mister Fox told him to hop onto his back and plunged into the river.' She shielded her eyes with a hand and, for the want of anything wetter, pointed to a far off gulley. 'Half way across, the scorpion stung poor Reynard on the neck.' She glanced at Heather and shook her head in an exaggerated show of tragic inevitability. 'As he sank beneath the waves, Mister Fox groaned, why did you do that Mister Scorpion? Now we will both die. Grrrrr . . .' She lapsed into a low pitched foxy growl, clutched her heart and staggered in ever diminishing circles. 'Our little scorpion begged forgiveness. I couldn't help it, he said,' she squeaked in her scorpionesque voice. 'I am a scorpion. It is my nature.'

Having concluded the tragic tale of neck-stinging betrayal, Lady Elizabeth sank to her knees and flourished an arm in the famous dying swan pose that was still talked of in the byways and spyways of The Kremlin.

'Aunt Elizabeth, do you have any idea how ridiculous

you are?' Heather said as she watched her aunt look for the cameras awaiting a round of rapturous applause from a figmentary film crew. 'Is it any wonder that I was always too embarrassed to invite friends home from boarding school?'

Lady Elizabeth picked herself up, brushed herself down and was about to embellish a triumphant curtsy when she remembered where she was. 'Darling Spriggy,' she said with a thespian sob in her voice. 'I have been a self-centered overbearing burden. How can I ever make it up to you?' She dabbed a crocodile tear from an eye and swallowed. 'The thing is, if I want something badly enough, I have to get it by fair means or foul. I am like the scorpion in our little story. It is my nature.' She gave Heather a doe-eyed look of begforgivess and sniffed back a tear. 'Simon was just another trophy to go with my Oscar, my Nobel Prize for Literature and my Playmate of the Year awards,' she said. 'I couldn't help myself. Temptation got the better of me. Can you ever forgive me?'

'No.'

'Not even of I give you a lift back to London in the Porsche?' When Heather turned her back and stuck her nose in the air, she said, 'what if I let you drive?' knowing full well that her niece would strip off to the buff and tango on red hot coals for a chance to get behind the wheel of her aunt's 911 GT3.

'No use trying to butter me up, aunty,' Heather said,

meaning you bet . . . you just pressed all the right buttons. 'If I say yes, it's only because I'm desperate to get home,' she fibbed. 'I suppose you're going to stay at one of your Westminster houses,' she said, anxious to know where the she-devil she knew would be staying so she could give her the widest possible berth.

'Not for long, my dear. London is such a bore. I am thinking of sailing round the world again. I could do with some time on my own and it will give me a chance to translate War and Peace into Inuit.'

Simmering like a slow dog's dinner, Heather left Lady Elizabeth to pack and took a last meander in the grounds. Like her *unspeakable* aunt, she had an awful lot on her mind. The previous evening, after her uncle-in-law had been driven away to a padded cell cackling like a duckmonkey, she sent Naff packing with a swarm of *unrepeatable* fleas in his ear. Left to her own miserable devices, she barely slept a wink, if that. Her spirits were hardly heartened when she rose to the mind-numbing prospect of trudging into New Scotland Yard's staff canteen at the eggcrack of morn the following Monday. Indeed, all ill-considered things considered, she was seriously tempted to hand in her notice. Having terminally shredded her deductive credentials, she doubted whether she would ever be granted an opportunity to rise above the yeasty confines of the Metropolitan Police canteen. The thought of Brillo-padding congealed grease off saucepans forever and a day was beyond contemplation. Uncompletational it might, or preferably might not, be said.

Fed up to the pinny strings with the prospect of kitchenary drudgeries into the unforeseeable future, Heather scuffed a pebble across the lawn. 'Sorry, Guany,' she shouted when she saw Guan-Yin rubbing a shin.

Pretty as a calligraph, Guan-Yin was wearing a tightfitting long-sleeved slit-skirted cheongsam dress over loose fitting coolie trousers and sockless sandals. Her tumbles of jet black hair were swept onto the crown of her head in a bird's nest bouffant, held in place with a cluster of ebony pins and an eye-catching gold clasp inset with the mother of all pearls. As always, her trademark pigtail - now plaited with snow white lilies - tumbled down her slight back to her boyish hips. With her porcelain doll complexion, high blushered cheekbones, swallow-winged eyes, pencil-tipped brows and cupid rosebud lips, to Heather's way of eye she cut a perfect picture of demure Mandarin maidenhood.

'Didn't see you,' Heather said apologetically. 'I have an awful lot on my mind.'

Guan-Yin clasped her hands, bowed her head and, in a rare moment of candour, said, 'what is done is done, Miss Heather. The situation cannot be restored to how it once was.'

'Yes. It's all been a bit of a disaster, hasn't it?' Heather agreed. 'Uncle Monty is probably going to spend the rest of his life in an asylum and may not get his knighthood. Aunt Elizabeth says she has never been so humiliated in all her life. I'm stuck in a dead-end job and to cap it all,

I just found out that my boyfriend has been cheating on me.'

'Bad fortune is more frequent than good, Miss Heather,' Guan-Yin said with a sophical sigh. 'Life does not come without risk, but risk of failure is not an argument for not trying.'

'I'm dreadfully confused,' Heather said, terribly confused. 'Why did Naff cheat on me? I love him and thought he loved me. Where did I go wrong?'

'Every girl loves to her own taste but if you love someone, you will love also the things associated with that someone,' Guan-Yin said. Then she went all Zen again. 'The waterside flower pining for love sheds petals, while the heartless brook babbles on.'

'You Chinese have such a handle on life,' Heather sighed.

'Ah-so.' With the incrutablest of smiles, Guan-Yin planted her hands on her thighs and bowed her head. Then she cast a quick glance over a shoulder and lowered her voice. 'Keep it under your hat, hunny, but I never been to China in my life,' she confided in a coarse South London accent. 'The name is Tiffany Kim – special agent 0069 to my buddies. My folks are good Godfearing Catholics. They run a Korean restaurant in The King's Road - makes a mint. I grew up in Chelsea but after that bit of bother with the Old Bill when I was fourteen - don't ask - mum and dad shipped me off to a convent boarding school in

Brackonshire. Believe me, it was brutal. So, I got pissed one night and told Mother Superior I couldn't be arsed with all that superstitious religious bullshit. Well, you can imagine - she blew her top. Talking of which, fancy a spliff?' She gave her arms a vigorous shake and a joint and a packet of prophylactics fell out of her billowing sleeves. When she saw Heather's jaw drop, she winked and said, 'be prepared, hunny.' She lit the joint, took a drag and rolled her eyes. 'Jeez, I've been gasping for a toke all day - you have no idea. See, I have to be stoned out of my box to do this bonkers job – as if you hadn't noticed.'

Tiffany Kim aka Guan-Yin tossed the roach on the grass and stubbed it out with an embroidered sandal. 'Where was I?' she said. 'Oh yeah . . .' She clicked her fingers. 'When I told Mother Superior I'd seen the light and gone atheist, she threw the mother of all hissy-fits. See what I did there?' She clicked her tongue and winked. 'Anyway, after that the only habit I was allowed was penguin drag and a wimple. Every night I was given bum-smacks with a wooden paddle in a cold shower to stop my mind straying to the dark side. Turned me onto the joys of discipline and bondage – no bad thing in my line of work.' She batted her luscious lashes suggestively and ran her fingers down her stomach-cramping, hip-nipping, bum-busting, tit-pinching, body-hugging cheongsam. 'When I lost my rag and laid one on the head penguin, I got expelled. Well, I'm a grafter and a grifter - never afraid of putting it about - so I shagged my way through sixth form college and wangled a scholarship to The University of Asian Studies. My God, hunny, I worked my butt off. For three years, I screwed all the professors in the faculty regular as clockwork - my physical curriculum, I called it. At the end of the course, I threatened to post a photoblog of my classwork online if they didn't play ball. Did the trick. I graduated summa cum laude with a post-coital degree in Oriental Sophistry. I was planning to go into investment banking, but after talking it over with Grandmamma Kim - she wears the trousers in the Kim household - I plumped for the secret service. Must say, it's been a hoot. When I'm not mincing about in goofy drag spouting inane nonsense, I get to rub shoulders with studs who make James Bond look like a choir boy. Fact is, I've been laid more times than Mata Hari. It's a key part of the job. You would not believe the training regime - can't remember when I last slept in my own bed. Pretty good going for a street-wise Korean sister, ain't it?' She snatched a breath when she heard the distant clunk of St. Mary of Our Nook church bell. 'Love a duck – is that the time?' she gasped. 'My helicopter will be here any minute to whisk me off to GCHQ. Just time to change into a suit and take off this bloody wig . . . weighs a ton and itches like a spinster's fanny. Cute though, ain't it? Turns fellas on like nobody's business.' She raised a lightbulb finger, struck by a thought. 'Tell you what, hunnybun, why don't we go clubbing next time you got a free slot in your diary? We can get dolled up and go out on the pull now you've dumped your scumbag boyfriend. Take it from me, you can do loads better than him. He's bloody useless in bed. I should know.' She twinkled an eye and smacked her lips. 'Look, I'll give you a bell. We'll hook up in Soho, pop a few pills, get pissed out of our skulls and paint the town red. Look out for a small blonde sister with a pixie cut, combat trousers, a leather bomber jacket and bovver boots. I'll have a couple of squaddies with me – one each. See you about, noodlehead.' She hitched up her coolie pants, flipped her pigtail over a shoulder, blew Heather a kiss and padded off to bid a fond farewell to the koi carp.

Heather was still shaking the surreality out of her ears when she heard the throaty roar of Samantha Ingham's Karmann Ghia careering down the drive. Of one mind, she strode across the carpark to confront her new worst enemy. Arms crossed, lips pursed, she steeled her nerves ready to say, 'don't call me and I won't ever call you. Guide's honour.'

'Glad I caught you, pet,' Sammy said sheepishly as she got out of the Ghia. 'I was going to tell you about Jaimie. Honest. Must say, she's not best pleased with me just at the minute. You don't want to know what she called me when we got home.'

'Think I care?' Heather tossed her head in a show of wanton disregard. 'You and Aunt Elizabeth have been making fun of me all week, haven't you? What with those absurd costumes, ganging up on me behind my back and everything.' She gritted her teeth so hard she felt the ivories tickle. 'Well, thought I'd play along. Didn't want to upset you. But really . . .' she narrowed her eyes. 'You slept with my aunt. That is unforgivable.'

'Whoa, hold your horses, sweetie.' Sammy raised her hands in a gesture of don't-go-there-pet. 'We didn't have time to sleep. Blimey, you are so uptight. Loosen up.'

'I will have you know I am as broadminded as they come.' Heather set her jaw and stuck her nose in the air. 'I went to boarding school, remember?'

Sammy reached out for Heather's hand, crestfallen when Heather spurned the proffered olive branch. 'Sweetheart,' she said. 'I wasn't taking the piss. Honest. You're like my innocent kid sister. I been up all night worrying about you. Wanted to take care of you, that's all.'

'Innocent?' Heather gasped. 'I will have you know, I am the most hardnosed copper you will ever meet. I hold the record for handing out parking tickets to unattended wheelchairs on the Holloway Road.'

'Copper-bottomed credentials, like them saucepans you scrub for a living,' Sammy sniggered, then begged, 'wait, pet. Didn't mean it,' when Heather stormed off to the house.

Assuming it was Sammy grovelling for forgiveness, Heather ignored the doorbell at the first time of ringing and ignored it at the second. But when the ring persisted like a nagging blister, she strode to the door, yanked it open and screamed, 'go away, you rotter.' Red in the face when she saw Inspector Obafemi staring at her, she clamped a hand to her mouth and garbled a stuttering apology through her fingers.

'No need to apologise, Miss Prendergast. No harm speaking your mind once in a while. But don't make a habit of it.' Inspector Obafemi cleared his throat and asked, 'is Lady Trevelyan in? I feel I should apologise for the disruption.' He nodded at a team of forensticians busying brushes over every immovable object in sight.

Heather lowered her eyes, in part because she was embarrassed at having misidentified a superior officer, but mostly because she was humbled by the great man's presence. 'Can't see it will be a problem, sir,' she mumbled. 'Aunt Elizabeth will be staying at one of her Westminster houses while she decides what to do. I'm driving her to London this afternoon.'

Obafemi turned to go, then paused as if he had something of import to impart. 'PC Prendergast,' he said with a hint of ominous foreboding.

'Heather,' Heather replied then bit her lip, embarrassed by her presumption.

As always, Detective Inspector Obafemi measured his words with all due care and attention. 'Don't take this the wrong way, Heather,' he said. 'But you're not really cut out for kitchen duties, are you?' When she lowered her eyes and fidgeted with her fingers, he said, 'but let me say how impressed I was by your presentation last night. It would have done Sherlock Holmes proud.'

'Most kind,' Heather mumbled. 'But I got rather the

wrong end of the stick. If it hadn't been for Guan-Yin, I'd be a gonner.'

'Not a bit of it.' Inspector Obafemi gave her a buckup pat on the back. 'At your age I wouldn't have known where to start with a case like The Murder on The Ordinary Express. And let's face it, you worked everything out to the last detail, apart from the actual perp. But two out of three's not bad.' He looked her over, tapped his chin and said, 'ever thought of joining CID?'

'I have thought about nothing else since I was ten,' Heather said with a lump in her throat as her ambitions crashed before her eyes like an inebriated unicyclist.

'It just so happens that I have a vacancy on my team for a trainee detective,' Obafemi said casually. 'Fancy giving it a go?'

Heather surfaced from her swoon to find Aunt Elizabeth wafting smelly-salts under her nose. Detective Inspector Obafemi was standing behind her with a chuckle in his eyes. 'So is that a yes, Heather?' he asked. 'Or would you like a little time to think it over?'

Not sure if she had died and gone to heaven, Probationary Detective Heather Prendergast of The Yard scrambled to her feet, elbowed her aunt out of the way and stood smartly to attention.

'So when do I start?' she asked and tipped an imaginary cap. 'Guv.'

If you enjoyed this journey to the mad side, please leave a review on your favourite booksite. It would be appreciated.

For more info on forthcoming novels, join the mailing list at www.em-thompson.com.

ALSO BY em thompson

ELLIEFANT'S GRAVEYARD
The Curious Case of The Throatslit Man
Book one of the Prendergast of The Yard Casebooks.

Convinced that two unexplained deaths on her London patch are murders, rookie police officer Heather Prendergast's unofficial investigation takes her to an isolated mill town on the Huddshire moors where she unearths a web of corruption that threatens her career – and her life.

What the reviewers say...

"Em Thompson's Elliefant's Graveyard is like stumbling upon a hidden door in a London alley, one that leads to a parallel universe where the tea is spiked with mischief and the fog has a mischievous grin."

"This book is a breath of fresh air. It has all the elements of a crime mystery but has a quirky and funny edge to it. It's the first book I've actually had a laugh at for a while!"

"This is one of those rare gems that hits you with its originality and charm. As someone born and raised in Yorkshire, the characters, landscape, and attitudes are all too familiar and Elliefant's Graveyard made me smile, wince, and homesick. Wonderful!"

"A uniquely fascinating read. Its narrative style is more akin to Lewis Carroll's works than your average detective thriller."

"If you love a fun, imaginative mystery, you'll love this book!"

"I absolutely loved this book! As Constable Prendergast delves into the mystery, the plot thickens with plenty of twists that keep you guessing."

"A must-read for those who enjoy novels that are as thought-provoking as they are entertaining!"

"A uniquely entertaining read. Perfect for fans of whimsical mysteries and aspiring detectives everywhere."

"Make a cup of tea and settle down for a fun read."

"This is a fun and well written story with mystery and suspense that will have you turning pages from the very beginning."

Audiobook available narrated by Billie Fulford-Brown.

THE HAPPY THISTLE

The Curious Case of The Katenapped Girl

Book Two of The Prendergast of The Yard Casebooks

When probationary police officer, Heather Prendergast, is enlisted by her estranged father to secure the return of her kidnapped stepsister, she is faced with the most baffling case of her short career – and her most deadly foe.

What the reviewers say...

A Hilarious and Twisted Mystery You Can't Put Down.

Reviewed in the United States on January 17, 2025

The Happy Thistle – The Curious Case of the Katenapped Girl is a brilliantly quirky ride through a madcap mystery that combines crime, chaos, and humor in a way that's completely unforgettable. Heather Prendergast, a probationary officer with her own family baggage, finds herself thrust into the most bizarre case of her life. From the very beginning, I was hooked by the absurdity and sheer originality of the plot. The book delivers a wildly entertaining mix of eccentric characters, including a mad professor with delusions of world domination, a kilt-wearing chef with a penchant for kidnapping, and a loan shark mob demanding payment in bitcoin and physics equipment. Despite the zaniness, the story never feels overly chaotic – it's cleverly plotted, with enough twists to keep you guessing. Heather's reluctant collaboration with her estranged father adds depth to the otherwise laugh-out-loud narrative. Her character development feels genuine, providing an emotional anchor amidst the over-the-top antics of the villains. And speaking of villains, the Proust Mob and their outrageous demands add a layer of tension and hilarity that keeps the pages turning. The writing is sharp, witty, and filled with clever observations. Even the setting – a Highland-themed restaurant that doubles as a front for a nuclear operation – is so vividly described that you can almost smell the haggis. The dialogue sparkles with humor, and the pace is perfectly balanced between suspenseful moments and laugh-out-loud absurdity. If you're a fan of dark humor, unconventional mysteries, or stories that refuse to take themselves too seriously, The Happy Thistle is an absolute gem. It's a whirlwind of wit, action, and sheer fun that left me grinning from ear to ear. Highly recommended for anyone who enjoys a unique and utterly entertaining read!

"This book is a laugh-out-loud, quirky mystery that combines British wit with a playful parody of classic detective tales."

"This book is very descriptive, very funny and very British. The characterization is stellar, her characters are so quirky and never behave in quite the way you'd expect."

"The story has mystery, suspense, adventure and twists and turns that make it difficult to put down."

"An absolute gem of a mystery novel that masterfully combines humor, intrigue, and heartwarming adventure. Thompson's storytelling style is delightfully reminiscent of Terry Pratchett, with witty dialogue, clever twists, and a richly imaginative world that leaps off the page."

PRENDERGAST OF THE YARD SHORT STORIES.
The Curious Case of the Kitnapped Cat.

For as long as she can remember, nineteen-year-old police cadet, Heather Prendergast, has harboured a burning ambition to become Prendergast of The Yard - the greatest detective the world has known since her hero, the late, great Sherlock Holmes hung up his dearstalker hat. If she becomes a national treasure in the process, so be it – it is a cross that she is prepared to bear. However, her career almost hits the buffers when she finds that her ambitions are sadly not matched by her abilities. A chance to rehabilitate her credentials arises when she is asked to find a stolen cat. As is her modus operandi, she embarks upon a bungled undercover investigation with hilarious consequences. Disguised as a tramp, she is arrested for tompeepery, her attempt to assist a citizen in distress backfires disastrously and her use of an artificially unintelligent drone almost results in a third world war. But all is well that ends well when she finds the missing cat and salvages her career . . . after a fashion.

What the reviewers say...

"Witty writing is amazing. I absolutely loved this book. If you love lighthearted detective stories with a comedic twist, this is the book for you!"

"Keeps readers entertained from start to finish. It's a perfect read for anyone who enjoys a blend of humor and mystery in their fiction."

"The banter is witty, and there are plenty of laugh-out-loud moments. The mystery-solving might take a backseat to the comedy, but if you're looking for a fun read with a bit of detective work mixed in, this book is for you. Perfect for fans of light-hearted, comedic mysteries."

"Roll over Nero Wolfe and tell Miss Marple the news! There is a new detective in town! And the place is on fire (literally!) A hilarious and well written book, a perfect vacation or weekend read."

KRILL

A disgraced businessman's chance encounter with an enigmatic stranger leads to a journey of political awakening and redemption. Set in a murky world of anarchist computer hackers, sinister secret societies, the Deepnet, quantum computing and ultimately a struggle for world domination, nothing is as it seems and no one is who they claim to be. Krill charts the journey of disgraced businessman, John Tucker from the verge of bankruptcy to the pinnacle of power. Enlisted by a shadowy political organisation, The New Praetorians, Tucker undergoes a political awakening as he watches his paymasters stage a democratic coup and put The People's Democratic Republic of Britannia on a war footing. A non-political Neutral, he finds himself in a murky world of political populism, computer hackers, false news and social media manipulation, cellphone spyware, computer server vulnerabilities, quantum computing, artificial intelligence and terrorist atrocities. As he sees the dictatorship he helped bring to power career headlong towards a cyberwar, he is faced with a dilemma - assist the New Praetorians in their lust for world domination or join the anarchist resistance and fight back.

What the reviewers say...

"A thrilling ride through a world of intrigue, technology, and political chaos. The plot is full of twists and turns, keeping you on edge as the story unfolds. The characters are complex, and the themes are disturbingly relevant to our times. A must-read for anyone who enjoys a suspenseful and intelligent political thriller."

"From the start, you see this is going to be one heck of a ride. And I wasn't wrong. This was incredible. I swear I felt like I was in the book with them. And it's scary in a way because this is something that could happen. Or maybe ... well. I couldn't put it down. I definitely recommend."

"Loved this book. Couldn't put it down. The many twists and turns make the book unforgettable. Some parts hit a bit close to home with a possible cyberwar looming on the horizon and political intrigue."

"Keeps readers on the edge of their seats, making Krill a thrilling read from start to finish."

"My friend recommended this book to me, she was totally into

it. I started reading and it totally hooked me. It's a gripping novel that keeps you hooked till the very end. I love unexpected twists and not knowing how the book will end. This book has it all."

"If you're into thrillers that mix real-life issues with a dose of fiction, this is a must-read. Trust me, you won't be able to put it down!"

"Whether you are drawn to its intricate plot, complex characters, or the chilling parallels to modern-day political dynamics, "Krill" offers a compelling read that lingers long after the final page."

"This was a great read...I couldn't put the book down!"

Audiobook available narrated by Malk Williams.

Special thanks to

Marc Dolley, Claire McKone, Philippa Donovan

Thanks to

Priscilla, Suzi, Jerry, Amelie, Kate, Kelvin, Lyndon Smith/ConsultingCops, Nicky Blewitt.

Cover by Amelie Ahern-Williams

9 798227 041890